STEL

M000283282

A PINK FRONT DOOR

STELLA Dorothea Gibbons was born in 1902 in London. She was educated first at home, then the North London Collegiate School for Girls, and finally at University College, London, where she did a two-year course on journalism.

Her first job, in 1923, was as cable decoder for British United Press. For the next decade she worked as a London journalist for various publications, including the *Evening Standard* and *The Lady*.

Her first published book was a volume of poems in 1930. This was followed by the classic comic novel *Cold Comfort Farm* (1932) which remains her best-known work. In 1933 she met and married Allan Webb, an actor and singer, the marriage lasting until the latter's death in 1959.

From 1934 until 1970, Stella Gibbons published more than twenty further novels, in addition to short stories and poetry, and there were two further posthumously-published full-length works of fiction. She was a fellow of the Royal Society of Literature, and was awarded a *Femina Vie-Heureuse* prize in 1933 for *Cold Comfort Farm*.

Stella Gibbons died on 19 December 1989 at home in London.

FICTION BY STELLA GIBBONS

Novels

Cold Comfort Farm (1932)
Bassett (1934)
Enbury Heath (1935)
Miss Linsey and Pa (1936)
Nightingale Wood (1938)
My American (1939)
The Rich House (1941)
Ticky (1943)
Westwood (1946)
The Matchmaker (1949)
Conference at Cold Comfort Farm (1949)
The Swiss Summer (1951)*
Fort of the Bear (1953)
The Shadow of a Sorcerer (1955)
Here Be Dragons (1956)
White Sand and Grey Sand (1958)
A Pink Front Door (1959)*
The Weather at Tregulla (1962)*
The Wolves Were in the Sledge (1964)
The Charmers (1965)
Starlight (1967)
The Snow-Woman (1969)*
The Woods in Winter (1970)*
The Yellow Houses (written c.1973, published 2016)
Pure Juliet (written c.1980, published 2016)

* published by Furrowed Middlebrow and Dean Street Press

Story Collections

Roaring Tower and Other Stories (1937)
Christmas at Cold Comfort Farm (1940)
Beside the Pearly Water (1954)

Children's Fiction

The Untidy Gnome (1935)

STELLA GIBBONS

A PINK FRONT DOOR

With an introduction by
Elizabeth Crawford

DEAN STREET PRESS

A Furrowed Middlebrow Book
FM60

Published by Dean Street Press 2021

First published in 1959 by Hodder & Stoughton

Cover by DSP

ISBN 978 1 913527 75 4

www.deanstreetpress.co.uk

TO

JENNIFER AND CLARE,

MY GOD-DAUGHTERS

INTRODUCTION

A Pink Front Door, advertised as 'a novel of contemporary London', was described by the reviewer in the *Marylebone Mercury* (27 November 1959) as 'a story that takes a cheerful look at changed social condition and the lot of today's highly educated young wives with next to no money and little domestic help'. Certainly the novel does centre on one such young wife, but the Oxford-educated heroine who lived behind 'the pink front door', has no such problems and, while sorting out the lives of '"drears', drifters, and muddlers', takes us into London's 'howling mid-century wilderness – without domestic service, enough house room or well-defined social customs', a world of distressed gentlewomen, of multi-tenanted houses in which the 'most persistent companion was the smell of boiled fish', and where for one woman the great fear was of never experiencing The Real Thing ('It was Love, of course'), while for another marriage, schemed for, was still the only acceptable goal. Of the novel the *Birmingham Post* (2 February 1960) commented that 'as usual Stella Gibbons tells a good story, combining a sharp eye for absurdities with pity for poor humans', while noting that it did not have 'the savage humour' of her first novel, *Cold Comfort Farm*.

For early success had been for Stella Gibbons both a blessing and a burden. Nearly thirty years after its publication, *Cold Comfort Farm* was still the standard against which all her subsequent work was measured. 'That Book', as the author came to call it, had been a great popular success, had received rave reviews on both sides of the Atlantic, and in 1933 had won the *Prix Étranger* of the *Prix Femina-Vie Heureuse*, much to the disgust of Virginia Woolf, a previous winner. An excoriating parody of the 'Loam and Lovechild School of Fiction', as represented in the works of authors such as Thomas Hardy, Mary Webb, Sheila Kaye-Smith, and even D.H. Lawrence, *Cold Comfort Farm* was also for Stella Gibbons an exorcism of her early family life. There really had been 'something nasty in the woodshed'.

Stella Dorothea Gibbons was born at 21 Malden Crescent, Kentish Town, London, on 5 January 1902, the eldest child and only daughter of [Charles James Preston] Telford Gibbons (1869-1926) and his wife, Maude (1877-1926). Her mother was gentle and much-loved but her father, a doctor, although admired by his patients, was feared at home. His ill-temper, drunkenness, affairs with family maids and governesses, violence, and, above all, the histrionics in which, while upsetting others, Stella thought he derived real pleasure, were the dominating factors of her childhood and youth. She was educated at home until the age of thirteen and was subsequently a pupil at North London Collegiate School. The change came after her governess attempted suicide when Telford Gibbons lost interest in their affair. Apparently, it was Stella who had discovered the unconscious woman.

Knowing it was essential to earn her own living, in September 1921 Stella enrolled on a two-year University of London course, studying for a Diploma in Journalism, and in 1924 eventually found work with a news service, the British United Press. She was still living at home when in 1926 her mother died suddenly. No longer feeling obliged to stay in the house she hated, she moved out into a rented room in Hampstead. Then, barely five months later, her father died, leaving his small estate to Stella's younger brother, who squandered it within a year. As a responsible elder sister, Stella found a new home to share with her brothers, 'Vale Cottage' in the Vale of Health, a cluster of old houses close to Hampstead Heath. These Hampstead years were to provide a rich source of material. Not only the topography of the area but friends and acquaintances are woven into future novels. One young man in particular, Walter Beck, a naturalised German to whom she was for a time engaged, reappears in various guises.

In 1926 Stella's life was fraught not only with the death of her parents and the assumption of responsibility for her brothers, but also with her dismissal from the BUP after a grievous error when converting the franc into sterling, a miscalculation then sent round the world. However, she soon found new employment on the London *Evening Standard*, first as secretary to the editor and then as a writer of 'women's interest' articles for the paper. By 1928 she had her own by-line and, because the *Evening Standard* was championing the revival of interest in the work of Mary Webb, was deputed to précis her novel *The Golden Arrow* and, as a consequence, read other similarly lush rural romances submitted to the paper. This at a time when her own romance was ending unhappily. In 1930 she was once more sacked, passing from the *Evening Standard* to a new position as editorial assistant on *The Lady*. Here her duties involved book reviewing and it was the experience of skimming through quantities of second-rate novels that, combined with her Mary Webb experience, led to the creation of *Cold Comfort Farm*, published by Longmans in 1932.

In 1929 Stella had met Allan Webb, an Oxford graduate a few years her junior, now a student at the Webber-Douglas School of Singing. They were soon secretly engaged, but it was only in 1933 that they married, royalties from *Cold Comfort Farm* affording them some financial security. Two years later their only child, a daughter, was born and was, in turn, eventually to give Stella two grandsons, on whom she doted. In 1936 the family moved to 19 Oakeshott Avenue, Highgate, within the gated Holly Lodge estate, where Stella was to live for the rest of her life.

For the next forty years, in war and peace, Stella Gibbons continued to publish a stream of novels, as well as several volumes of poetry and short stories. In 1959, as she nursed her husband, ill with cancer, she was writing *A Pink Front Door*. He died, still comparatively young, four months before its publication. During this harrowing time, Stella looked back to a setting which had given her such pleasure in her younger days. It was to 'Vale Cottage' that, over thirty years after her tenancy, Stella gave a pink front door and made it the home of Daisy Muir, her husband and baby son, part of a generation of 'young prosperous artists, dress designers, advertising executives, rising Television personalities and a few bright young business men and their families' who were 'eagerly buying and moving in' to the area. Daisy, a variant on Flora Poste, who in *Cold Comfort Farm* brings order to the lives of the Starkadders, is endlessly busy with the good works that take her all over north London and into a variety of inadequate lives, while failing to notice the effect that her activities, apparently selfless, are having on life at home. With its cast of shrewdly-drawn characters, *A Pink Front Door* captures a society on the cusp of change.

After Allan's death Stella never remarried. Although avoiding literary and artistic society, she did hold a monthly 'salon' at home, attracting a variety of guests, young and old, eminent, unknown and, sometimes, odd. She continued to publish novels until 1970 and even after that wrote two more that she declined to submit to her publisher. As her nephew, Reggie Oliver, wrote in *Out of the Woodshed* (1998), his biography of Stella, 'She no longer felt able to deal with the anguish and anxiety of exposing her work to a publisher's editor, or to the critics.' She need not have feared; both novels have subsequently been published.

Stella Gibbons died on 19 December 1989, quietly at home, and is buried across the road in Highgate Cemetery, alongside her husband.

Elizabeth Crawford

CHAPTER I
"To haunt, to startle and waylay"

"Is THAT a taxi?"

The instant after she had said it, Ella Furnivall wished that she had kept quiet. Of course it was a taxi; she and her cousin Marcia had both heard it; and although she did not put down her book nor Marcia lift her eyes from the pages of *The Times*, both were now listening. In a moment, Marcia got up, with an energy that suggested controlled impatience, and went across to the open window.

The taxi had stopped. They could hear it panting in the road below; they could hear, too, coming up to them, that high, clear voice like the fluting of a distant blackbird handicapped by just the hint of a lisp, which they had known for the past twenty-five years; and it was saying, with an intonation of nurse-like cheeriness that caused them both the strongest forebodings: "Here we are. Come along."

Marcia slid up the massive sash-window to its full extent with a vigorous movement of her long arms, and they stared down into the road.

They could not see everything that was going on, because the black branches of the monkey-puzzle growing immediately below obscured the view; but they could see that the taxi was now ominously silent and prepared to wait, they could see three figures crossing the road and approaching the house, and they could hear Mrs James Muir chattering. Her companions were silent.

There wasn't any other sound in the road. The railway cutting, drowsing deep in smoky purple vapours which even the strong sunlight of this September day could hardly penetrate—trainless, and suggesting as it often did to Ella one of the Circles of the Inferno temporarily out of action during repairs—was, as usual, the most conspicuous object in view; beyond it, the long, broad, sober avenue of very large houses built in brick a shade lighter than the fumes in the cutting seemed as if it were asleep, stupefied with the warmth of the fading summer's afternoon.

Now Daisy was standing on the little lawn under the monkey-puzzle. Looking down, they could see her long, pink, delightful face smiling up at them, between the black branches. She was long altogether; a streak of black and white dress, long legs, long sunburnt arms with a round, smooth knob of brown head on top of all.

"She's brought James Too," Ella murmured in her soft, uncertain voice.

"That white thing? I thought it was a parcel. She drags that child around too much."

"Do modern babies mind it, do you think?"

"There aren't any modern babies."

Ella was silent. Marcia had her nursing experience; Marcia *knew* more than she herself did about babies—liked them better, too. All the same, Ella did think that babies appeared larger, calmer, and yet more 'forward' than they had done sixty years ago.

"Hullo!" Daisy's voice soared joyously through the scaly, sooty old boughs. "Can we come up?"

"Of course. I'll throw you down the key." Marcia, who liked to spare their maid Annie's sixty-two year old legs whenever possible, drew in her head. "Is that James One with her, that man?" she muttered. (Ella could see things so much better than she could; always had.)

"No. It looks like a foreigner."

"How very tiresome," Marcia said and absently handed her cousin the key, attached to a large white label (probably it was one of Daisy's customary unfortunate protégés, in need, as usual, of help).

Ella, having taken a wavering and uncertain estimate of the distance between the window and the intervening boughs, cast the key wildly forth. It landed on a branch some eight feet above Daisy's head, teetered tantalizingly for an instant, and settled into place.

"Blast!" called Daisy cheerfully. The other girl and the man were laughing, but Ella thought that, if it had not been Daisy who was in charge, they would have appeared depressed and cross. Their shapes looked depressed.

Ella, who had never known how to 'get on' with human beings, had in her seventy-odd years formed the habit of judging them by quite other pointers than what they said or the expressions they put on their faces, and although she never, or hardly ever, told anyone what her conclusions were or enjoyed having them confirmed by other people—often, so surprisingly often, they turned out to be right.

"You know where the bean pole is," Marcia was calling.

Daisy, putting her white bundle into the arms of the other young woman, who curved over it protectively, ran across the garden and down a passage at the side of the house, where she pushed open a door with a latticed top, all newly painted green, and made her way to a neat shed. She emerged with a seven-foot bean pole, and ran back to the monkey-puzzle.

Marcia and Ella, not bothering to watch what had happened many times before and would happen many times again, withdrew into their sitting-room, and Marcia went through into the kitchen to tell Annie to get the tea. Annie did not smile as she acknowledged the order, and Marcia returned to Ella with the realization, which she kept to herself, as she did all things likely to trouble or alarm her cousin, that the tiresome old creature was in one of her sulky moods.

"I'll take him now," Daisy said, as she led the party quickly up the stairs, carpeted in drab drugget, past white walls and closed doors, through the quiet, fresh, old house.

"Oh, do let me keep him, he's so cuddly," implored Molly Raymond in her sugariest voice, clasping the baby closer.

"All right, if you enjoy it . . . but he can be a swine," Daisy said, with a threatening look at her son.

The man, meanwhile—the man whom Ella had described as looking like a foreigner and who was in fact a refugee—was looking about him as they mounted the stairs: taking in the size of the house, the prosperous, orderly garden visible through the windows, the air of refinement over everything (prints of Rome, and of English cathedrals, in wide, worn, gilt frames on the staircase walls, fresh flowers on the polished old tables placed at every landing . . .), up he went, on light deprecating feet, after the girls;

wary, hopeful, and ready to take advantage of anything coming his way.

The two old cousins were standing to receive them.

"This is Molly Raymond," Daisy said, when she had kissed them both, "and this is Mr.—" She clearly pronounced a mouthful of z's and y's and p's, which she had mastered early on in her acquaintanceship with the feckless being who bore it, simply because she thought it hard luck enough for him to have lost his job and his home and his nationality, without losing as well the right to have a careful and correct pronunciation of his name. But as his first one was Tibor, and as he looked, with his triangular face and slanting, thickly lashed eyes and wide mouth, very like a tom-cat, she and Molly had soon taken to calling him Tibbs.

Marcia said, "How do you do", repeating the z's and y's and p's without a stumble, and, as he bowed and smiled, he looked gratified (poor man) and surprised.

"Miss Furnivall knows your country," said Daisy, "she nursed there in the First World War, didn't you, darling?"

"I was mostly in Serbia. But I do know it," Marcia said. Her voice was strong, for all the fact that in three years' time she would be eighty years old, and it matched her height, her upright carriage, and the dark silvery grey hair arranged in heavy loops on her small head. Her commanding easy manner and her little Roman nose, however, were set off by a pale, flowery silk dress and some lace at her neck, while the other Miss Furnivall—Ella, her cousin and Daisy's aunt—although at the first glimpse more feminine in voice and air, was covered, merely in as nondescript a collection of fading, aged and shrunken garments as ever affronted a connoisseur of female dressing. Her hair is like the seeds of a thistle, thought Tibbs, and with those wild, round eyes she is like a crazy Koala bear from Australia.

When introductions were over, Daisy began at once:

"We can't stay, darlings, we're on our way to Laurel House. I've got a room there for Molly, and then I've got to dash over to Brondesbury to a junk shop to buy a jug . . . and I want to borrow *The Lord of the Rings*, Ella, please. Only the first volume, if you'll be an absolute angel?"

Her smile was affectionate but it was also business-like and confident. Ella would do as she was asked. In twenty-five years she always had. Yet when anyone ever said to Daisy, "I expect your aunt and her cousin spoil you, don't they?" her answer was invariably: "No-o—I wouldn't say so. Not *really*."

Now Daisy had given *The Lord of the Rings* to Ella for a birthday present only three weeks ago, and Ella was savouring it, so slowly that she was still only half-way through the first volume. But she knew that time must pass more quickly for Daisy than it did for herself, and perhaps Daisy felt that she had given her the book several months ago. In any case, it would not have occurred to her to announce that she was still reading it; that would have been, she felt, rather rude.

"I'll just get it," she said, and went out of the room with her rocking gait, knocking into a table as she did so.

"Marcia," said Daisy next, "can I speak to you a minute?"

"Of course." Smiling an excuse at Tibbs and Molly Raymond, Marcia led the way out of the room. Annie could be seen through the landing window down in the garden, hanging out tea-towels; Marcia went into the kitchen and shut the door.

As soon as they were alone, Tibbs looked across at Molly and began to smile. That pretty Daisy! He would always remember her leaning forward so earnestly, with such a grave face, while she repeated the syllables of his name. She had great style, authority and charm, yet she was so 'kind' as really to be something of a fool. But she had never troubled to flirt with him (and he knew that she could be provocative; he had seen her sparkling with other men) and this had offended, even a little hurt him. He was just a refugee, was he, to Daisy Muir?

And as he was not one of those men who find a woman proportionately desirable as she is unattainable, he did not find Daisy irresistibly attractive; he kept to his conviction, held now for some three months, that the little Molly was the nicer girl of the two; with her cap of thick fair hair that hid half her forehead, and her air of being an indoor girl fond of an easy chair and the fire. He also enjoyed her voice, coming muffledly out of her thin vulnerable lips, and her habit of looking right into a man's eyes while she was talking to him.

Molly sat in the sunlight near the window and kept her big dim grey eyes cast down on the imperious sleeping face of Daisy's eleven-months-old son. She liked Tibbs to see her holding a baby, although she did not really like babies. But she did not want to give way and look at him.

She resisted as long as she could, and then, when she just darted one glance at him from under her fair lashes that always had a matted, sleepy look—just one, so quickly—he was smiling; that unkind, well-known smile.

Trembling, she rearranged the baby's clothes. She felt the quiet to be unbearable. But if she did say something, it was sure to be something it would have been wiser not to.

"Have they deserted you?" Daisy's aunt asked suddenly in her soft voice—too *haughty*, Molly thought it was, to be really pleasant—as she blundered back into the room, and she came over and sat down by her. "Did Daisy say that you are going to live at Laurel House?"

"Yes, and am I looking forward to getting out of the place I'm in now! I can't tell you."

"You will like it there, I am sure. My brother has lived there for many years, and he finds it very quiet and comfortable."

"Yes, Daisy told me Colonel Furnivall speaks highly of it." Molly pronounced the name of Daisy's father, as always, with a feeling of pleasure. "It's terrible where I am now; no proper bathroom and the toilet is unspeakable. And only one, for a houseful of twelve people."

"Is it an old house?" enquired Miss Furnivall, with a gleam of pleased interest which, Molly felt, was an odd response to her unpleasant revelations. Then Daisy's aunt, appearing to recollect herself, added in a lulling tone, "How uncomfortable. I am sure you will be very glad to get away."

"Oh, I shall." The baby stirred, awoke, gazed around him with a wild, toothless smile and went off to sleep again, and they turned their attention to him for a moment, Molly commenting upon his size and beauty and her companion studying him with a detached expression in her widely-opened pale eyes.

Tibbs, covertly studying *her*, decided that his first impression of a clumsy, eccentric, painfully nervous old oddity had been superficial. What was more marked about her than her queerness was a delicacy and fineness; the straight hair falling about the full, round face actually was as fragile and sheeny as the thistledown to which he had irritably compared it; the skin made him think of the petals of some fading white flower; how moistly the wide eyes shone! But it was with—not intelligence, exactly, but with a kind of awareness, he now realised; they wandered about the room (at least, they did the moment Molly Raymond ceased to look at her), paused, darted their stare at some reflected gleam or a shadow. But most of the time she kept them fixed upon the visitor's face, in a quiet, attentive way that contrasted strongly and strangely with their darting, eager movements when she believed herself unobserved.

'What an old freak,' thought Tibbs. 'Even as a young girl she could never have been a real woman. Yet how exquisite that skin must have been, at eighteen! And it's strange, I like to look at her.'

"Laurel House *is* very clean," Ella was saying earnestly, "and there are some nice restaurants at Belsize Park. Marcia and I walk up there to lunch sometimes, when we are going to Daisy and the car is being repaired. (It is always going wrong; it is so little and old, you see) . . . And how will you manage about *breakfast*?" She leant forward slightly, and looked intently—glared almost—into Molly's surprised face.

"Oh. . . ." Molly was a little embarrassed; she did not like people to get behind her barriers of drooping hair and muffling scarf and expose, so to speak, her face to the open air, and that was what she felt they did when they looked at her as closely as this old lady was doing; a cold wind seemed to blow into her face.

Yet Daisy's aunt couldn't have sounded more interested. "Oh, there's a kitchen we can all use—more than one kitchen, I believe, and then I don't go in for cooked breakfasts; I just have Continental style." She wished that Miss Furnivall would turn away those great eyes.

She didn't want the poor old dear worrying about her. Evidently worrying about people 'went' in Daisy's family. "I'll be all right once I'm out of that hole in Glenister Road," she ended.

Miss Furnivall nodded.

"I mean, the landlady won't be troubled with meals or any cleaning," Molly enlarged. "Just lets the rooms to whoever could put down a week's rent in advance—artists (well, I don't mind them when they're genuine but these weren't) and students— more like teddy-boys, if you ask me . . . and . . . some very . . . queer types." She broke off, then went on quickly, "Playing the tape-recorder until three in the morning, sometimes. My *nerves* got so bad. Sounds silly, but I'm the nervous type. The least thing, and I can't sleep."

Miss Furnivall was nodding again.

"Yes . . ." she said in her weak, cold voice, " . . . the nervous system . . . that can inflict terrible tortures."

Molly barely caught the words, but she just did, and for a moment they absolutely silenced her. Tortures? She looked away from the old, soft, ravaged face. Daisy had never *said* anything about her aunt being a bit mental. But then Daisy never did warn you about anything.

Tibbs crossed his legs over to the other side. The taxi must be ticking up at a fine rate. But Daisy would see to that. He need not worry. When you were with Daisy no one need worry.

Why did she do so much for people? Rush around, find rooms, arrange introductions, put people up in that pretty little cluttered house of hers, cook large meals for droppers-in, dispense advice by the hour over the telephone? Was it an excess of the maternal instinct? (Tibbs made it a rule always to discover what was the ruling passion in each new acquaintance he made; such information could be useful.) And what—he was an inquisitive man—what could she be saying now to her alarming old cousin? He had a feeling that it might concern him.

Marcia, standing by the kitchen table, wished that Ella had not chosen this moment to disappear. She needed her support.

The kitchen was a small high sunny room painted a clear yellow and overlooking through its heavy sash-windows the lawn of the walled garden far below; down there everything was in order and quiet, and the big yellow leaves floated off the chestnut tree on to Annie's red hair as she hung out the tea-towels.

Marcia had that feeling, increasingly familiar during the past two years, of being imprisoned inside an aching, creaking, slowly-moving machine that refused to work properly any more. Sometimes, when she had been driving for too long, or sitting up late in vehement talk with old friends, she could almost feel herself—her true self, whom she had known for seventy-seven years—banging about inside that machine like some trapped and rebellious bluebottle against a window pane. And *her* particular machine used to be so unobtrusive, so biddable and efficient! That made its recent insolent refusals all the harder to bear. It was the turn of the machine, now to tell *her*, the real Marcia, what to do, and if she refused, it dared to turn upon her, and hurt her.

She did not want to have to refuse Daisy anything. But before Daisy began to speak, she knew that she would have to.

Daisy sat on the table. Her upturned nose needed the powder that girls did not use nowadays, and her lovely mouth was painted an improbable shade of sickly pink.

"Darling, I'm going to be a nuisance again. Will you have Tibbs (that's Mr P . . . z . . . y) for a night or two? Oh"—as Miss Furnivall, prompted by strategic motives, began to disengage herself from the long young arm wrapped about her waist—"I know you won't *want* him. But it's only until I can find somewhere more or less permanent for him, and just now he *literally* hasn't anywhere to lay his head. He was living in that ghastly house where Molly was, you know, and then there was some kind of trouble—I really don't know what happened—and he came to us for a bit. But . . ." Daisy faltered, and her cousin said, with an impassive face: "But James wouldn't put up with him."

"Well, yes. (James really *is* rather naughty sometimes about my friends; he simply will *not* make an *effort*.) But he and Tibbs parted quite amiably (at least, I *think* James was amiable; it all happened in rather a hurry). Then the Lloyds took him for a week and that was all right, he had the studio at the end of their garden, only he had to clear out. because they had some sickening person coming to stay. So I persuaded Sue Ruddlin (you remember Sue: my worst friend; married to a bright young film-man; lives at Canonbury) to have him. She's got *masses* of rooms in that vast house of hers, and nearly all empty; it was only a question of a *bed*. Tibbs does get a grant of some kind and he's ready to do *any* kind of work; he's been harvesting, and hopping, and waiting in a seaside hotel. He isn't a *sponger* or a *loafer*; you would have *thought* Sue could have coped. But *no*, it didn't work—"

"Why didn't it?"

Marcia put the question quietly, easily, even, but behind it was the weight of her years, her relationship with this child whom she and Ella had helped to bring up, and the authority that was a legacy from certain public positions of importance which she had formerly held. It pulled Daisy up short in the full flow of what her husband uncharitably called her sales-talk. She looked quickly at her cousin, and began to laugh.

"Oh, he made a pass at Sue, actually. Awfully silly of him, he ought to have seen that she isn't that type (at least, not with a refugee who she'd *given* a bed to!). But he does make the oddest clangers now and then, although he has been here more than three years. Anyway, Sue was furious. She socked him one, as a matter of fact, and he cried—"

"Cried?" Miss Furnivall was grave; not because she did not find the story rather ludicrous but because this afternoon she felt old, and she felt tired, and she did not want to alarm Daisy by showing it.

"Oh yes." Daisy nodded her smooth brown head. "Cried buckets, and told her she was a Fascist cow."

Miss Furnivall's eyebrows lifted. "A different world," was all she said.

"He isn't *naturally* a nice person, poor Tibbs, I'm afraid," Daisy went on. "He had a very bad time in the Revolution (he's a chemist—a very good one, I believe; he was doing research for some firm or other and he lost *everything*) and of course his pride was hurt as well . . . Sue had to call a policeman to get rid of him at last."

"Thank you for being so frank with me," said her cousin, and they both laughed.

"Oh well, darling," the arm was back again around the brittle old waist, "I should hardly ask you to have him without telling you what he can be like . . . but he'll be as good as gold with Ella and you. I've put the fear of God into him."

She began to slide off the table, with the manner of one whose task is accomplished.

But Marcia was *pulling herself together*.

It was something that she had not very often had to do during her long lifetime (always, of course, with the exception of that winter spent in the mountains of Serbia) and the rarity of the exercise made her resent it the more.

She detested feeling dismayed at the prospect of having a troublesome foreigner under her roof for a couple of nights (she, who had marshalled and managed hundreds of wild Serbs) and she very definitely did not want Daisy to get the idea that she was now, suddenly, about to become a helpless old woman. Daisy had always relied upon her and Ella (although Ella's support had been passive) since her mother's death ten years ago, and Marcia wanted her to go on relying; she needed the advice and the support of elders, with the amount that she took on her silly young shoulders. . . . 'But,' Marcia suddenly, exhaustedly, thought, 'I can't do it. I *can't* have the man here; I absolutely cannot.'

She said without hesitation:

"We can't have him, Daisy."

Daisy stared, red colour rushing up into her long, vivid face.

"Oh . . . can't you?" She was very taken aback. "But there is the spare room—and I *know* he won't be any trouble—unless of course you've got anyone coming to stay?"

"Mary Lowndes is coming to us for a few days, if her arthritis will let her. But that won't be until late October, I expect. It isn't that—"

"Was Delia Huxtable the last straw? You didn't take to her, did you?" asked Daisy, recalling the last protégée whom she had thrust upon the cousins.

"I thought she was deplorable. Unhelpable, too, I am afraid, Daisy."

"Oh—well—poor Delia, she's had a rough time. . . . But I did think you would *want* to help Tibbs! He's educated—he's got a degree from the Sorbonne! And he *was* in the Revolution! He *did* fight the Communists! Of course, I must say"—Daisy's natural honesty frequently compelled her to speak at moments when, to gain her own ends, she would have preferred to remain silent— "he sometimes seems a bit Communist himself. I expect he got indoctrinated almost without knowing it. But—"

"That has nothing to do with our not wanting him. I respect him, of course, if he has suffered for his convictions. But you know that I stopped being interested in politics in 1919, when I realised that the majority of women voters was not going to use their new privilege intelligently . . . it's simply that I don't want the bother of someone extra in the house."

Daisy had been looking closely at her, and gradually her tragic, baffled expression had changed. She said suddenly, in the off-hand voice Miss Furnivall knew concealed alarm:

"You aren't ill, are you, Marcie?"

"Not in the least," snubbingly. "We had a delightful time in Brittany and I'm looking forward to the winter. It's just that—we can't have him."

"May I put it down to bloody-mindedness, then?" impertinently.

But Daisy was looking relieved.

"Certainly you may, if you don't mind using the expression. Bloody-mindedness it shall be."

"I'd sooner it was that than your feeling ill." She put her soft crimson cheek, still hot from the rebuff, against Marcia's sallow drooping one for a moment. "All right then, darling. Sorry I asked."

"I am sorry that I had to refuse."

In a very few minutes, Daisy had collected her charges, reassumed the care of her son, and farewells had been made. With Molly now carrying Volume One of *The Lord of The Rings*, they made their way down to the waiting taxi.

"Damn, now there won't be time for me to come up with you," Daisy said to her, glancing at her watch. "I'll drop you there and try and look in tomorrow—if I can manage it, I've got a pretty full day . . . Tibbs," turning to him with a rather desperate expression as he stood, looking proud, by the open door of the taxi, "*what* about you?"

How glad she was that she had not told him about the plan for letting him stay! (But he had probably guessed; her husband's unkind words—'as sharp as some rusty old razor blade'—would recur.)

He shrugged.

"I can go to Grania again."

Daisy caught a dismayed sound from Molly, who was now seated amidst her luggage in the taxi.

"Don't worry about me, my dear," added Tibbs. "I always fall upon my feet."

Like a cat, again . . . though James would say that he usually fell 'upon' other people's.

"Well, if you really think you'll be all right—"

"I shall be all right. And I'll telephone you tomorrow."

"Oh yes, do." But Daisy couldn't help rather wishing that she need never hear Tibbs make that particular threat again.

"Here's your case." It was Molly's voice, very muffled in scarf and hair; she had managed to disengage the cheap, shabby thing from her own possessions He pulled it out, and braced himself, noticeably, to carry it.

"It isn't far to Grania's," he said. "Thank you, darling. *Auf wiedersehen.*"

The taxi moved off.

"He's so *gallant!*" burst from Molly.

"Yes, well, I hope he'll be all right—" Daisy muttered. "Of course, Grania . . . ."

"I never liked her. I don't admire that very dark type. What is she—Jugoslavian?"

"Rumanian, *he* says."

"She's got a terrible temper. Of course, *I've* always—thought she was sexshually attracted."

Daisy, thinking it wiser to ignore this contribution, created a diversion by kissing the top of James Too's pate and asking him if he wasn't a wavishing wabbit?

Molly looked sadly out of the window at Primrose Hill Road going by. She imagined Tibb's arrival, in the increasing bustle of late Saturday afternoon, at Grania's hot, crowded, steamy café near Swiss Cottage; his jaunty pleading with her to let him occupy, just once more, the stifling little room next to the kitchens that always reeked of frying fat, his delighted recognition, later in the evening, of compatriots of both sexes who had dropped in for a coffee and a gossip . . . she never felt so far away from him as when he had been compelled to go for a few days to Grania's.

"Of course, sexshually—" she began suddenly.

"Now *have* you got anything for breakfast tomorrow morning?" Daisy demanded.

CHAPTER II
Bottle Court

LATER that afternoon, when the sun was setting into the evening clouds over south-west London, James Muir cautiously put the key into his front door.

It was a pink front door; a clear, bright, soft colour, a little weathered, now, from the frank Shocking Pink that it had been when he had carried Daisy over its threshold four years ago, but still startlingly pretty amidst the cream stucco and brown brick of this tiny courtyard high up in the village of Old Hampstead, in North London.

In those days, the Muirs' cottage had been the only one so transformed and painted; now, the tenants who had lived there for many years were gradually dying off or being tempted by specu-lators to sell their charming inconvenient houses for large sums, and tenants of another type were eagerly buying and moving in; young prosperous artists, dress designers, advertising executives, rising Television personalities and a few bright young business men and their families.

There were three or four dazzlingly white cottages further down Bottle Court, with bright doors and flowery window boxes and blue-painted balconies of wrought-iron, but the Muirs' front door was still the only one painted that unusual shade of pink.

Space was not one of the amenities offered to prospective tenants in Bottle Court. Big cars belonging to its residents had to be garaged in wider streets lying immediately below it or wherever they could find room nearby to park, for there was no way of approaching it directly save by thirty or so shallow eighteenth-century stone steps leading up from the High Street, or by a kind of lane between the houses too narrow for any but the smallest vehicles to pass. Oh, a madly inconvenient, unbelievably picturesque, passionately sought-after residential quarter was Bottle Court, N.W.3.

James's gesture with the key was cautious because he was not always sure of who or what he would find in the hall when he got in. It might be someone in tears, or someone asleep while they filled up time waiting to catch a train, or someone drunk. Once it was an elderly stranger who had chosen Daisy to collapse on in the preliminaries to a fit. But of course the visitors were not always so dramatic; usually they were some young woman on whom she had been besought to keep an eye in London, or a child parked on her for the day, or perhaps one of what James called The Soft Core: a group of inconsolables who were pulled out of one misfortune by Daisy only to slide into another the instant her guiding hand was relaxed.

The lock, as usual, stuck: this was because the anti-burglar device which Daisy had insisted upon his installing tended to keep out the occupants as well as the burglars. He looked up critically at the smoke-coloured facade that always struck him as having a *squashed* appearance; next year, it really must be re-painted. That would be expensive. But then everything to do with the house with the pink front door was. For such a small house, with such small rooms, it did cost the hell of a lot to keep up.

The key suddenly worked. Still cautiously he pushed open the door. But he was met by a reassuringly savoury smell, rather than the defiant reek of frying sausages, bath-water was running in the distance, a Mozart aria suddenly leapt into brilliant sound from somewhere upstairs, and the light was on in the basement. He was smiling as he put his clubs down on the ironwork table with the mosaic top. Daisy was home.

But if she was upstairs bathing James Too and playing Mozart, she did not need the light on in the basement. So James, having shouted up the stairs and received a welcoming thrush-note in answer, went with his leisurely step down the very narrow descent into the kitchen, where two 200-watt lamps sent their radiance up the well and into the hall, and turned them both out. He lifted a saucepan lid, peered in, muttered with satisfaction, turned off a dripping tap, shut a window because the gas might blow out, and went upstairs again to the top of the house.

"Hullo, darling. What did you go round in?" Daisy looked smiling over her shoulder; she was kneeling beside the big bath and supporting James Too in the water; he was looking apprehensive but when he saw his father he smiled.

"Eighty. Whatcher, tosh," and James snapped his fingers at his son.

"Better than last week. You're steadily improving, aren't you?"

"I was in form today," he said merely, and, bending forward from his seat on the bathroom stool, pushed aside the hair at the nape of her neck and gently bit her.

"Don't, James," said Daisy, dodging, "I can't join in or he'll drown."

"Hasn't he lain down *yet*? He is a little shower."

"He is not. If you were the size he is, that water would seem twenty feet deep. Give me that towel, will you?"

"Did you have a good afternoon?" he enquired, as he gave it to her.

"Oh yes . . . that is . . . fairly." All Daisy's features saddened and drooped; it was as if a light had gone out. "Something rather worrying—not very, only a little bit—Marcie wouldn't have Tibbs."

There was a pause. Daisy was deftly drying James Too.

Then: "You don't mean that you *did* ask them to have him, Daisy, after I said you were not to?"

"Well—" her expression was self-conscious—"I *actually* didn't remember *exactly* what you said; I was so *desperate* to get him in somewhere. But it was all right really, James. I didn't argue or anything. I couldn't, even if I'd wanted to: Marcia was so definite about not having him."

She paused. In the little silence, the music sprang and rippled in brilliant showers. She turned James Too over on her knee and began to dry his back.

"But what I *really* minded," Daisy went on, "was—well, she was so . . . funny . . . about it. She hardly ever has refused me anything, but if she does she *always* gives me a reason. This afternoon she just said that she and Ella didn't want the fuss." She looked up at James; the afterglow shining through the window was reflected in her wet eyes. "Do you really think it's what you said last night? Are they beginning to get old?"

"I've told you what I think." James's beautiful square face displayed only common-sense, an expression which his wife never found comforting. "You won't have them for ever, darling. You'll have to get used to the idea."

"Yes, I suppose so." Daisy did not want to talk about it. She picked up the baby and carried him into the next room.

James walked to the window and looked down at London lying spread out under the sunset.

He was so lucky, he thought, in his wife's relations; in her father, who was generous and charming as Daisy herself, and never any trouble, in his reserved and orderly widowerhood, to anyone; and in the two old cousins, living in such a way in the house in King Edward's Road that their life was a peaceful pleasure to think about. That big old house of theirs, the suggestion of country pursuits in the background, was the kind that James really liked; more, actually, than he did this expensive, brilliant, cluttered little box humming with untidy life, with its pink front door, where he was almost perfectly happy with Daisy.

It was Daisy's lame ducks and protégées who were largely responsible for that 'almost'.

His expression, as he stared down at the roofs and chimneys in the glowing evening light, was just a little cross.

Marcia and Ella ought not to be worried with troublemakers, chronic telephones, and demanders of time, sympathy and attention. It was too bad of Daisy. She did it often enough to make him very definite with her about how much he disapproved of it. Marcia was well over seventy-six, Ella was in the early seventies. They had surely come to a time of life when they might expect tranquillity and rest? The friends of their own generation were, apart from the inevitable worries of failing health—and even so they seemed far better physically than the people who were now in their middle fifties—a source of pleasure to the Misses Furnivall, as friends (thought James) should be; the two other flats into which their house was divided were let to prosperous professional people with whom Marcia and Ella were on terms of pleasantly cool neighbourliness and mutual respect. The younger people whom they occasionally met respected them too much to intrude upon them with confidences or claims on time and money.

No; if it were not for Daisy and her demands on behalf of Delia, Tibbs, Molly, poor David and heaven-knew-who-else, the house in King Edward's Road would always have presented that front of unruffled harmony which he most admired.

In the background of the cousins' life, never obtruding but supplying the last touch, in James's eyes, of desirability to their way of living, were the spires of Oxford. For they were the daughters of two brothers who had lived and lectured there, their houses standing side by side in a wide, quiet, shady road, in the nineties, and Ella and Marcia had grown up in the old city. The roots, the framework, of that life he so much liked—and rather envied—went back further still; deep into the Oxford of the sixties.

One day, but in another country, where the horizons were wider, he would like that kind of life for his own children. It would be difficult to achieve but it was what he would like, and as for difficulty (thought James unfashionably), it was there to be got over by planning and hard work.

He turned away from the window and went into their bedroom, where Daisy, to the last strains of 'The Marriage of Figaro's' first act, was putting James Too to bed in the powder-closet that had been built in the same year that the opera had been written.

"Did you get your seduced friend settled in?" he enquired, beginning to change his clothes.

"I dropped her at Laurel House by taxi but I hadn't time to see her in . . . she isn't really *seduced*, James."

It did not in the least surprise James to hear that Daisy had been in a taxi. He said:

"What is she, then?"

"Well, it isn't quite so serious . . . I mean, she isn't . . . she has had one or two affairs that got as far as sleeping . . . but you make it sound so *Victorian*."

"The facts are the same," said James.

Daisy looked at him, then turned off the first act of 'Figaro' and shook her fist at James Too, who was staring steadily at her out of his bed in the powder-closet.

"He can hardly keep his eyes open. It's only bloody-mindedness. Bring that down for me, will you, lovey," she said, meaning the white portable gramophone that went with her everywhere that she could take it, and she ran downstairs.

James put on his old coat. He had had a pleasant game of golf and had also met on the course a man who might bring to the advertising firm in which James's job was consumer-research some useful business . . . if James and Daisy had been living anywhere but in the house with the pink front door it could have been said that he was doing well. But Bottle Court easily swallowed most of what he earned. Even the fact that the house with the pink front door had been a combined wedding present to them from his family and hers did not make as much difference as it should have done.

Nevertheless, as he finished his dressing he began to whistle. The seduced character was safely bestowed in Laurel House and the Communist type had been given the firm brush-off from King Edward's Road. And Daisy had a free weekend.

He insisted upon her having one, more frequently than she really liked, telling her that the secretarial agency in Kensington which employed her as a 'temporary' and paid her twelve pounds a week for being available for work at odd hours, could now and then find someone else to take down the letters and run the errands of Greek shipping magnates and Texan oil tycoons.

The training which she had taken at a first-class secretarial college on coming down from Oxford combined with her personality, intelligence and looks to secure for her a choice of the best jobs on the agency's books, but James did not like her working at all. He said, frequently, that he earned enough to keep them all in comfort.

"I like to spend it on my lame ducks."

"Well—I can manage that too. I'd rather you spent it on scent or stockings, but if you want to have a spending spree with my cash on bedsocks for the seduced character, I don't really mind."

"I like to spend *my* money, that *I* earn, on *my* lame ducks."

"Oh, very well."

And the subject remained unsettled, a source of slight friction between Daisy and James.

Before he went downstairs clasping the gramophone, he saw that James Too was asleep, with both arms flung up behind his square golden head.

Daisy lit a fire after supper, more for cosiness than for warmth, and they settled themselves contentedly on either side of it.

James was full of excellent food, for Daisy was a more-than-good cook. Janine, the young Frenchwoman who helped Daisy to run her home and who had been recommended by that Susan Ruddlin always referred to by Daisy as her *worst* friend was out, as Daisy frequently said that she could be after supper, and he had his pipe and his *Evening Standard* and they had the house to themselves.

Daisy, in the sturdy little chair which had originally been made without arms to accommodate the billow of a crinoline, had the sewing which she did not do well but which she enjoyed. Through the window, between the parted curtains of striped silk, London displayed itself as a pattern of light, glittering away behind the dark crooked chimneys of the houses lower down the hill. James glanced at his wife; she looked fine-drawn. Thank God for absent friends, he thought. Delicious, thought Daisy; just me and James and James Too goodly asleep upstairs.

How was Molly getting on, though, at Laurel House? Her room was very small; up there on the third floor among the long dim winding corridors where Mrs Brogan's collection of poor old people lived, who would sacrifice warmth, convenience, even food, for the privilege of living in a nice house in a nice road among nice people.

"What's up now?" asked James.

"Did I sigh? I was just wondering—I do hope Molly won't go making herself a nuisance to Daddy."

"Didn't you think of that before you got her the room?"

"Well, I *did*—but not *really*, you know."

"I shouldn't worry. He's had thirty years in the Army in India; he can take care of himself," and James returned to his paper.

That was all very well, but Molly was so *interested* in him; if you mentioned any man whom you happened to know to Molly, she always was interested, especially in what she referred to as 'his love life'.

It was true that she had not, so far, ventured to imply any interest in that department of Colonel Furnivall's life, but she had shown a sadly sympathetic face whenever she referred to his being a widower. 'Your father's great loss', she called the death of Daisy's mother, and Daisy knew that much of her willingness to leave the squalid house in Glenister Road for the room with a higher rent which Daisy had found for her was due to the fact that in Laurel House Colonel Furnivall would be living on the ground floor.

The rest of her willingness was accounted for by the fact that Tibbs was being turned out of Glenister Road because he could not—or would not—(he had strong views on the rights of land-lords) pay his rent.

Daisy painstakingly tied off an end of cotton. It would be really frightful if Molly did make herself a nuisance to Daddy. 'I ought to have realised that she might, before I got her the room,' Daisy thought, 'but I was so busy trying to get her *off* Tibbs.'

"It won't *lead* to anything," she had warned Molly, meaning Molly's interest in Tibbs, and she had marshalled all that she knew about him, as well as all that she suspected, to support her earnest arguments. No use.

"But, Daisy, he *has* got charm! You must admit that."

"I don't see it. Besides, even if he has—a person can have charm, and still be bad."

"Oh, poor Tibbs! Aren't you being rather unkind?"

"I daresay . . . Molly, do you honestly attach so much importance to charm in a man that you'd go on seeing him, and risking things getting into a worse and worse mess, even though he'd already showed you that he was a tick?"

"I know I'm hopeless. But I'm simply a pushover for charm."

Molly's eyes had looked out pleadingly from under the hair, and Daisy, thinking that she was a pushover anyway, had temporarily left the subject. After all, the tapering off of this affair could really safely be left to Tibbs, who was not a pushover for anything except himself. He had been steadily contemptuous to Molly ever since the twenty-fourth of August, Daisy had worked out. She decided that the night of the twenty-third was the one that they had spent together.

It was a great nuisance (Daisy re-threaded her needle) that she could not find for Molly a young man who only wanted from a girl abject devotion, generosity without safeguards, and a romantic temperament. And yet, if such a young man could be supplied, would Molly's troubles be over?

She did not seem, as she often said, 'all that keen to get married', and—rather surprisingly, in such an ultra-feminine young woman—she appeared to shrink from the thought of bearing children. She avoided James Too on those rare occasions when he was sick, and she did not care to assist at his pot-training ('which is *interesting*, whatever other disadvantages it may have,' Daisy thought indignantly). Housework and cooking Molly found 'squalid'.

So it would have to be a young man wanting an eternal girlfriend who would never tire of romance or grow old. But Molly was thirty. She did not look it, yet she was. She would have to hurry up. Not that she seemed to mind being thirty; she dressed as if she were nineteen and shy, and ignored her years.

The two girls had met when Molly had been sent up from the typing pool to help Daisy in the office of the director to whom she was temporary secretary, in a large firm for which she occasionally worked. 'A scarf in this weather!' had thought Daisy, 'flying around in sheer black nylon, and all that hair! It looks like a *deformity*.' But it was impossible, after a time, not to like Molly. She was so amiable and humble and good-natured. And she did suffer from sore throats. Soon she was telling Daisy about Wilfred Mortimer.

Daisy heard about David Pinner; then about Reg, and the boy in the post office at Harrow, where Molly's parents lived, who was so good-looking. But after Tibbs had been introduced to Daisy, at a party given by one of her wilder friends, and after she had casually recommended to him, in the way she did, the house at Glenister Road because it was near the Heath and cheap, she heard no more from Molly about anyone except Tibbs, his gallantry and his charm.

And, as usual, it had 'led' nowhere, except to Molly's being set a little deeper into the pattern of her fate—sometimes, when she thought of Molly, Daisy wanted to cry with rage, against whom or what she did not quite know.

Tibbs had been wrong when he believed that Daisy might possess an excessive maternal instinct, but perhaps, as a foreigner, he could not be blamed for his mistake. Chivalrous women are rare; when they do occur, they are so often Englishwomen.

Daisy put down her sewing and looked thoughtfully, without seeing it, at the blue jug bought that afternoon from the junk shop in Brondesbury. It now stood in the window against a background of the immense plain of London spread out below, quite dark, and seamed and sprinkled with a myriad lights.

The front door bell rang.

CHAPTER III
"Yea, beds for all who come"

"CURSE," said James with self-control, putting down his paper, "I'll say you're out, shall I?"

"Oh yes, do, for heaven's sake, I'm so tired."

He looked at her searchingly, then went out into the hall. Both of them took it for granted that it would be one of her friends.

'I hope it *isn't* anybody,' thought Daisy, straightening her back. 'I'd like to go to bed.' Then she began to listen.

It was a man's voice, deep and blurred in tone. She did not recognize it and yet it was familiar. She could not quite make out what they were saying.

"It's Don Hulton." James, suddenly reappearing, looked ruffled.

"Don Hulton?" Daisy shook her head and looked blank.

"Says he was up at Oxford with you."

"What's he like?"

"Enormous—rather grubby—needs a shave," muttered James, whose rufflement was now explained.

"Oh, heavens—I'd better come."

Before supper she had put on a black silk skirt shaped like a bell. It rustled stiffly as she got up and went out into the hall.

The young man standing in the doorway, as if afraid to come into the house, was so broad that he seemed to fill it and so tall that his head was almost touching the lintel. His dark red face and his thatch of black hair and his broad chin—which certainly did need a shave—seemed vaguely familiar to Daisy, and yet she could not supply him with a background.

"Daisy?" he said, in that hoarse, blurry voice. "It is Daisy Furnivall, isn't it? I don't expect you remember me. At Oxford. Don Hulton."

"Of course!" Daisy cried (she just stopped herself from adding 'The Hulk'). "You were in your first term the year I went down. You used to go to Johnny Diss's parties." *(And sit in the corner the entire evening with that little Katy MacRae.)* "How nice to see you again."

She stood under the hall light, her greenish-hazel eyes bright with welcome, her wide pink mouth smiling, her simple evening clothes filling The Hulk with irritation. In the background stood James, looking not too forbidding. There seemed to be no doubt that she at least was really pleased to see him, yet the visitor hesitated.

"I'd better tell you straight off, Daisy—I want you to put me up for the night."

"Oh—er—" James moved into action. But he was not quite quick enough.

"I haven't any money now. I walked from King's Cross," Don Hulton added.

"Yes, of course we can," Daisy was saying. "We'd be delighted ... do come in and James will get you a drink while I make up the bed."

'His gloves—his black wool gloves with holes in—I can't bear it,' Daisy was thinking. 'And why hasn't he any money *now*? Mysterious! And James is going to be cross.'

"Thanks, Daisy," said The Hulk.

He came in, seeming to fill the hall with his shoulders and his dirty duffel coat and his green velveteen corduroys. (Nothing about 'hoping he wasn't being a nuisance'.) Pulling off his beret, he shied it down the hall so that it landed on one of the gilt pegs at the far end, and followed James into the living-room.

Daisy, rustling after them, remembered both his trick of making himself instantly at home by some such gesture and also his habit of continually using people's names in conversation.

"*Don't* keep calling me Daisy, *please*."

"It's your name, isn't it?"

"Even if it is I don't want it roared at me every three seconds." And then, unexpectedly, The Hulk—thus nicknamed by herself and her third-year friends—had said, "All right, Daisy, I'll try not to. I'm sorry, Daisy," and she had had to laugh, and from that evening (it had been at one of Johnny's parties) she had always said that The Hulk was not so utterly hopeless as he pretended to be.

She drew the curtains, trying not to see James's expression. The whole thing was quite maddening, and rather ominous too, for supposing he asked to stay on tomorrow? But in spite of the threat of a spoilt Sunday, James really *must* make an effort. He now appeared so unwelcoming that his manner was really rude.

She was certain, herself, that The Hulk was in some kind of trouble.

"Sherry?" enquired James, unsmilingly.

Daisy turned quickly. "Oh . . . I'm sorry . . . this is my husband, James Muir."

"Hullo," said The Hulk, nodding. (Trust him not to have changed, in five years, his chosen manner of greeting.) Then he said, smiling for the first time: "Well, I took that for granted, Daisy—judging by the set-up."

"Sherry?" patiently repeated James.

"I'd sooner beer, if you've got it. But what I could really do with is some food. I haven't eaten since breakfast."

"I'll get it . . . no, it's all right, thank you, James . . . we've got some beer, haven't we? and will soup and French bread do?" The Hulk nodded.

Daisy was half pleased to get out of the room and half wondering whether James would do or say something in her absence that would prove beyond all doubt that he was not even *trying* to make an effort.

She heated the soup, dirtying again the saucepan and bowl so carefully washed two hours ago, hunted up cheese and butter and a loaf; beer and a glass; loaded a tray, toiled up the tall narrow stairs.

They were sitting down, and apparently, thank goodness, James had not been outrageous.

"Mr Hulton is married to a friend of yours," he said at once, getting up to take the tray from her.

"Don," said The Hulk. "I've no time for gracious living." He began to break bread into the bowl of soup.

"Don," repeated James carefully, "is married to a friend of yours."

"Oh?" said Daisy. "Which one is that?"

"Katy MacRae," said The Hulk, and smiled for the second time, with his mouth full. "You remember Katy? That's right. Yes, we're married. Been married over five years now. Got three kids to show for it," and he laughed.

"You've beaten us," said Daisy. "We've only one, so far. He's asleep upstairs. But do tell me, how did you find us?"

"Katy kept your letter telling her you were married, with your address of this place."

"She never wrote to tell me *she* was married."

"No? Well, you know Katy. She hasn't kept up with her Oxford set much; she took it rather hard she didn't get a First."

"She took Chemistry, didn't she?"

"That's right. She didn't do too badly; second-class honours; but she was so dead sure she'd get a first, and she didn't want people talking to her about it. So she dropped out."

He paused, wiping bread round the empty soup-bowl. Neither of his hearers said anything. Daisy was wondering why Katy, most promising student of her year, had failed to do what everyone had expected her to.

"She took her finals at the end of my first year, if you remember. Then we decided to get married, and Mark started almost at once, and we couldn't live on my grant, so I chucked Oxford, and we came to London. I decided I'd get a job, and work externally for my A.R.I.C." ("Associate of the Royal Institute of Chemistry," explained James in an off-hand way, in response to an enquiring glance from Daisy and she, not for the first time, thought how many things he knew in comparison with herself.)

"I got a job on the strength of my work at Oxford, only naturally no one there was too pleased with me for marrying and starting a family, and it isn't a very good one (the job, I mean, not the family!). But when I'm qualified, I can get something much better."

"Who are you with now?" asked James.

"Eastern Electric. I'm an analyst. But it doesn't keep us anything like decently, and Katy can't get anything well-paid either. She could if she was single, of course, or even if we hadn't the kids. She was with a milk processing firm for some months early on, and that was decently paid, but then Mary started, and she was sick all the time and said she couldn't concentrate. I suppose"—rather grudgingly—"it must have been difficult. So she thought she'd try something a bit easier. She learned typing and shorthand in six weeks, and got a job with an estate agent in Brondesbury. It was shockingly paid, and they wouldn't keep her on when Maggie (she's our latest) started and Katy was sick all the time again—she'd been with them eighteen months by then and they seemed satisfied with her, but I think they were fed up her not being up to the work with the sickness. But they treated her better than the milk people did, on the whole; her boss there gave her a nice little lecture, all about how they preferred their women workers to be devoted to the firm and not distracted by divided interests (otherwise a family) and so forth—they seem to want a special breed of woman at that place, kind of a scientific Vestal Virgin or something." He glanced at the saucepan containing the soup, and Daisy, starting from painful thoughts about that little Katy MacRae turning out to work in the morning feeling sick, hastened to refill his bowl and hand him more bread.

"So you're both working in London now?" James said, passing the beer.

"I am. Katy isn't, not now. She was working, up till two months before Maggie was born—"

"Oh, is Maggie quite new?" Daisy cried.

"I don't know what you call 'new', Daisy. Maggie's six weeks. Katy's just out of hospital."

"But *six weeks* . . . did she have her on National Health? They usually only keep you in for ten days. Did something go wrong?" Daisy was beginning to feel that The Hulk's story was leading up to some disaster. James was thinking about the two spare rooms upstairs, which happened, for once, to be vacant.

"I'll tell you. It was our bitch of a landlady at Kilburn. Katy had Maggie on National Health, see, and normally she *would* have been out in ten days, but this old so-and-so—we'd been in these digs for over a year and Katy kept it dark, her being pregnant, as long as she could, because the landlady didn't *like* Mark and Mary, but even she couldn't say they were any trouble—they're good little kids, really, Katy's seen to that, and they've had to be, always in furnished rooms, poor little blighters—Mrs Watts wasn't too bad with them, at first. Katy was only working mornings, then, helping in a greengrocer's—"

"You mean, serving—vegetables and things?" demanded James.

"Yes." The Hulk's face, for a moment, as he glanced deliberately round the warm, pretty, luxuriously cluttered room, had a sour look. "She didn't like it and neither did I, but what else could she do? At least it did leave her the afternoons to get a lay-down, if she could, or be with the kids . . . Mrs Watts would give them their elevenses, and pot Mary, and that . . . and I'm bound to say nothing ever went wrong except the time Mark got at the matches . . . Mrs Watts found him playing with them—he didn't strike one—and she went yaketty-yak to Katy, of course, and Katy whipped him—pants down and cane and all."

Daisy was staring at him. He gave a not altogether comfortable grin.

"Yes . . . I thought it was a bit much, myself. But you know Katy. It isn't any use talking. Well, then she had a fall—"

"Katy?" said Daisy, swallowing.

"Yes, the stairs at that place were beastly dark and the old cow never would have the light on and there was a hole in her bloody carpet. So down Katy went. That started Maggie off two months before her time, and Katy had to get Watts to get the ambulance. Well, when I got back that night—while Katy was still in labour— the old so-and-so met me in the hall. She told me straight out, yelling at me like a fish-wife, that we must go. She wasn't having any squalling new babies in *her* house, not she. She gave me until Katy came out to find somewhere else, but when Katy did come out, yesterday it was (they kept her in so long because Maggie was so small and she was born with jaundice, too, as premature kids so often are, and she wouldn't feed properly, and I think myself they weren't satisfied with how Katy had come through it all)—well, as I was saying, old Watts was as good as her word. She turned us out."

He paused, and emptied his glass, which James at once refilled. He was wondering if Katy, Mark, Mary and the premature, jaundiced and pernickety Maggie would be in the spare rooms by ten o'clock that evening or delay their arrival until the following morning. It was now half past nine, and he had missed a particularly good boxing match on the Light.

"We hadn't anywhere to go," The Hulk went on. "I started straightaway, looking, the day Katy went in, but not a hope, not a smell of a hint of a hope. *You*—" he turned suddenly on James— "just try looking for digs, with two kids under five and a new baby. They won't even give you a trial. We might have been lepers. (I s'pose if we'd been dope-smugglers, or childless perverts, we'd have got in with no trouble.) I've been at it almost every evening and most weekends, when I ought to have been working, it's put me back weeks . . . oh, it has been a caper, I can tell you." He shook his head, like a horse bothered unbearably by flies.

There was a silence; on James's part from sheer apprehension, on Daisy's because her head was busy with plans.

"Is Katy very weak?" she asked at last, refusing to catch James's sombre eye.

"Katy's all right, Daisy. She's very strong, you know," The Hulk said, and James felt distinct relief at the news; he was sure that Katy would need to be. He glanced again at Daisy; she was gazing at their visitor with a flushed face and an expression fatally familiar. When he heard her ask: "Where are Katy and the children now?" he expected to hear that they were at the foot of the thirty eighteenth-century steps, awaiting the order to move in. But his fears were not realized.

"They're down at a hotel in King's Cross just for tonight, Daisy," said The Hulk. "A filthy place, but it was the only one we could get at our price—I had to have a taxi to get us away this morning, we haven't much, but there are my books and the kids' things—Katy hasn't had a new coat for six years," he added irrelevantly—"and that cleared me out . . . they did let the kids go in with Katy—charged for the baby, too, the bastards—but they drew the line at me. So I walked up here."

He paused. He seemed to be struggling with an impulse to say something apologetic, but all that finally came out was:

"Katy thought I'd better come to you, Daisy. You're the only person she knows in London who's got a house. She chanced your having a room."

"I'm so glad you did," Daisy said. She got up, and began to collect the plates on to a tray. "And tomorrow I'll see what I can do . . . I'll go and make up your bed."

"The water is hot," said James. It was bad of him, but he felt bad, in more ways than one. It was a bloody shame that these Hultons couldn't find anyone who would take them in because they had three children—but three in five years! It did seem rather—

unnecessary, surely, and haphazard. If there was one thing you did have to plan ahead for, it was children—not that he liked, or approved of, small families himself.

"Righte-o . . . I could do with a bath; the washing facilities and the plumbing at Watt's were pretty bad, and I feel filthy," Don Hulton said. James felt ashamed, and led his visitor up the narrow red-carpeted stairs in silence.

"What's his background?" he asked Daisy when they were in bed with the lights out.

Their undressing had been conducted almost without exchange of words but he had not seen her lower lip protrude or her long white neck rear up in silent defiance, and so he ventured to hope that the message he had been signalling—*don't make any rash offers, for God's sake; do think what you'll be letting yourself in for*—throughout their half hour with Don Hulton, might have penetrated.

"His father keeps a little news-agency in Reading—you know, cigarettes and newspapers and Aspro and a notice board outside where you put up things about charwomen for sixpence a time. He once won fifty pounds on the Pools and sent Don twenty-five pounds of it and that's really all I know about them."

"He doesn't sound too bad. Can't they go to him?"

"They really are poor, James, and I think Don's mother is rather a horror; she didn't like him marrying Katy and having all those children, he says. She's *ambitious*."

"Good lord," said James sleepily.

"Oh, only for money; she wanted him to get a very good job and look after her in her old age."

"He really is clever, then, is he?"

"Oh yes. He's pushed himself along entirely by scholarships. I don't think he's as clever as Katy, and she's a natural passer of examinations and he isn't. That's what we all thought when I was up, anyhow. That little Katy—imagine her in a greengrocer's! She could have been a don, we all thought . . . I expect she minds it like mad, not using her brain."

"I should hardly think she notices she isn't using it, in the kind of life she has to lead. It made my hair rise."

"Mine, too. With a new baby, too. (I wonder if she's nursing it herself? I hope so . . . getting the right feed heated in a ghastly dirty hotel . . .) Poor Katy. Not that you can *really* think 'poor Katy', somehow. She's *fanatically* independent. And she can be very prickly, too, in a cocky kind of way . . . I don't know . . . funny. She's so *serious*. I think," said Daisy, in a voice both portentous and struggling against sleep, "she's a really *good* person. She comes from a poor home—I don't mean low, I mean high-think-ing and just plain poor; her father is a minister in Glasgow, and she never had any clothes; she used to wear two frightful home-made dresses all the year round."

James made a lulling and sympathetic sound; so long as Daisy had not actually proclaimed an immediate occupation by the Hultons, there was hope.

"Tomorrow," added Daisy, and his heart sank, "tomorrow I must ring up Daddy about them."

"Why?" he asked, apprehensions on his father-in-law's behalf replacing those about the spare rooms.

"I want to ask him about a woman he's known for years. Mummy used to know her, too. Mrs Cavendish. She had a house in Charlotte Road and the top floor was empty."

'Thank God,' thought James, and diplomatically did not point out that it might not be empty now.

"She kept it empty," Daisy's voice was a series of fluting notes growing drowsier, "while she was looking for the right kind of furniture to furnish it really *beautifully*."

"Oh well, one sees her point, I suppose." (Bravo, Mrs Caven-dish. You have whatever furnishing notions you please, Mrs Cavendish, so long as your top-floor provides an alternative to our spare rooms.)

"So I thought I'd just . . ." The voice died away.

"He doesn't seem quite so bad as I thought at first," James said presently.

There was no answer, so he gently pushed his chin into her shoulder and went to sleep.

His first opinion of The Hulk was further modified next morning when they awoke to find him gone. There was a dirty cup and saucer on the draining-board, three eggs missing from the rack in the cupboard, crumbs on the kitchen table, and a note:

'O.K. Be seeing you. K will 'phone. D.H.'

"I hope so," said Daisy. "I'd like to see that little Katy again."

"Don't worry," said James, "I feel that you will."

CHAPTER IV
"Old footsteps trod the upper floors"

WHEN, after some days, 'K.' had not telephoned, Daisy thought that she would not, after all, trouble her father about Mrs Cavendish's empty rooms.

The Hultons might have managed to find somewhere to live after all; and also there was a strong feeling in the family (so strong that it had even conveyed itself to Daisy, in spite of her conviction that everyone should rally round to help her unfortunate protégés) against troubling Colonel Furnivall about anything.

He—content, useful in his unobtrusive way, with voluntary social work, even his holidays arranged for at the houses of old friends living in the country who had known his wife—should certainly be the last person to have his routine disturbed. It was such a blessing nowadays, said everybody, to find a person on the wrong side of sixty who was neither ill nor lonely nor in some way needing help! For heaven's sake, they all chorused, leave him be, and find some other way of getting information or advice.

Tibbs did not keep to his threat (Daisy regretted having to think of it in those terms, but there you were) of telephoning, and after a day or two she began to feel uneasy about him. Then, one morning about a week after Don Hulton's visit, she called up Molly Raymond and had news for her.

"And Tibbs? Have you heard from him lately?" Molly enquired, before Daisy could ask how she was settling in at Laurel House.

"He's all right. He telephoned this morning, actually. I was just starting to wonder if he'd been deported or something . . . Sara and Joe have got him."

"Those Jewish friends of yours? But—has he had another row with Grania?"

"I expect so . . . he's only with them for a fortnight but it will give him time to look round, he says."

"Oh yes . . . and it's all *copy* for him, isn't it?"

"What?" asked Daisy sharply.

"Getting into so many English homes, I mean. Copy for his book."

"What book? This is the first I've heard of it."

"Well, I don't suppose he wanted to bother you with it, Daisy . . . he's very *shy* you know, but he has his dreams . . . though it was my idea, actually," Molly ended, sounding, Daisy thought, exceedingly smug.

"What was?"

"Him writing a book about England. From the Continental angle, of course. I thought it was such a good idea—he's so witty, you know, and he says such amusing things about England, every so-when."

"Oh, does he?" said Daisy grimly. "Well, I think it's a perfectly futile idea and I shall discourage it all I can . . . how *could* you be such an ass, Molly? He'll never get it finished; it will hang around for *years*, and it will just be," Daisy's voice deepened warningly, as she uttered the gravest phrase in James's repertoire, "One More Thing."

"Oh . . . well . . . perhaps nothing will come of it . . . it was just an idea . . ." said Molly, placating and a little scared; Daisy was such a dear but she could be quite masterful sometimes. "How is he? Did he sound cheerful?"

"Perfectly. But he always does." ('Only it isn't real cheerfulness, it's a kind of sneering imitation of the English kind,' thought Daisy. 'Still, it's better than grizzling; anything's better than that.')

"He's so brave. It breaks your heart."

"Yes. How are you getting on?" Daisy asked.

"It's rather quiet after Glenister Road. But beautifully clean, of course. I haven't met your father yet."

"He isn't all that easy to meet. He's always busy."

"But I thought he had retired?"

"So he has. But he does two days' voluntary work a week with the London Council of Social Service, and he plays bridge a good deal, and he reads, and listens in quite a lot, and he often goes away for weekends."

"Has he got television?"

"James and I are giving him one for Christmas." Daisy felt that the ensuing silence implied disapproval. Molly's private picture of Colonel Furnivall did not present him as sitting glued to the Little Screen.

"I see a light in his sitting-room most evenings," Molly said at last. "His red curtains look so cosy . . . mine are very thin. I don't know what I'll do when the really cold weather sets in."

"Yes, all Mrs Brogan's seem to be." Daisy was wondering if she could find Molly a pair of thicker ones, but the house with the pink front door had not been "going" long enough to provide a store of disused, worn, warm curtains.

"But the bed's comfortable—I put my coat on it, nights—and I love my view across the trees."

"I'm so glad."

"Any chance of your coming in for a coffee one evening? It does get a bit lonesome."

Daisy said something promising and kind. She was thinking that it need not have got a bit lonesome if Molly had managed things better with Wilfred Mortimer and David Pinner and only heaven knew how many more . . . But she had to admit that her first impression of Molly flinging herself upon these gentlemen like a—what Daisy called to herself a *man-eating cobra*—had not been quite accurate: they had all apparently warmly welcomed the flinging, and in more than one case it had been Molly who had inaugurated and implemented the 'dropping' that had inevitably followed. Molly, Daisy had decided now, was not quite the typical problem-girl. And she was certainly no Delia Huxtable—Delia specialised in married men.

"Have you seen your cousins lately?" Molly asked. "Give them my very kind regards when you do, won't you? Not that they'll remember me, I expect."

Daisy made a soothing and incredulous noise.

"I thought there was a wonderful atmosphere of the gracious Past in that house. It was quite something—for me, at any rate."

"Yes, they're darlings. Look, Molly, I must fly—we're going to the theatre—I'll ring you up next week. Bye-bye."

"God be with you," said Molly.

She replaced the receiver and turned away from the telephone.

It stood on a massive table of black oak, heavily carved, on the black and white marble of the hall, and everything that she could discern in the dimness on either side, beyond the faint light of the lamp, was on a similar scale. It was the biggest house that she had ever been in; as big as a hotel, with a great staircase whose wide, shallow steps and iron handrail curved up and away into the maze of corridors, little flights of steps, and small rooms that filled the space about the great central well. After the autumn dusk had descended, it was so black up there! The weak light which could be switched on from below only burned for three minutes, and Molly would always finish the climb up to her room on the third floor in complete darkness.

A railed gallery ran round the head of the stairs, under the big skylight so thickly encrusted with the dust and the rain-drippings of years that strong sunlight could barely penetrate its glass, and along beside this rail she would creep, her natural slowness of movement increased by her fear of stumbling against something in the dark, holding fast to the ironwork which still bore a few faint traces of the gilding that had gleamed there ninety years ago.

Sometimes she would hear a door quietly open in the blackness, a ray of light would shine out, and a head would appear round the crack . . . only Miss Cazalet, or the old clergyman, Mr Plumtre . . . and although she resented, a little, the almost frantic inquisitiveness which had prompted the action, in another way she welcomed the beam of light and the silent, stealthy inspection. It did at least show that they were still alive up here, and, gradually, she was getting to think of these four or five poor, and usually invisible and silent, old people as her neighbours.

But her most persistent, if also invisible, companion, was the smell of boiled fish.

"They all live on it, I think. It's cheaper than meat and easier for their poor old stomachs to digest," Daisy had said carelessly, on the occasion of her darting up to inspect the room which Molly was to occupy. "But the *real* thing is that it reminds them of cats."

"Cats?"

"Yes . . . they all adore them, Mrs Brogan says, but of course she *can't* let them have them in their rooms (well! can you *imagine* what it would be like?), so they eat boiled fish and think about cats instead."

The smell haunted only the upper floors, never penetrating to the lower part of the great house where Colonel Furnivall and the two other prosperous tenants had their rooms (if it had, something would very soon have been done about it); lurking in the well-brushed but ancient carpets and the curtains, and settling steamily into the worn brocades of the settees on the landings; clinging along the wide expanses of wall where the ceiling brush, however vigorously out-stretched by the stout arms of Mrs Brogan's Irish maids, could never reach, and hovering in the airless regions under the lofty ceilings.

Molly tolerated it. Her nose was not very sensitive, and, also, she was usually smelling so sweetly herself that disagreeable odours were not noticeable to her. She bought scent much more frequently than most English women buy it: she was continually experimenting, never certain which flowery or spicy or 'sophisticated and challenging' perfume really suited her personality. Her dressing table always had two or three half-empty bottles, of which she had either grown tired or decided that they were 'not really me'.

This evening she accomplished the climb to her room surrounded by the smell of 'After Rain', which brought to you all the intoxication of a garden wet with a summer shower. She unlocked her door and turned on the light.

The small room had a kind of cosiness. There was no fire, of course, and the autumn night stared in suddenly through the dark windows, but the solid Edwardian pieces which Mrs Brogan had bought at second-hand were polished, and the carpet was swept. Molly had put flowers—from a man—into a ghastly vase with blobs on it. She looked around with a faint feeling of home-coming and comfort, and thought that she would re-read David's letter, which was in her pocket.

Wanting to start things up again. Wanting to take her to that new club where all the models went.

She threw her coat on the bed (she had paused to answer Daisy's telephone call on her arrival in the hall, as she got back from work) and lay down on it and took out the letter.

'Miss you still . . . started something in me that I can't put out . . . "Night and Day" . . .' and so on.

David certainly wrote a thrilling letter; the sort of letter, really, that girls wanted young men to write. 'But when you were with him,' reflected Molly, 'he wasn't all that . . . well, wasn't like his letters, that was all. Now Tibbs was just the opposite. Never said much, never wrote you even a p.c., but . . .'

Oh, *Tibbs*. Molly got up quickly and put away her outdoor clothes, then lay down again . .. And David, she was certain now, could never give her The Real Thing. (Her feet hurt. The new shoes were not comfortable.) Tibbs had been beastly to her ever since that night, and he would go on being. He did not want to give her The Real Thing, even if he could, and she did not think that what she felt for him was that, either; *she* didn't know what it was; she just knew that she felt, in a desolate way, that she belonged to him; and she yearned—yearned, repeated Molly softly—for his eyelashes and his cat's face and his thick, dusty-looking black hair.

She reached across to the dressing table without moving and thoughtfully re-drenched her face and neck with 'After Rain'. So he was with those Jews of Daisy's, was he, in Dean's Walk. It was only just the other side of Rosslyn Hill. She would treat herself to a supper out somewhere, this evening, and she might as well stroll down Dean's Walk afterwards. She could look up at the windows of the Meissners' house and wonder which was his.

There was a restaurant on one particular corner of Rosslyn Hill where, for the last few years, Colonel Furnivall had gone for his dinner on those evenings when he was not at his club or dining with friends.

This evening, on his way back from a few days' fishing in Herefordshire, he had decided—more from principle than from economy—not to pay the dwarf's fortune demanded by British Railways for a meal on their train, and had repaired by taxi to Laurel House, deposited his fishing rod and luggage, and come on to his usual table. He was now engaged in making up his mind between roast chicken and a mixed grill.

The white tablecloths, the waiters, the pink lampshades and the absence of a wireless and a modern decor made a suitable background for the spare man of sixty-odd, of medium height and dressed in thin greenish tweed, with white hair crowning a face whose skin had been yellowed by the Indian suns and whose round hazel eyes suggested, in their misleading expression of candour mingled with pensiveness, those of the late Sir Max Beerbohm.

He had a book on the table in front of him and, having chosen his dinner, he propped the volume against the thick glass water carafe—a small art in which years of reading while he dined in solitude had made him an expert—and began to read. He soon became absorbed. He did just notice, with the mild wonder that years of repetition of the experience had not lessened, when a young woman hesitated between four or five unoccupied tables and finally seated herself opposite to him; but he thought no more about her until, in the midst of an agreeable smell which he had for some moments been half-unconsciously inhaling, he became aware that she was mumbling at him.

Now Colonel Furnivall disliked mumbling, even as it irritated him when people, out walking, crept along the streets instead of keeping up a good smart pace. 'Speak up, please', was a phrase very frequently used by him in the past, and it would be again. So he said now, not testily, but rather unusually clearly:

"What did you say?"

"Excuse me, please . . . I said, could I just have the water, please."

"I beg your pardon," and he removed his book.

"Oh . . . thank you so much . . . but please don't let me disturb you." She was beginning to smile.

"If you are to have the water, I must be disturbed," said Colonel Furnivall, but *he* did not smile, and he allowed her to pour the water into her glass without any 'Let me do that, won't you?' When she had replaced the carafe, he propped up his book again and began once more to read.

Molly slowly ate her way through the plate of chicken which cost more than she had intended to pay for her evening meal. It had been a failure. She would never have come into this expensive place if she had not caught that glimpse, through the net curtains, of Daisy's father sitting alone in the glow of a pink lamp at an empty table.

She had expected him to pour out the water; then she would have introduced herself as a friend of Daisy's and he would give her a twinkling smile and say, "Oh, so you know my daughter, do you, young lady?" and *she* would go on to say that he was very like his sister, Miss Ella Furnivall, wasn't he? (he was, too; they had the same round eyes, only his hadn't got that almost mental look) and he would say, yes, people always noticed the likeness; and . . .

But it had all gone wrong; no water-pouring, no twinkling, nothing but what Molly called a straight look from those eyes whose expression was . . . not exactly sad. What was it?

Molly didn't know, and, sitting opposite him like this, she felt too embarrassed to indulge in those dreams about having coffee with him in his cosy den and seeing all his Indian Treasures, much less wonder about his being a widower and leading an unnatural life (she did not really like to think of his having a girl friend, preferring to imagine him as faithful to the memory of Daisy's mother); and now she would not even be able to say hullo to him when they met in the hall at Laurel House; she would have to get Daisy to introduce her formally.

She finished her peaches and cream in a choke, and hurried out.

'Thank goodness,' thought Colonel Furnivall. 'Smelt very nice.' He extended his legs more comfortably beneath the table.

In another quarter of an hour he finished his coffee and his chapter, paid the bill, and went out for a breath of air near the Heath before going home to bed.

As he went down Dean's Walk with his light, quick step, he was thinking about Daisy.

Although he loved her, it was perhaps more because she was so like her mother in appearance than for her own qualities, some of which he simply failed—he admitted it—to like or understand. He was alternately irritated and bewildered by her quickly aroused emotions and her lack of foresight, to say nothing of her violent prejudices in favour of the people she championed and succoured. Marcia had amused him once by telling him he expected Daisy to behave like a nice public schoolboy of twenty-eight.

Perhaps it was true, though, that he would have understood a boy better, and been fonder of him, too; they could have done together the things which they both enjoyed doing.

But the truth was that, since his wife's death, he had not been very close to anyone. Since Claire was no longer there, he preferred to endure the lack of her in loneliness; that was, in itself, in some way a kind of link with her, and he had never been a man who made intimates outside his own family. His younger brother Ned had been his closest friend, and he had been killed at the battle of Alam Halfa.

It had been staggering, losing Ned and Claire in the same year, utterly shattering, like the experience of being wounded almost to death in battle, to find, when he came home from India with his Army life behind him, that nothing was left of his marriage but Claire's grave, and the lovely, lively girl of eighteen, living in the care of his sister and cousin in the house at Primrose Hill.

'Daisy . . . I suppose,' he thought, 'I'm not always grateful enough that Claire left her for me . . . I've got loneliness because I prefer it, but if there weren't Daisy and James and the boy' (he meant James Too) 'I would *have* to be lonely, whether I preferred it or not. It's quite possible to imagine that you like something more than you actually do, and probably I find my life livable—enjoyable, even—because know I can run over to that pink powder-box of Daisy's whenever I like.'

He had, though—he had returned to thoughts about Daisy's character—he now believed, been 'slack' about the way that she had been educated.

He had given way to his conviction, secretly felt rather than openly expressed, that women knew how girls should be taught and brought up; and when Marcia and Ella (particularly Marcia, of course—poor old Ella could not be expected to have favourable views on the higher education of women but she had naturally supported her cousin)—when Marcia had insisted that Daisy must try for Oxford, he had outwardly agreed.

But his private opinion had been that Claire had managed very well without Oxford, and as for Daisy's *brains* . . . Marcia had said, *of course she can do it and she will*, but he believed that she was secretly surprised when Daisy had got in. She would not admit it, any more than she would admit to any disappointment when Daisy, emerging from three years of university life with a poor third, proceeded at once to fall in love and marry, showing throughout these experiences few, if any, signs of possessing a trained mind.

Colonel Furnivall admitted to a prejudice against the higher education of women—although nowadays, of course, when the future of any girl was under discussion, it wasn't even called that; it was simply called 'being properly educated'—and he knew why he had it: it was because of that miserable business, it must be all of fifty years ago, with Ella.

It had made on a ten-year-old heart what was to be one of the impressions of a lifetime. Night after night, he remembered, turning sleepily in the small hours to put away the volume of Henty or Rider Haggard that he had been reading by the light of a smuggled and forbidden candle, he had seen through the window, open to the summer darkness, *her* light burning across the courtyard; still burning, with an unquenchable glare that had vaguely frightened him, when he at last settled his head into the pillow and shut his aching eyes. There had been that wretched whisper—he could see her young, pallid face now—"I've been so sick again, Mother"; he could remember painfully clearly her expression of terror and strain.

No one, of course, had talked to *him* about it. He was the youngest but one; a small boy well-loved but also well-snubbed, with his own unimportant affairs at day-school and at home to keep in unobtrusive order; who should bother about him? But he had overheard things from time to time. Sitting at the school-room window, perhaps, on a summer evening, with, in front of him, the Latin grammar that had never given him much trouble, while his father and mother paused for a moment on their stroll through the gardens below.

"Thornton says there is no organic weakness."

"And it isn't as if there were even a trace of it on either side." That was his mother, her soft skirts trailing on the stone path as she paused to stare critically at the roses.

"It's incomprehensible to me," said his father and he sighed.

"She does *try*, Godfrey. Indeed I sometimes think that's part of the trouble. I've no patience, as you know, with the word 'nerves', but—"

"I should hope not." His father's thin, clever face was all distaste. "Well, we will give this new treatment a fair trial—say a month?—and then, if she is no better, I suppose any idea of Somerville must be abandoned."

"I'm afraid it will have to be." His mother's face, with its expression of intelligence and calm, was all puzzled sorrow and regret. "We can't go on like this. Apart from the unhappiness of it, people are beginning to talk."

Colonel Furnivall's love for his cousin Marcia dated from that troubled time, too.

Until that summer, when she came out as the champion of Ella, she had been to him an object of remote admiration, the beautiful grown-up cousin, clever (not that he thought much of that, because the Furnivalls all took cleverness for granted) and bold, and brave, who rode a black horse, and sculled on the river, and bowled overarm like a man.

He seldom saw her, for she was in her last year at College and led an extremely busy and crowded social and academic life, but on the occasions when he did, at some family party, he venerated her from his obscure place among the small fry and the hot milk and the buns, and felt gratified by her casual notice.

It was Marcia, he now knew, although neither she nor Ella ever 'reminisced' about the affair, who had burst like a comet, he imagined—because in early youth that was what, in her energy and beauty and fire, she had most suggested—into her cousin's affairs and bullied?—yes, there had probably been something of that—his parents not only into letting Ella give up all idea of working for admission into Somerville, but—a far more serious decision—any attempt to be formally educated at all.

It was thanks to Marcia that she had been able to decline—in a state of exquisite relief and content that soon began to shine in her manner and face—into being, first, the daughter at home, 'the home bird', in the words of the less intellectual cousins and aunts of the family, and then, by gradual stages and through the passings and changes of the years into 'Miss Furnivall, the younger one, who paints'.

If, when his father and mother were dead, and his uncle's family scattered, Ella, living on in the old home at Oxford with their servant Annie, had become in the eyes of strangers, 'that dotty old thing at the house on the corner', Colonel Furnivall did not know it. When you have lived side by side with someone for more than sixty years, you see them only with the eyes of the heart, and it would not even have occurred to him that anyone could find Ella so much as odd.

She could 'paint', too. He possessed one of her tiny watercolours, a sketch of his wife, smiling over her shoulder in a white blouse with a double row of pearls, that was *she*, herself. He very seldom took it out to look at it.

For all her scattiness, Daisy was a good child. But she would not be what her mother had been.

The Colonel was very well content with his daughter's marriage. James seemed to him rather a prosaic chap, for all his looks (if he had been a girl, the Colonel thought, his mind touching seriously for an instant upon this unlikely metamorphosis, *he* would have wanted something a bit more exciting); but James took good care of Daisy, and he worked hard for that advertising firm of his, and he was bringing the boy up to do as he was told. Well, I should hope so, reflected the Colonel, in whom thirty years of military service had left no theories about the glamour of disobedience.

He paused in his brisk walk. Across the road there stretched away into dimness and faint moonlight the expanse of the Heath. Autumn winds had swept the leaves from the great drooping branches of the willows bordering the road, and the dim light of a waxing moon fell across the distant pond, with golden lights reflected from the houses along its brink. And, hullo, there was somebody snivelling.

He peered into the shadows cast by the bushes in some gardens nearby. There seemed to be two figures standing there, a man's and a woman's, and he was quickly glancing away when the man, detaching himself from an outstretched hand, turned in at the gate of one of the houses and ran up the steps. The other figure turned, and in a moment began to walk slowly towards the light cast by one of the street lamps, while what Colonel Furnivall thought of as the snivelling grew louder. It was a heartbroken and a wretched sound, at that hour, in that light, and the Colonel could not bear it.

He stepped forward, and as he did so encountered a familiar sweet smell.

"Don't cry, please," he said, raising his cap, then: "We have met before, you know. In the restaurant, this evening. I passed you the water jug."

The fair hatless head lifted, large eyes smiled waterily among the folds of the muffler into which she had been crying.

"Oh—you're so kind!"

Colonel Furnivall made a soothing sound. It was exactly the sound he would have made to a distressed cat, in which light he regarded his present companion. Nothing but 'poor pussy, there, there' was omitted.

They stood, with the wind sighing around them. She had extracted a handkerchief, and was wiping her eyes and sending waves of scent out into the autumn-smelling night. Colonel Furnivall waited. (Never do to run off now. In for a penny.)

"This isn't as unconventional as it seems," she said at last. "I know your name, you see, and I'm a friend of your daughter's, and you—I—we live in the same house. So it's quite a coincidence."

In the same *house*? The evening suddenly seemed darker and the wind more chill.

"Indeed," he said. "Well, may I see you home? I was just on my way there."

This was not quite the reception of her news for which Molly had hoped; it lacked warmth even as it did pleased surprise; but her disappointment was overcome by pleasure.

"Oh . . . Colonel . . . you *are* kind. I was just feeling . . . but it's all right. Please don't worry about me. I'm sure all this must be most embarrassing for you."

"Not at all." Colonel Furnivall was now annoyed, rather than embarrassed; not only because it appeared that an inscrutable Providence had decided he should make this silly young thing's acquaintance but because her 'all this' implied more involvement in her affairs than he either wanted or was prepared to put up with.

But a woman crying in the dark—no.

"Come along," he said, and stepped briskly away.

"I *do* feel like an escort, I must confess," Molly said in a moment, wondering if she dare take his arm. (Better not, the first time, perhaps. How did he like his coffee? she pondered.) "And at least I shan't be taking you out of your way, shall I?"

"No," was the brief and joyless answer.

"I don't expect you've noticed me, because I only moved in Saturday week. But I saw you in the hall, Monday. And anyway I'm up on the third floor, way, way above your head. It's such an *enormous* great place, isn't it? Laurel House."

"Yes, very large; it has thirty rooms, I am told." They were now walking at a slower pace than the Colonel liked, because he thought she might need time in which to recover herself. But she seemed to have recovered rather quickly. She had put away her handkerchief.

"Fancy. The *servants* it must have needed, when it was in its prime. There are lots of little rooms up where I am that I don't expect *you've* ever seen, Colonel, all let out to poor old souls living on about tuppence a week. And it's so *lonely,* somehow, when you get home from business, evenings. That spooky great hall. And never a soul about. But it *is* all beautifully clean, isn't it?"

"Oh—er—yes, I suppose it is." If a few native quarters visited in the course of duty be excepted, Colonel Furnivall had never been inside a house that wasn't.

"It was so kind of Daisy to recommend it to me. She's a charming person, isn't she?"

"Have you known her long?" he asked, when he had recovered from this, wondering if the young woman was a typical specimen of Daisy's friends. (The ones whom he had actually met at the house with the pink front door had all been carefully screened by the prosaic James, and such rumours of Delia Huxtable, Tibbs and the rest of the Soft Core that had reached him were, so to speak, muffled—both by distance, and by his lack of personal experience of the post-war London jungle.)

"About six months. But it seems much longer—I always say she has 'the gift of intimacy'. We met at an office where we were both working. I'm a 'temp.' too."

"What is that?" The Colonel quickened his step; she seemed perfectly restored, even cheerful, and it did no one any good to crawl along at this pace.

"Oh, I'm sorry." Molly explained, then went on, "It's all right in summer, of course, when all the regular girls are on holiday, but round about November things get slack, and that's just when you want the work. Then what you pray for is a nice long 'flu epidemic. Have you escaped this Asian 'flu, Colonel Furnivall?"

"Yes, thank you. Er—have you?" (Rosslyn Hill, Glenister Road, Brynhilda Road, Laurel House. Not long now.)

"Oh yes, thank you. I don't get 'flu. With me, its nervous. The least thing, and I don't sleep. This last business—just now, you know, when you so kindly spoke to me, I mean—I don't suppose I've had a good night's rest since late August."

"Sleeplessness is very bad." Colonel Furnivall did not wish to discuss it, or sleep either, but the alternative was 'this last business', which would be worse. It was not that he really grudged giving the poor thing a few moments' polite attention; it was *what it will lead to*, as Wilmet Underwood used to say in his sisters' childhood favourite, Miss Yonge's *The Pillars of the House*. This young woman might come down from the third floor, and find some doubtless amiable pretext for knocking on his door. He did not get so far as imagining her actually gaining entry to his rooms; there were limits, even to pictured discomfort.

"It's funny your saying that, because your sister was saying much the same thing to me Saturday week," Molly said.

He could only stare at her. Ella? How on earth had she, of all people, come to be exposed to this style of thing?

"I expect you're wondering how I happened to meet her," said Molly humbly, being an adept at reading the slight changes of expression on a man's face, and apprehensive at what she now saw, by the light of the lamp beneath which they were passing, on her companion's. "But actually Daisy was so kind" (So it was Daisy; he might have known it) "as to give me a lift by taxi to Laurel House with all my bits and pieces and we called in at your sister's to borrow a book. Daisy wanted to lend it to someone she knows who's ill—fish-poisoning, I believe. The . . . the . . . you know you saw me with someone, when you so kindly came up just now? *He* was there, too," she added, as if compelled to make a confession.

There was no reply beyond a murmur proving that she had been heard. They were now passing through one of the maze of squares, avenues, gardens and roads which lie west of Rosslyn Hill and are all named after the former manor of Belsize, and on either side of them enormous houses of red brick, turreted and porticoed and gabled, towered up against the dim autumnal stars.

"*I* didn't like him being there, I can tell you," Molly went on rather desperately. "I know *you* won't be pleased to hear about it, Colonel Furnivall, either. He knows some very funny people. He isn't your sister's type of person at all, I know that; why, I don't suppose she's ever met anyone like him in her life before. But it isn't altogether his fault, you know—him having such . . . I mean, he's a refugee, you see, and he's had a very hard time . . . he's clever, really, he's a kind of chemist in his own country but . . . he doesn't seem to be able to stick in a regular job here, I don't know how it is . . . I suppose," she ended almost inaudibly, "he's got a difficult temperament. More the artist, really."

There was no reply. They were crossing the road. She felt the lightest of firm guiding fingers on her elbow.

"He hardly spoke to her, really. Just to say good-afternoon," she ended.

"A lot of these refugees are . . . very good types," said the Colonel, his indignation a little softened by her unexpected perception of what he was feeling, and by her defence of one who, judging by the evidence of this evening, had not treated her well. Poor girl, he thought. Loyal. No longer very young, either.

But he really had not known what commendatory adjective to apply—out of mere kindness towards her poor silly self—to this fellow she was defending. What *did* one say, collectively, about refugees? One could not even feel content to say that they were brave; a lot of absolute perishers were as brave as blazes. (But women always thought that if a man was brave he must be all right in other ways.)

"Here we are," he said, with a relief in his voice which Molly was now too disturbed to notice. Laurel House, looking square, white and enormous, with its brass knocker and letterbox winking deep within its shadowy porch, loomed above them.

"Oh . . . yes . . . shall I get out my key, Colonel, or will you?"

"I will," said he decidedly; the subject, with its intimate undertones, had no charm for him.

When they were once in the vast, dim entrance hall, they both glanced towards the great oak chest where stood the telephone, to see if there were any messages; she allowed him to pick up the sheet of paper which lay beside it, and in fact it was for him.

'*Colonel Furnivall.* Mrs Muir 'phoned at 8.15. Will you please 'phone her directly you get in. Important.'

Crumpling the sheet, he pocketed it without comment. The girl, he was relieved to see, was already standing on the lowest stair. He compelled himself to ask gently:

"All right now?"

"Oh yes, thank you. 'All better', as the children say. *Good-*night, Colonel . . . and thank you. You've been so very kind. It's . . . just made all the difference. I felt so *alone*."

She went up another stair, half-turned, looking down at him; Molly loved to see women poised on staircases in films, and this one was such a wide, romantic old beauty! Lucky to have the chance of it, really . . . "Oh, by the way, my name's Raymond. Molly Raymond" (slowly; yes, it was a pretty name) "Miss."

He should have said, 'Good-night, Miss Raymond. We'll be seeing something of one another from now on, I hope. Sleep well.'

But, now looking rather irritable, he merely nodded, and turned away down the short passage that led to his own rooms.

He was annoyed with Daisy. Dubious refugees . . . young women who made scenes with men in the street . . . thrusting them upon the household at King Edward's Road . . . he wasn't *going* to ring her up this evening, 'important' or not. Ten to one it was only some waster wanting a bed or a loan. Oh, she didn't often bother him directly with her lame dogs, but he knew. James might be a bit of a stick, but he had his head firmly screwed on where spongers and loafers and whiners were concerned and James had dropped hints . . . the Colonel knew that, on this subject, he and James were allies. James would approve this postponement. Daisy could wait.

Molly lingered at the foot of the stairs for a little while after she heard him shut his door. How dim the hall was, how chilly; how forbiddingly the lofty shadows towered up the well of the staircase into the regions hidden above. From far away in the basement, where Mrs Brogan lived in warm and comfortable widowhood, there came faintly the cachinnations of her television. Molly went slowly on up the stairs.

How cruel Tibbs had been; cruel and really *low*. It took a foreigner to say things like that; no Englishman would demean himself. Could you imagine Colonel Furnivall stooping so low? You could not.

He had been so kind, so gentle, so chivalrous. She could remember every note in his voice and every word that he had said. No wonder he had not liked the idea of Tibbs going to see the old ladies. You never knew what Tibbs might do to people, really.

No, there was nothing to beat Englishmen, after all, especially—Molly put out her hand, in the blackness, as the light on the landing below which only burned for three minutes abruptly went out, and began to grope her way up the top flight of stairs with the aid of the iron rail—especially English *gentlemen*.

CHAPTER V
Voice from Reading

ON THE day before her father's return to London, Daisy had been about to leave the house with the pink front door for the office where she was working that week, when the telephone bell rang.

'Damn,' she thought. But she could not resist halting upon the very doorstep while Janine toiled up from the kitchen to answer it, her mind running like lightning through the recent activities of the Soft Core. Delia?—recovering from that peculiar fish-poisoning. Tibbs?—comparatively safe with the Meissners and a job at Foyle's—she had got thus far when Janine appeared.

"Eez—Mrs—Ulton," she announced rapidly.

"Ulton?" Daisy irritably searched her memory.

"I—tell—'er—you—are—out?"

"No . . . I'd better come . . . it may be about those curtains . . ." She darted back into the house.

Ulton? She lifted the receiver and said, "Hullo?"

"Daisy? Is that you?" It was a low voice, with a slurred, faintly Scottish accent.

"Oh . . . *Katy*! That's Katy MacRae that was, isn't it? How nice, after all these ages. How are you? I've been hoping you'd ring up; you know Don came to us for a night, some weeks ago—and he said—"

"Yes." (Daisy remembered how one had always expected Katy to say 'Aye'.) "But we've been away. We're all right. Maggie's been ill. But she's better now."

"Maggie's the baby, isn't she?"

"That's right."

There was a pause. Daisy was thinking about the time, but she was also thinking how much she would like to see that little Katy again. The very individual voice, which three years of University life had never succeeded in modifying in the least, had recalled all the inexplicable attraction which Katy—her direct opposite in character, appearance, aims and tastes—had had for her in those days.

The pause went on, and Daisy remembered how Katy either took her time about telling you things or else, in her rare moods of exultation over some academic triumph (her triumphs over young men—and they were many—she never referred to), ran along at a great rate in a cocky way that was rather irritating. Now she was evidently going to take her time. But there was work to be thought about . . .

"I'd love to see you," Daisy said. "How about lunch today?"

"I can't, I'm only up for the day and I've got things to do."

"Oh . . . well . . . up where from?"

"Reading. We're staying with Don's people. That's why I rang up. I thought you could find us somewhere to live."

This time the pause was different. *Oh heavens*, was implied in Daisy's silence, and perhaps Katy felt it.

"You always knew so many people at College," she said; it was a mere addition to her previous sentence: purely explanatory, containing not a hint of apology for the absolute point-blank, unmodified nature of the demand, but at least it was an addition. 'Marriage,' thought Daisy, 'must have done *something* to Katy MacRae.'

"Well—" she began, trying to keep from her voice the depressing awareness of the successive dingy, icy, expensive attics and damp, dim, over-furnished expensive basements which she (of course it would be she) would have to inspect—and then she remembered Mrs Cavendish's top floor.

It must be brought forward at once. Never mind if it had been triumphantly furnished with Sheraton and Chippendale ten years ago, or if old C. no longer lived there at all—or if the roof had fallen—trot it out. If Katy were given some helpful fact to chew upon immediately, she was more the likely to feel that Daisy had done her share and could be let off further efforts.

To such an attitude had four years of helping her unfortunate friends begun to reduce Daisy Muir.

"I do happen to know of just one empty place," she went on, in a strong, cheerful tone, "at least, my father does—it belongs to a friend of his. He's away at the moment but I'll—"

"Unfurnished?" the voice seemed to pounce. "That's no good to us."

"I think it's partly furnished . . . or used to be . . ." Daisy tried to recall her impressions of the nest of small, shapely rooms grouped around a central landing, last seen six years ago, but could remember only the outline of an elegant, dark old chair against a white wall, a threadbare Persian carpet, the curved scroll-ends of a sofa covered in striped silk, and a general impression of bareness and airiness and chill.

"It'll have to be furnished," Katy warned, "we've hardly a stick of our own."

"Yes . . . I'll remember. The trouble is," Daisy's mind was now almost entirely on the flying time, "Mrs Cavendish, the woman who owns the house, wouldn't *dream* of letting rooms, I'm sure. She—"

"And it'll have to be very cheap," the grim young voice went uninterruptedly on. "Don's got to stay in this job until he takes his finals in January, and passes, and can try for something better . . . and it's got to be quiet, too. He works every evening."

"Yes—furnished (the difficulty is to find anywhere *unfurnished*), very cheap, quiet. I'll remember . . . look, Katy, I have to fly now, I'm late for work, but can't you *possibly* lunch today? Green Park tube station, Park side, half past twelve?"

"I can't do that, Daisy." Pause.

"As—as my—*with me*, of course," Daisy babbled.

"Thank you. But I can't," on a harder note.

"Blast you for a proud-stomached Scot, Katy MacRae!" burst out Daisy, with angry laughter, and was rewarded, amidst a rush of memories of similar occasions at Oxford, by hearing a faint, reluctant laugh from the other end of the line.

"Look—" she said, "how long are you going to be at Reading?"

"They can have us for another fortnight. Then it's stock-taking."

"And what's your address?"

"It's care of Mrs Hulton, 26 Dropmore Street, Reading, 6."

"All right. I'll get in touch with my father as soon as he gets home (you see, I *can't* really approach old C. about *letting rooms*— her name's Cavendish, by the way—when I haven't been *near* her for years), and as soon as there's *any* news, good or bad, I'll telephone you. What—"

"They aren't on the telephone."

"Oh—well, write you, then. By the way, isn't Don working in London? If I find you somewhere, couldn't he come along and look at it?"

"No. He's got to study every evening or"—Katy's tone was very calm—"he won't pass. And that would be—" She broke off, then went on, "But of course he'll pass. He's got to. You get on, Daisy, you'll be late for work. Good-bye then. I'll be hearing from you, and perhaps," her voice changed slightly, "I'll be able to manage lunch next time."

"Good-bye, Katy, and good luck."

'But it's me that will need the luck,' Daisy thought, as she flew down the thirty steps and out into the High Street. 'That little Katy! What a set-up. "They can have us for another fortnight and then it's stock-taking"—and Maggie "ill" at nine weeks . . . but *why* must she always sound so prickly? And never a word about sorry she's being a nuisance. Which she certainly is. Not that I want people to be *grateful* (disgusting word). But it does make doing things for them a bit easier if they'll only *realize* they're being a nuisance, and occasionally *say* so. Of course, The Hulk never apologises, and I suppose she's caught it from him. I don't remember her ever sounding quite so grim at Oxford. But I suppose she's had enough in the last five years to make her grim. I must telephone the aunts this morning and find out exactly when Daddy will be home.'

Here Daisy, having learnt from the clock on the tower of the former fire-station that the time was a quarter to ten and decided without dismay that it would be imperative to take a taxi, was fortunate enough to see one descending the High Street; and hailing it, sank upon its welcoming seat and was borne swiftly away.

It had not occurred to her to tell Katy that she could not find them somewhere to live.

CHAPTER VI
Ella

"WHO was that just now?" Marcia Furnivall enquired of her cousin, as she came into the living-room later that morning carrying a tray. The weather was fine and sunny, and Ella's preparations to take sketching materials out into Primrose Hill had been interrupted by the telephone.

Ella accepted the glass of wine and a slice of the rich dark cake. "Thank you. It was Daisy."

"What did she want?"

"She asked me if I knew when Godfrey will be home."

"It's tonight isn't it?"

"Tomorrow evening. I looked in my book and it was written down." A faint note of satisfaction sounded in Ella's voice. "This is one of Annie's very good cakes."

"Isn't it excellent. Did Daisy tell you why she wanted to know?"

"Yes. She wanted to ask him if Mrs Cavendish is still alive. You remember." Ella frowned slightly. "Mrs Cavendish," she went on, speaking slowly, "used to live in that thin, high, white house with marigolds all over the front garden, in Charlotte Road, didn't she? She had a daughter with a pretty name."

"Anthea. A very neglected garden; she detested gardening."

"Yes, Anthea. That was it. Anthea," said Ella.

"Claire used to know them."

"Yes, they were friends of Claire's."

"Not a close friend," Marcia corrected her. "Claire used to say that she *kept an eye* on Minta Cavendish . . . I really don't know why, I should say that she was eminently capable of keeping an eye on herself. I never liked her."

"Claire was afraid she wouldn't ever get . . ." As Ella's mouth was full of cake, her sentence was almost inaudible, and then she began to choke.

"What?" Marcia, from her graceful, lounging position in the chair that was always regarded as her own, looked with indulgent love at the odd small figure sitting upright opposite her. "All right, don't hurry, darling."

"Get . . . be a nice kind of woman, I think." Ella had gone red, presumably as a result of the choking. She sipped some wine.

"The last time I saw her," said Marcia, when her cousin had recovered, "I made her angry by telling her she ought to have had that girl properly educated."

"Didn't she go to school?" Ella asked, interested, as always, in hearing about any girl whose education had been improper.

"She went to an *excellent* school," with energy. "She was at Claregates. But her father died suddenly when she was only sixteen, you may remember, and her donkey of a mother, instead of scraping together every penny she could to have the girl trained for earning her living, talked about wanting her at home and marrying her well and that kind of thing, and took her away. And she hasn't married—at least, she hadn't when I last heard of them from Godfrey, and she must be twenty-seven or twenty-eight now—and she has a miserable little job teaching dancing at some place in Knightsbridge."

"Is she clever?" Ella asked, after a long pause in which thoughts about what the house in Charlotte Road might contain in the way of consolation for one whose education had been improper mingled with others, guilty as they were unhappy, about that broken-off sentence which had caused her to choke.

"I should think it very unlikely. Her mother is a fool; sharp, don't you know, and a fool. I have been out of touch with them for years. But I believe Godfrey hears from them at Christmas."

She broke off, not wishing to utter her next thought aloud, but Ella looked across at her wisely out of her round pale eyes.

"Is that because she hopes that Anthea might marry Godfrey?" she asked. "I expect it is."

"*I* think so," Marcia confessed, laughing and looking at her with her own eyes full of love. Bless her, she could always sweetly see through you; it was like living with a fey, self-absorbed, contented child. And her health was good, too: she never ailed in body. With one touch of her will, Marcia put a certain thought aside.

"She is a vulgar woman," she added, musingly.

"Mrs Cavendish?"

Marcia nodded. "I don't blame her for wanting Anthea to marry 'well'; I suppose that's perhaps part of a mother's duty; but I do blame her for wanting to secure such a poor type of man for her (money and social position appeared to be everything) and for not seeing to it that she was equipped to earn a decent living if she didn't marry. Of course, for all I know she may *be* married. She used to be unusually pretty."

"As pretty as Daisy?"

"Ah, no. Not so pretty as Daisy—though in fact Daisy's prettiness is mostly vivacity and health; she has a *funny* face, by the standards of our day, although funny faces are fashionable . . . Hadn't you better be off, if you don't want to miss the best of the day?" The cousins always lunched lightly and early, while Annie was out collecting the house-hold shopping, and dined, with some formality and the donning by Ella of an old necklace of sapphires, at seven; this gave Ella a long afternoon for her painting.

Her large sunny room next to Marcia's overlooked the green slopes of Primrose Hill. It was crowded with the tiny watercolours, the painting of which had been her chief occupation since childhood; some of them were little larger than those tail-pieces which decorate the blank spaces in nineteenth-century volumes of verse or adorn, in the shape of a panel in which a capital letter is contained, the opening of a new chapter in some forgotten novel.

The little pictures were nearly all landscapes—street-scapes, rather: rows of the crumbling brown or white houses which, with their curtained secretive windows and their flight of grey stone steps leading up to a dark and heavy door, belong typically and unmistakably to older London. But there were other subjects too: lengths of ancient wall, expanses of grey paving stones wet with rain whose every crack was depicted, great aspen trees whose myriad silver leaves almost covered the paper from edge to edge, gutters where orange peel glowed, roads paved with damp cobbles. Sometimes Ella painted sparrows or a stray cat; sometimes a dog;

very rarely people. Her tiny landscapes were usually as bare of human life as if everybody were indoors and fast asleep. An astonishing delicacy of treatment, the reduction to a miniature size, and also a quality, difficult to convey in words, of each picture being dominated by its own particular light, was common to all.

Painted upon a smooth, thick paper, glowing with colour and marked with precise, delicate shapes, thousands of them were falling out of the rows of shabby brown portfolios arranged against the walls of her room. Boxes in her wardrobe were filled with the little things. A view of London from Primrose Hill, clear and grey and tiny as if viewed through the wrong end of some fairy telescope, looked up at her now, as she opened the dressing-table drawer to look for a hairpin. None were framed or displayed in any way in the cousins' flat. The only picture on her wall was Henry Holiday's famous one of Dante's meeting with Beatrice.

Annie called the little paintings 'Miss Ella's rubbish'.

This morning Ella did not feel as happy as usual while she walked slowly up the short ascending road that leads on to Primrose Hill. The board which served her as easel felt awkward in its position under her arm, the forty-year-old schoolgirl's satchel, holding her paint-box and water bottle, tapped against her shoulder as she walked. This morning the sensation, so familiar as usually not to be noticed, was irritating.

Claire was afraid she wouldn't ever get to Paradise. It was the last two words of that rash sentence that had caused her to draw in a breath of alarm, and choke over her cake. *(Deceiver. Liar, Sneak.)* There was also something, wasn't there, about 'bearing witness'? Oh dear. And if she *had* gone on, if she had finished that sentence without choking, what would have happened? Nothing; except that Marcia would have supposed she (Ella) had been reading *The Divine Comedy* again, as she did three or four times a year, wandering through a shelf-full of translations by many scholars which she had beside her bed. Marcia was used to quotations and stories from that book being brought into Ella's conversation; the words might vary according to what translation she had read last, but Dante's thought, Dante's people, remained.

Marcia, who read Italian as easily as she did English, loved to hear Ella quoting Longfellow's or Burton's or Sayer's version, and Ella knew that she loved it, and sometimes when the longing to speak of heavenly things was strong upon her, she would speak of them to her cousin through the voice of him of whom his fellow citizens said: "There goes the man who has been to Hell."

Coward. Deceiver. Cheat.

Ella plodded on up the rise. Behind the black trunks of the trees bordering the road, each laden with its fragile golden leaves that the first frost would send silently floating earthwards, the panorama of London was beginning to unfold, bathed in a noble clarity by the autumn light.

Hobbling, panting slightly now, guiltily allowing her guilty thoughts to fade before the stillness and beauty of the morning, Ella reached the summit of the hill, and began to set up her materials for work.

The picture was of the highest branches of a mighty aspen, whose leaves, scarcely moving in the wind that came straying through the soft air dimmed and thickened by London smoke, yet sent down an almost inaudible rustling from up there in the deep blue. Its likeness began to grow; Ella's gift had been patiently trained by good masters, and the branches were drawn in with the surest of light strokes. Now, as she loaded her brush with rich gold, the feelings of guilt and shame had almost passed, and while she put in her first minute touches of colour and washes of clear blue, she began to murmur to herself; always lines of poetry and always about the season of autumn. "A spirit haunts the year's last hours, Dwelling amid these yellowing bower"—"Heavily hangs the hollyhock, heavily hangs the tiger-lily"—"Conspiring with him how to load and bless" . . .

Her strange old face, that was so often agitated by moods of terror and secret amusement and delight, gradually became as calm as the scene around her, and when, now and again, she looked out from under the hat bought for her thirty years ago by her mother at Scotts', at the soiled and trampled grass, the fading leaves choked with soot, the dilapidated ancient houses at the foot of the hill now being steadily shaken towards complete ruin by the passing traffic, and the sodden newspaper and stained cardboard scattered on the paths, they carried her, by their marvellous beauty, into an exquisite dream.

Occasionally someone drew near and peeped at the little picture over her shoulder. "Life-like, isn't it?"

"That's effective."

"Come and look at this, Jean." They were mostly young mothers with children, out for an airing. Ella took no more notice of them than an occasional half-turn of the head and uneasy smile; she did not make her boredom and her dislike obvious, yet soon the visitors drifted away. There was something strikingly unwelcoming in the air, the silence, of that dumpy figure in its almost grotesque clothes.

And when they had gone, Ella felt guilty again. "And thou shalt love thy neighbour as thyself."

Love? She feared and disliked her neighbour; she did not understand them; she never could. In over seventy years she had learnt—with how much effort and pain!—to behave kindly to them in public, but in private her mind's eye continued to see them as mysterious and slightly unpleasant creatures, whose inexplicable behaviour and motives were made the more bewildering because they could talk.

Courtesy to these beings, however, was another matter. Ella was courteous to everything living—because she had been properly brought up in a gentle home.

Sometimes, in her anxiety to use courtesy as a substitute for love in her dealings with her neighbour, she 'overdid it', and the oddness of her concentrated glare and her eager enquiries after their welfare slightly alarmed her hearer, as they had Molly Raymond.

No one, on the strength of the fact that she was almost unfailingly polite, had ever called Ella a dear old lady.

She was a stranger, and content to be. She had known it since that morning more than seventy years ago when she had suddenly *woken up*, at the age of three, to find herself bathing one of the tiny wooden animals belonging to her Noah's Ark in a saucer of milk at the nursery breakfast-table. The exquisite sensation of absorbed content in what she was doing, *mingled with the knowing that she was doing it, and happy,* had arrived at the same moment. Dawn! She was in this world, and she knew it.

She leaned forward now, and just touched the underside of a twig with a colour that would make it look shadowy. There, that had gone exactly right. She began to feel happy again.

But then, she usually was happy, unless someone from outside was compelling her to learn something.

Oh, those summer evenings in Oxford more than half a century ago! Even now, fifty years later, the memory in her mind's eye of certain women's clever faces, of certain stained, rubbed pages in certain books, caused her head to grow hot and feel as if it were beginning to swell; as if it were all yesterday . . .

She used to sit in her room with the book in front of her on her desk and her head in her hands. Godfrey's room was just opposite her window, in the little wing that projected across the garden, and she would watch his light burning; very late, it would be, the leafy road outside silent and still, the many clocks of Oxford tolling now and again—loudly and near, or faint and far away—the passing hours of the warm night.

Godfrey's light would go out. (He had been reading; she never 'gave him away'.) The tears trickled down again between her fingers, making the cruel, mysterious, alive symbols dance and blur on the page. One—two—three rolled out from a distant tower. Very soon it would be light—and then again the hopeless questioning, the failure, the agony of guilt. Poor tears, so weak, so burning. She wept again for their helplessness.

Sometimes there would be people out there, talking under the two great elms—"And groups under the dreaming garden-trees"—friends of Walter's of Ned's, a girl or two who might be staying with Alice. Ella could see them from the other window in her room, and their voices and laughter floated up to her; then the sound of her father's voice or Marcia's, and a hush, followed by yet livelier conversation.

Only—on the evenings that Marcia was in the garden Ella did not stay up in her room. Her cousin would stride upstairs, with her full white skirts rustling along the bare boards of the passage

as she came, and unhesitatingly open the door and put round it
her tall head with its thick loops of brown hair.

"Darling? Come along out."

"I must learn my Chemistry."

"Not this evening." She was all decision and straight shoulders
and energy, like a young soldier. "I saw a moth you would like
just now; he's still there, hovering about. So down you come!"

"Oh, Marcie—" Tears again. But the book was put away and
the desk shut, and Ella bathed her face and smoothed (as if that
ever did any good!) her hair. And as they went along the passage
side by side, with the bearded faces in the photographs of cricket
teams in which their fathers had played looking gravely down at
them from the walls, strong fingers would link with Ella's and
swing them blithely.

"That moth must be quite two inches across; we'll have to
look him up."

"I love you."

"Hush . . . I love you, too."

Too; as well; I also love other people. Ella had had to share. If
Randolph Gurney had not been killed in South Africa she would
have had to share with a husband and children. But he had been
killed, at twenty-six, 'in circumstances in which he displayed
gallantry of an outstanding kind', and as a result Ella had only
had to share with nursing, and forty years of public work, and the
entire nation that, before 1914, had been called Serbia. She had
been fortunate in having a very large share, throughout her long
life, in the only human creature she had ever loved.

Because it could not really be said that she had 'loved' the
Reverend Arthur Currey, whom after all, she had only known for
four hours. Yet when she thought of him, as she often did, she
always repeated to herself 'I love you,' and perhaps it was only
in the eyes of human beings (those incomprehensible creatures)
that her feelings for him would not have appeared as love.

Marcia was so *clever*. The pages of cruel and mysterious
symbols, filled with their own spiteful life, that caused the poor hot
tears to run down Ella's face, caused Marcia to exclaim "Ha-ha!"
like the war horse scenting battle, in the Old Testament. Marcia's

clothes fitted her tall upright figure, her hair was always smoothly looped and shining. She not only seemed comfortably at home in her body; she managed it, and controlled it, and made it do as it was told.

Ella, moving uneasily, became aware that one of her suspenders had mysteriously detached itself from its stocking, which was beginning to descend. But she was too contented to pay much attention to it yet.

For she was very used to such tiny personal mishaps. There never was a creature less at ease in her own body—and even uneasier in her clothes—than Ella.

Her hair, for example: in youth it had been an unmanageable pale mass of greenish gold, whirling about her face at the lightest invitation from the wind. (Ella still did not like to think about those balls of frizz resulting from the 'good strong perm, miss' prescribed by Annie when they had been living alone together in the house at Oxford.) Now, in old age, it hung about her face in short, limp strands as unbecoming as they were unsuitable.

Her petticoats broke their supporting straps and slipped from her shoulders, her blouses escaped from the most carefully adjusted belt, her stockings 'went' mysteriously into holes, great 'potatoes' and 'ladders' that caused other women to stare in amused surprise that sometimes had a hint of distaste.

Formerly she had had her clothes chosen and bought for her by her kind, clever, handsome mother, and, as they were always of the very best quality, many of them, surviving Ella's habits of sartorial misfortune, had fingered on to be worn in the atomic age. Faded, old-fashioned and shapeless, they covered her stout form warmly in the winter and coolly in the Summer. Indeed, they were her old friends, and it was not her fault if, while she was wearing them, they were exposed to grave risks. They ought, she often mused, to be used to that by now, but they never seemed to learn any better.

Presently she heard a distant bell, and, looking up, saw that groups of children were beginning to idle along the paths running across the foot of the hill. That would be four o'clock; school was out. She cleaned her brush for the last time. The little picture of golden leaves against a blue sky was almost finished; it could be completed at home, and tea was at half past four and Marcie would be in. Now put away the box and the water jar.

Now the stocking; it would have to be rolled down and arranged just above her shoe (made, by hand, from brown calfskin). The day was warm; she would take no harm from walking through the streets with one leg bare, and she was accustomed to being stared at. While she was adjusting it, she looked, not down at her foot, but out across the slopes of grass faded to soft fawn by the summer heat and, beyond, to the white terrace behind the trees. A faint mist had crept into the air with the declining of the sun; the peach colours in the sky were reflected back from the leaves, and the humble paths winding across the thick pale grass, and the frail old countenances of the houses. *'I'll come out early one morning next week; it's at eight o'clock, the church notice-board said. I can be home by nine if I hurry, and I haven't been there for six weeks.'* She saw a picture of Marcie, sitting back in her graceful, 'un-womanly', lounging pose (that had come in for some criticism, fifty years ago) behind the silver teapot and the Japanese cups. *Well, did you have a good afternoon, darling?* Her tall, bright, protecting girl. Ella saw the loops of brown hair shining in the evening light. She had said, "I will always take care of you," and since she had said that so many years ago, Ella had never really felt frightened again.

Suppose Marcie knew? Suppose she found out? *Would* she be angry? She had never been angry with Ella in all their lives long, but she *could* be angry; Ella had seen her angry with other people, and the sight had as nearly frightened her as anything could since she had been taken into Marcia's protection.

It had been going on for such a long time! More than forty years. That was not like a deception which started last week . . . such secrecy, maintained for so long, was enough, were she ever to find it out, to shock even someone who loved Ella as much as Marcie did.

But as she hurried down the path through the fading autumn light, under the great misty London sky of orange and apricot and dim rose, it was, as usual, not sensible reflections, and conclusions about the facts of the situation, that gradually turned Ella's thoughts into their usual happy groove but the beauty of the streets, and their lonely, pale, bare paving stones.

CHAPTER VII
Daisy looks so like her Mother

"He's annoyed with you."

"Why, in heaven's name?" It was an indignant flute-note, but Daisy herself had been suspecting that very thing. Two days had passed since she left her message at Laurel House asking her father to telephone, and there had been no sign.

"Because," pronounced James, with whom she was having this conversation at breakfast, "you unloaded Tibbs and that seduced character on King Edward's Road. You may remember I told you not to."

"It didn't upset them, and it's not the first time I've taken people there who were in a hole."

"It would have upset them all right if they'd had Tibbs to stay. They'd have had to boot him out, I'll bet."

"You haven't any *right* to say that . . ."

"Doesn't he always have to be booted out?"

Daisy was silent.

"Well, doesn't he? Where is he now?"

"He was at Joe and Sara's, but—"

"But they had to boot him out. Exactly."

James, with an expression whose careful lack of smugness was infinitely more infuriating than any indulgence in it, lit the after-breakfast cigarette.

"Why are you so down on Tibbs, James?"

"Don't like the type."

"He isn't a type, he's an *individual*. That's just his trouble. That's why he came over here three years ago. He couldn't stand having to live like everybody else. He was sick of being *regimented*—"

"He came to the wrong place, then," muttered James. "Don't be so *ridiculous*. Just because the pubs close at certain hours . . ."

"I am no pub-crawler, Daisy, as you know. What I complain about, in England—" began James luxuriously.

"Darling, I *do* want to listen, but I'm booked for twelve o'clock at the Dorchester today and I simply do *have* to hurry . . ."

"—is the food tasting the same everywhere, and the people all doing the same things everywhere, and the newspapers all sounding the same everywhere. Now in France . . ."

"James, I *must* fly. I'll argue with you about France this evening."

"Women always start an interesting argument and then say they have to fly. And we're going to the Ruddlins' this evening."

"I am *not* 'women'!" Daisy's voice came back indignantly as she darted up the narrow stairs.

James laughed. But as he looked round the gay little room where the canary was trilling in the sunlight, the laugh was replaced by a frown. The electric fire was burning to capacity—not necessary on such a warm morning—and there had been three bills in the post: telephone, repairs to the house's two-hundred-year-old roof, and seventeen pounds-odd to a firm for what he rudely thought of as 'slinging a few bucketfuls of earth into the garden'.

He put the envelopes away in his desk on his way out to the front door. The roof experts and the telephone should be paid at once, with an effort; the landscape gardeners could damn well whistle for a month or so.

The hall, with its narrow exquisite proportions and its walls painted the soft golden yellow of a Mermaid rose, seemed to shut him in this morning. The house felt too warm. When he opened the pink front door, he saw the smoke blown sideways by a strong wind in the fast-moving sky. He picked up his bowler; it needed a brush.

"James?" Daisy ran down the stairs.

"Hullo. Where's the clothes-brush?"

"Down behind the table, I expect . . . yes . . . here you are, hat. Let me do that." She took the hat, then glanced at him. "What are you thinking about? Sailing?"

"That, and other things. The sea, anyway. What a morning to be stuck in Thretton Street talking about consumer-research."

"Poor poppet . . . We might go and walk somewhere on Sunday."

"I don't want Buckinghamshire, I don't want anywhere in England at all, I want thousands of miles, with the sea as well." He opened the door, which he had shut while Daisy was attending to his hat. A crowd of dead leaves ran past in an orderly flock along the pavement, tinkling dryly as they ran.

"I'll see you at the Ruddlins', then, about six," Daisy called after him, and he turned to wave to her. Pretty thing . . . darling Daisy. But wasn't that a new dress? The wind, blowing up from old, smoky, crowded London, met him full in the face as he set off down the street.

The dress, in fact, was a suit. But it was certainly new; Daisy had bought it only yesterday.

This week her services as temporary secretary were bespoken to an American business man with a very great deal of money and she thought it only good policy to look her best. (Daisy scarcely knew what it was to feel shy or ill at ease, and she did not need to rely on clothes to give her the confidence which she never lacked.)

The purchase had, strictly speaking, been a piece of extravagance and she knew it. She owned a large wardrobe, of which she took good care, and hardly ever found that she had not right clothes for an occasion. The fact was that buying clothes was one of her great pleasures, and although she did not go to the most expensive shops, she did go to a great many; and when she was going to a party at Sue Ruddlin's there was this business of never letting Sue see her in the same thing twice . . . she could not yet really *compete* with Sue, of course, who was beginning to go in for mink and diamonds, but she could at least never let Sue see her looking anything but immaculately elegant and prosperous.

There was occasionally playful talk of James Too being later on betrothed, in spite of nearly three years' seniority on her side, to Susan's Vanessa. 'Over my dead body,' thought Daisy, as she came out into the hall again, 'she'd eat the poor poppet alive; those carroty girls are always madly possessive . . .'

About half past four that afternoon, Colonel Furnivall, who had just come in from one of his days with the London Council of Social Service and was changing his street shoes for slippers while awaiting the arrival of tea, heard a taxi draw up outside Laurel House. 'That's Daisy,' he thought, for taxis were not wont to stop there and he had been anticipating some such swoop upon himself.

"Hullo, Daddy. Cross with me?" asked his daughter, giving him a cheek to kiss that smelled faintly of scent and air-cooled girl.

"Not cross. Mildly annoyed. You know I don't like your worrying your aunt and cousin with these people of yours."

"So that's it . . . James said it was. Is that why you didn't telephone?"

"I presumed you only wanted to worry me about some lame duck or other." He settled his left foot more comfortably into a neat slipper.

"But how did you know about it? They haven't been complaining have they?" asked Daisy, letting his insinuation—how fatally true!—slide past unanswered.

"I haven't seen them since I got back. I—er—a young woman, a Miss Raymond, who seems to be one of your friends, has come to live here. She told me that you had taken her to King Edward's Road."

"James warned me that she would get on to you," said Daisy, looking suitably concerned. "How do you mean—*told* you? Did she come up and introduce herself?" in a steely tone. Molly would have to be given a rather large rocket.

"Not exactly. She came and sat opposite to me at Orsini's, while I was having dinner, and asked for the water-jug, and afterwards I was able to—I came across her in some sort of trouble, crying and that kind of thing, at the bottom of Devonshire Hill, and I saw her home."

"*Crying?* What was the matter? Really, she is . . . was there a man with her?" *(I'll bet that was Tibbs.)*

"I believe so. Yes, there was—or so she said. I didn't really see him. She did make some reference to troubles, but it wasn't my business . . . I didn't encourage her, I'm afraid."

"I should think not . . . I'm sorry, Daddy."

"It hardly matters. I see her only very occasionally; in the hall on my way out, and when the telephone rings. That sort of thing."

He was not going to say, when he recalled Molly's manner and expression, that it did not matter at all. But, studying his daughter as she leant back in his armchair, with long legs crossed, and breeding, intelligence and authority in every line, he did rather wonder what she could possibly 'see in' poor Miss Raymond.

"You mustn't let her cling. She is rather a clinger."

The possibilities implied in this remark seemed sufficiently remote to Colonel Furnivall to justify him in ignoring it. He glanced at the clock.

"You wanted to talk to me about something important. Is it still important?" he enquired, with the 'twinkle' for which Molly had looked in vain. Daisy looked such a satisfactory young married daughter this evening; just for a moment, he was off his guard.

"Oh yes . . . very important." Her eyes followed his. "I've got to get home . . . bath James Too . . . do my face . . . but I *must* tell you. Can you spare a minute?"

While she was pouring out his tea, which one of the Irish maids now bumped down upon the table and which she declined to share with him, she told him briefly about the Hultons and their plight. She kept her eyes fixed on his face while she was talking, and what she saw gradually settling there was not encouraging. But she had expected strong opposition, and she was prepared to overcome it. She added, forcefully, at the end of her tale:

"You see, they really are in a terrible hole, Daddy, and they're the kind of people one *ought* to help—what you would call 'our own kind'—educated and with the right values, and then three small children . . . they aren't selfish or vulgar or greedy . . ."

"Yes, yes. But what do you want *me* to do about it?" he asked, with a trace of impatience. "Do you want money? I can let you have a cheque; not much, but something. Would a fiver be any use?"

"That's so kind of you, darling." (Poor Daddy; his generation never could realise how tiny a drop, in how terrifyingly large an ocean, a fiver had become.) "But I'm afraid I want something far more difficult than just money. Do you still hear from Mrs Cavendish?"

"Minta Cavendish? I get a card from her every Christmas. But I haven't seen them for—it must be getting on for four years."

Colonel Furnivall paused. He was wondering very much what could possibly be coming.

"Didn't she have three or four empty rooms at the top of her house?"

"I believe she did, yes; kept them empty because she hadn't the right sort of stuff to put in them. The rest of the house was full of really good things; there were some fine old pieces, I seem to remember."

"And wallpaper by William Morris."

"Yes, in the drawing-room. You have a good memory."

He looked at her approvingly, but now he was on his guard again.

"And Anthea taught dancing."

"Yes, a very pretty girl. But what's all this leading up to?" He looked at her steadily out of round, calm eyes that were just a shade lighter, in their clear greenish hazel, than her own.

"I thought she might let those rooms to the Hultons," Daisy said.

He did not say anything for a moment, and she, too experienced in asking people favours on behalf of her protégés to keep her eyes fixed irritatingly upon his face, looked out of the window.

How extraordinarily difficult communication with the older generation could be. Why, for instance, did she have to tell him that the Hultons were 'our own kind', an expression which made her feel slightly sick. Wasn't it enough that they were poor, and had three small children and nowhere to live?

"I'm pretty sure she wouldn't want to do that, Daisy," he said at last.

"You see"—eagerly—"I thought of her partly because we *know* her, and I shouldn't have to go chasing all over London looking for somewhere for them (I'm so busy now I don't know *how* I manage to fit everything in each week, and all the time it gets *worse*). And I expect she'd be glad of the money. Didn't you say something once about her being left not very well off? And she's a lady—well," as he slightly moved his head, "near enough, and that will make her nicer to them—easier to deal with. And the house is in a quiet neighbourhood and I expect they would be the only lodgers, don't you? (It *must* be a *quiet* house,

because Don—that's the husband—is working for an examination, as I said.)"

Daisy paused. She still had not got around to the most difficult
part: the request she had come there to make.

"Minta must be getting on, you know," he said suddenly, as
if in comment on the entire scheme.

"Oh, I don't mean for a minute that she should do
anything *for* them. Katy would do everything. I just meant that
she might let them have the rooms."

"It is just possible," he resumed cautiously, "that she might be
glad of the money. She lives on a fixed income; her husband left
them moderately well off, but his death was very sudden and it
was thirteen years ago . . . fixed incomes have taken some nasty
knocks since then, and the girl's work can't bring in much. But
as for taking in lodgers—frankly, Daisy, I can't think of anything
that would horrify Minta more. And I still don't see—where do I
come into all this?"

"You might prepare the way by writing to her for me," Daisy
said very quickly, glancing at him and then away again.

"*I* might? Really, Daisy—"

"You needn't say anything about *lodgers*, of course. Just tell
her that I want to see her about something and it's so long since I
saw her that I feel rather nervous about approaching her. (I don't,
but it's a question of not being *rude*.) Say, can I come and see
her one evening next week. That's all I want you to do, Daddy."

There. It was out. Daisy leant forward and slowly helped herself
to the last congealing piece of tea-cake.

Her father was silent, looking down at his slippers. He felt a
strong inclination to sigh. There certainly was no one like Daisy
for putting you into a difficult position. If there was one thing
that he was quite sure he did not want to do, it was to resume
his acquaintanceship (*she* had always called it a friendship but
he did not think of it as that) with Minta Cavendish.

She had never, even as a young married woman possessing
all that she could want, been a likable or even a pleasant person,
and she had never been really intimate with his wife—in fact he
had always had to suppress an unkind suspicion that young Mrs

Cavendish had 'cultivated' the young Furnivalls because of their social position rather than just because she liked them. (Certain other embarrassing suspicions, not unconnected with Anthea Cavendish and manoeuvrings for marriage with a financially and socially desirable widower which had once or twice entered his head, had been dismissed as 'old man's vanity'.)

He had scribbled polite vague excuses to all Mrs Cavendish's gushing invitations, and silenced his conscience by sending her a card bearing the arms of his old regiment at Christmas, and a cheque to the girl on her birthday every January. A perfectly satisfactory situation.

But these people who had nowhere to live . . .

"*I* think," Daisy suddenly said vigorously, "that people who can remember the world before 1939 ought to make it their *duty* to help people like the Hultons. After all, old Cavendish has *had* her life. She ought to be helping other people to have theirs."

"No doubt. But it doesn't strike me in quite that way, you see, and I'm pretty certain she wouldn't see it like that either."

"Aren't you *sorry* for them, Daddy?" Daisy's tone was not pathetic; she trotted out her appeal with briskness. But she knew perfectly well that this, and no other, was the moment to trot it . . . .

"Of course I'm sorry for them; don't be silly," irritably.

"Well, then. And when it's a question of *duty*, as well—"

"I don't see where duty comes into it. I'm not related to your friends. If there's any question of 'duty'"—he leant forward and deftly put a large lump of coal on to precisely the right part of the fire—"I feel it towards that poor woman—left a widow, completely unexpectedly (immediately before the war broke out, with all that to get through), and not as much money as she had the right to expect, and a girl to bring up and educate. She may have her little affectations, and attach too much importance to things like birth and possessions."

"Yes, she always was a fearful snob, wasn't she? 'My husband's mother was a Barton, you know.'"

"That's putting it too strongly," he said sharply. "You don't realise what it's like to live in a world gone socially topsy-turvy, because you've grown up in one, and you take it for granted. Your friend, Miss Raymond—" He broke off. "Anyway," he went on, "because poor Minta has her weaknesses, that's no excuse for treating her with less than—er—customary politeness."

"Well," said Daisy reluctantly, after a pause, "I do in a way see what you mean."

"How can I ask her a favour after ignoring her for years? It's so—blatant." The Colonel moved uneasily in his chair.

"Not really a *favour*. Just asking her if she'll let me come and see her one evening. I'll do the rest," coaxingly.

"It's such a cheek—letting the poor woman in for the possibility of a . . . a . . . crowd of strangers in her house."

"She can always say no."

"How do you know that they'll behave themselves properly if she has got the rooms empty, and does agree to have them? Suppose they're noisy—won't pay their rent—that sort of thing?"

"I'm sure they won't."

"You're sure, but you don't *know*. You—" he looked straight at her as he spoke—"you never seem to anticipate any unpleasant possibilities when you undertake these schemes to help your friends. Now if these people aren't the right sort, and misbehave themselves, I shall feel personally responsible to old Minta."

"She'll take it all much better if they've been recommended by us," Daisy said coolly, with a very shameless smile.

"All the more reason for not recommending them," he said, not returning it.

There was a pause. Deadlock seemed to have been reached. Daisy, leaning back in her chair, looked out of the window, and her father looked at her.

What a world this was, this howling mid-century wilderness—without domestic service, enough house room or well-defined social customs—in which a man could find himself in such a dilemma.

It would have been simple, for some fathers, just to tell Daisy to set to work and find somewhere else for her friends to live. But he did not want to add any more activities to her life, which was (he knew from his cousin Marcia and from James) already too full of 'this sort of thing'.

She 'over-did it'. She always had, as a schoolgirl; joining more societies, playing more games, taking up more hobbies, seeing more friends, than any one person could properly manage or enjoy. He knew that it had begun, just before her death, to worry Claire. If he sent Daisy off, by his refusal to get in touch with old Minta, on a chase through London in search of cheap, clean, quiet furnished rooms with a landlady who would accept three small children (yes! and he had forgotten the children—they made things even more difficult), it would be to impose on her, already overburdened, one more exhausting task. He was certain that that would have worried her mother.

And this afternoon it was one of those days when she looked so like Claire, even to the continuous play of expression across her face, suggesting the swift flight of cloud shadows over a brilliant landscape, that he felt doubly moved to give her what she wanted. He allowed himself the threatened sigh. 'I'm getting old and selfish,' he thought. 'Perhaps it will do me good to get involved a little with other people's affairs. But I'm damned if I like the prospect.'

She was looking at him expectantly.

"Very well," he said. "I'll write to her. I'll just say that you want to come and talk to her, shall I?"

"Thank you, Daddy. You are *extremely* kind, and good, too," Daisy said solemnly.

"Nonsense." He got up, and glanced again at the clock; it was the evening on which he went to play bridge with friends in St. John's Wood, and he always liked to rest for an hour before he went out.

Daisy laughed. "All right, darling. I'm going. Sorry to have been a bore."

"I do wish you would use words in their proper sense . . . you haven't 'bored' me at all; I only wish you had."

"And you'll write to her tonight?"

"Yes, I will. Go away. I want to go to sleep."

"Good-bye, then." A kiss dropped on top of his head. "And thank you very, very much."

The door shut. It was just as if a light had been turned off in the large, lofty room with the red curtains at the windows and the dim blue and red Indian carpets on the floor; the shadows in the corners seemed to take one long step forward. But Colonel Furnivall preferred it as it was now. He was tired; he had not really wanted Daisy to stay. He leant back in the deep armchair, covered with striped Arabian stuff, in which he had settled himself when she relinquished it, and, before he dozed off, looked across at the mantelshelf.

There was the seated figure of a *bodhisattva* that he had bought in Tibet, when he had gone there as a member of a mission some years before the war; carved from milky soapstone whose transparency seemed almost to allow the last reflection of sunset lingering above the marble shelf to penetrate its paleness. Faintly the lips were curved in a smile that was like the reflection of a greater peace than that of the figure itself; bathed in an infinitely comforting calm, the hands and limbs lay along the lines of their immemorial pose. 'Yes,' he thought, as he looked at it, 'if ever the peace that passeth understanding got itself embodied, there it is.' He looked at it for a moment longer, then shut his eyes.

'Good,' thought Daisy, skimming towards the taxi-rank at Belsize Park. 'Got what I wanted . . . but now I shall have to go and see Old Cavendish. Oh Lord.'

It really was rather frightful to think of being tactful and pushing and persuasive with that old acquaintance. When Daisy was compelled to pause for a moment amidst the whirl and noise of her life—while she was sitting under the dryer, for instance, or flung back, with limp body and closed eyes, for ten minutes on the seat of a taxi while speeding from here to somewhere else—she felt tired enough to *die* . . . And now there was going to be Old Cavendish.

And *now*, too (Oh Lord, again), here was Molly Raymond creeping towards one.

Daisy did not slacken her pace, and although her wave of haste and dismissal as she approached her already beaming protégée was sweetened by one of her best smiles, it was unmistakably a brush-off.

"Can't stop—flying home to bath James Too—off to a party," she cried.

But fatal are the habits imprinted by a first-class girls' school and a kind heart. When Molly paused, Daisy paused too.

"How lovely. What a thrilling two-piece . . . that's the first beetle-backed jacket I've seen actually *on* anyone . . . is it new?" Molly's tone held not a hint of envy; she certainly was disarming.

"Just, yes. How are you?" Daisy was poised, almost on tip-toe, half of her already at the taxi-rank.

"Oh, so-so. I got lots to tell you, but if you really can't stop . . . have you been to see your daddy?"

"Yes . . . *oh* . . ." Daisy's expression changed. "Molly, *have* you been seeing Tibbs again?"

"I just happened to run in to him the other night, as a matter of fact. That was what I wanted to talk to you about—he's decided not to write his book about England after all. And I've met your father! (*Through* Tibbs, actually.) Did he mention it to you?"

"He just said that he had seen you home." This was not the way Daisy would have wished to report the incident, but she was, as usual, in such a hurry.

"Didn't he tell you how kind he was to me?"

Daisy shook her head.

"Oh, he was quite wonderful . . . but it's a long story. I won't keep you. I've been hoping to get a peep at his Indian treasures, but no luck so far."

"All that brass; awful to keep clean . . . I really must dash, Molly."

"Maureen doesn't mind cleaning it one bit; Colonel Furnivall has made quite a conquest *there*."

"Good . . . I'll ring you . . . bye-bye," and off Daisy flew, pursued by a "God be with you."

'If Daddy has made a conquest of Mrs Brogan's housemaid and you've been nattering with her in the intervals of hanging round Sara and Joe's in hopes of running into Tibbs, why don't you get her to let you have a peep at Daddy's Indian Treasures while he's out?' Daisy was thinking furiously as she sank back in the taxi. 'Or perhaps you *have*?'

But then she felt ashamed. She was annoyed because Molly seemed bent on ignoring all the plans made for her own good: Tibbs she wanted and Tibbs, apparently, she meant to have (except that he might have other views). But because she was irritated with Molly, that was no reason for being unjust. She knew perfectly well that Molly would have been horrified at the idea of peeping into Colonel Furnivall's rooms when he was not there. Molly's faults were not of that kind. She was devoted to delicacy, refinement and fine feelings—God help us, she is, thought Daisy, putting up her feet.

"Chandeliers, now!" was her first remark to James on getting back from the Ruddlins' party. They had been given a lift to as near the pink front door as it could get in a car belonging to a fellow guest, and his presence (he was a stranger to them both) had restricted their comments upon the Ruddlin hospitality and decor.

"I must say I thought they looked rather stunning," Daisy went on, "but that girl Susan—she does see to it that she gets the lot, doesn't she?"

Her speculative eyeing of the living-room ceiling was interrupted by James.

"No," he said.

"No what?"

"No chandeliers for the Muirs."

"One would look wonderful in the hall . . . I can *see* it . . . it would reflect the walls and look like a *mass* of Brazilian diamonds. Why not?"

"Because we owe seventeen pounds for your little experiment in ornamental gardening."

"I can't help it, I didn't know I shouldn't enjoy gardening; all my relations do."

"Well we know it now. The knowledge has cost us seventeen pounds and"—James was rummaging in the desk—"two shillings and fivepence ha'penny, if you'd like the exact figures, for a sack of earth and two socking great pots full of dead begonias."

"I thought they would *do* there; the book says they like plenty of sun . . . would you be just the least bit tiddly, darling James? Always makes you fractious."

"The only thing to do at that kind of party is to get as near the gin as possible and stay there . . . I say, why do you suppose that character who brought us home was ever invited? His was the smallest car there. Can Sue and Chris be slipping?"

Daisy gave a disloyal giggle. "And it wasn't even the *right* kind of smallness, was it? Nothing vintage about it . . . just *frugal* and *neat* . . . I expect he's a brilliant young something or other who's going to make a lot of money out of some new thing and he hasn't started yet . . . I trust my Susan. She wouldn't invite anyone without a good reason."

"Or just because she liked them, of course."

"I say, that's a bit smug, isn't it?" But Daisy's tone was absent; she had seated herself at the desk.

"I daresay. What are you doing now? Starting a novel?"

"I'm writing to that little Katy MacRae (you remember?) about those rooms at old Minta Cavendish's."

"Who on earth's she? No . . . don't tell me . . . I'd rather not know. Is there going to be any food? I only had two of those filthy little canapés and an olive, and my stomach's rumbling."

"Poor Jamesey . . . I'll tell Janine to get us masses of cheese and beer," said Daisy, yawning. Her long fine-skinned face was drawn with exhaustion. "Yes, wasn't the food boring . . . and not enough of it . . . of course, Susan's got a *plan*, like she has for everything, about the food at her parties. She's going to stick to lots of drink and not much, rather dull, food until she's got rid of all the people who go to her parties *now*. (You see, that's what *they* like.) Then, when she's got to know the kind of people she really *wants*, she'll have the kind of food *they* like, which is marvellous, and plenty of it."

"I see. Upward and onward with clever Susan."

James, from his collapsed position in the deep chair, looked at Daisy, sitting sideways at the untidy desk with her legs coming out endlessly, in thinnest black nylon, from a dark silk tunic ending just below her knees. She would have been so surprised to know that he was imagining her, in those pointed shoes and that bandeau, in the middle of a pine forest . . .

'I am going to see the rooms I told you about some time next week, I *hope*. Will let you know the instant I hear something definite.' Daisy finished her postcard and stamped it with a theft from James's personal hoard. 'Now,' she thought, with a rending yawn, 'it's up to Old Cavendish. (Oh *dear*.)'

CHAPTER VIII
Marcia

MARCIA Furnivall very seldom took the car into London. The reason she gave was the difficulty of finding parking space; her real reason was the fact that she found it, in her mid-seventies, increasingly exhausting to drive in heavy traffic, while, apart from her own feelings, she felt her responsibility as a social unit. On any day, at any time, she might be betrayed by her years into a failure of eye or hand or quick reaction that would kill someone.

So, avoiding the Underground, where the advertisements and the faces (Marcia was not an easy-going woman) both irritated her intensely, she would, on those days when she went to the London Library or to lunch with a friend, travel either comfortably by taxi or, rather adventurously, by bus.

She liked to ride upstairs, climbing to the upper deck with a sensation of pleasure in the loose, unstiff way her body 'gave' to the careering movement of the great thing, as if she were a woman thirty years younger; she did not mind the conductor's 'dear' or the occasional 'ma' that was called forth by her grey hair, and she liked to see the conductresses, with their curls and their lipstick and their pearls, at work on a man's job. *That*, whether on a bus or in a laboratory or in the study, was something that had always given Marcia a small thrill of pleasurable triumph. But she did not find the conductresses' endearments so inoffensive as those of the conductors' (she had always—at home, at college, while she was taking her nursing unit through the horrors of the war in Serbia—'got on' better with men than with women); and she

'drew the line' at being 'dear'd' by a West Indian. Marcia's toler-
ance of foreigners stopped short at her own wild, loyal, dirty Serbs.

Some days after Daisy had sent the postcard to Katy Hulton,
Marcia was coming home from London on the top of a 68 bus.

She had passed the morning reading a play of Držić's in the
large, lofty quiet room reserved for readers at the London Library,
for, although she had at home a shelf-full of Serbian grammars
and poetry and biographies, she sometimes liked to range over
a wider field than she herself could command. She had also been
looking through the epic *Osman*.

But—she had *lived* through an epic: in the savage icy Serb
mountains in the autumn of 1918. Pictures, sounds, faces kept
rising before her mind's eye, and with their intense life making
the pictures conjured up by *Osman* seem faded and dim. Soon,
she realized that she was remembering, rather than reading,
and that she had been giving way (not for the first time, of late)
to the peculiar lassitude that nowadays assailed her in the early
afternoons. She shut the book and went upstairs in search of Sir
John Bowring's *Servian Popular Poetry*.

Dame Marcia Furnivall, G.B.E. (and at home, in the leather
case faded now from its first bright sapphire, was the gold Serbian Military Medal, 'For Valour', and in another case the Order
of the White Eagle) went with straight back and swift step up the
red carpeted stairs, and through the swing doors and over those
perforated steel gratings which, running between the narrow
lanes lined with thousands of dusty volumes, cause the thoughts
of the most absorbed female student to turn to undergarments.
Heads, occasionally encountered, turned admiringly to watch
her as she went.

Her suit, the French turban of black jersey set well back on her
head, and the ornaments of heavy silver in her ears and on her
wrists, were set off by her air of authority and her easy, unself-
conscious charm. There was a little of the pleasure, in seeing Dame
Marcia, that there is in seeing Royalty: both provided something
assured, gracious, comforting, in the midst of an anxious age;
and with her, too, as with Royalty, there went the suggestion of a
life given to public service, an aura of civic virtues and detached

good. She was one of the characters, one of the 'sights' (though of course in no unpleasant exhibitionist sense) of the Library.

And she stood now before the shelves looking for a book of poems about war (war poetry was the only kind of poetry that Marcia had ever liked); this vigorous and beautiful old woman was remembering—and as the words came back yet again with their touch of chill, her lids with the sharply-cut corners drooped for a moment over her eyes—something said to her by her mother when she had been about nine years old:

'It is only like going to sleep, Marcia, and never waking up again. You aren't afraid, I suppose, every time that you shut your eyes to go to sleep?—at least, I hope you are not.'

How ashamed of herself she had been! and how determined in her nine-year-old heart never to admit to fear of anything—*anything*—again, as long as she might live.

She had fought the battle with her fear of death in secret and by herself from that hour. She had been defeated, and as the years went on she came to know it, but she had kept her vow: never to another human creature—not to Randolph (although he, she believed, had guessed), not to Ella, even, had she ever confessed the terror with which the thought of death increasingly filled her.

She had sometimes wondered if her father's attitude of serene agnostic acceptance concealed something rather like her own feelings. He spoke of death rather too often, and always with that acceptance and tranquillity which has been called 'mellow' and 'ripe'.

"'Ripeness is all'," he would say, and, "'It sinks, and I am ready to depart.'" But what were the fruits that should have ripened? The Christian believer would say, 'sacrifice, humbleness, love'. Marcia's own 'fruits', she supposed (but she was only intermittently an introspective woman), were courage, and an overriding sense of duty. As for Christianity—it had been gracefully tolerated, in the household of her parents.

"If you have served humanity up to the limit of your powers," she could remember her father saying authoritatively to some-one—an uneasy one amongst the numerous female cousins, perhaps, given to good works, and scruples in the Roman Catholic sense—"you can certainly go to sleep with a good conscience. If you *must* have comfort—I do not see the need for it but I suppose that a woman might—then you can think of Jesus's words: 'Well done, thou good and faithful servant.' *That* was a man who knew how to comfort people, before his delusions became too powerful for him to master. He would have made a first-class specialist in nervous diseases."

Marcia stood in front of the long shelf of dusty books; there was a hushed, oppressive sense in this place of many a life's work finished and the poor forgotten results silently displayed. The building was very quiet; the long rays of late sunlight poured in through the bright windows; she was alone. Her eyelids fell again over her eyes.

It came in so many ways: bombardment, starvation, the hellish cold of a mountain winter, the knife in the hand of a man sent mad by misery . . . more than once, oh, twice—thrice—many times, if she let herself remember, it had been so near to her. And had not struck.

But now she was nearly eighty years old.

Four o'clock sounded from somewhere outside. She roused herself with impatience and went across to the assistant at the table in the window: would Miss Prince be so kind as to see that this went back to the right section upstairs? Miss Prince, who was very young, received the commission with a blush and a smile of pleasure and Marcia had gone out through the swing doors wondering where the child had been at school and if she had gone on to a university. Such reflections were always her first ones on any casual encounter with a young girl.

. . . She became aware of voices in the seat behind her. A woman's, of piercing raucousness, was saying:

"Never get a minute, do you?"

"That's right. So, 's I'sayin', I packed it up."

"Don't blame you."

"She created about it, course. Went on about me being there three years. Well, I says, you give me another bob an hour and we'll see about it."

"Some of them never think you want a minute to yourself, do they?"

"That's right . . . that's the place, on the near corner," the second speaker said, "all that stuff on the door to do every day."

"Plenty of stairs."

"You're telling me there are. And the *stuff* she's got there, all bits of silver, and wants them done once a fortnight. I ask you."

Marcia had glanced idly out of the window as the bus swept past, feeling a moment's sympathy for the lady with too much silver and, now, no daily help. She then saw that the tall white shabby house the woman had indicated belonged to an acquaintance: Mrs Cavendish.

She was not at all surprised that *she* had lost her 'char'; when she recalled Mrs Cavendish's standard of housekeeping it was only surprising that nowadays she had been able to retain the services of one for three years. And nobody, Marcia reflected, was less fitted to support such a commonplace misfortune, for Minta Cavendish was afflicted—but really it was an affliction, and it was quite absurd too—with what Daisy and her friends called 'a thing' about domestic help. Any crisis or lowering of household standards connected with it had always made her quite hysterical.

Marcia was interested in the wider aspects of this contemporary problem . . . she recalled a passage recently read in which it was pointed out that not until the hard pioneering work in a new country had been done could people find time and energy to cultivate their minds. But in the early years of the century, when she herself had been something of a pioneer in more fields than one, she had had far more opportunity to cultivate her mind than she had today, when, in spite of her good luck in commanding the services of Annie, there was always a certain amount of catering and ordering and domestic telephoning to be done . . . housekeeper's work, in fact.

There was no longer anything remotely approaching the number of even untrained domestic workers that there should have been . . . it made life for the highly-educated woman, especially the married graduate with a family and a job, almost unbearably hard . . . so many working-class women now 'went out', as a matter of course, to work . . . Marcia, who had been interested in the early stages of the Women's Movement, was able, though not *willing*, to admit that *this* particular situation was undoubtedly due to the activities of herself and her fellow feminists . . . it was a situation, she supposed, full of irony, but she did not inwardly smile over it.

Servants. The word repeated itself inwardly in a tone of acerbity, and it sounded none the sweeter because she had to admit that life for herself and Ella would have been very different if they had not 'had' Annie.

Annie March had come to the Furnivalls at the end of the century, from an orphanage, when she was fourteen years old. She had probably been born 'on the wrong side of the blanket', for she had been left in the garden of the orphanage on a cold March night that had given her her second name. There had been a scrap of paper with 'Annie' printed on it, pinned to the ragged shawl. She had grown into a gaunt girl with large features and that dark red hair which, in spite of admiration for the paintings of the Pre-Raphaelites, was still considered ugly, and, it soon became apparent, a dower of great physical strength.

There had been no one, even if Annie had wanted it, to prevent the Furnivalls taking complete possession of her; and, indeed, it was agreed both at the orphanage on whose Board Mrs Furnivall sat as a Governor and below stairs at Newton House, that the girl was lucky; she had that little room above the attics all to herself—and the mistress wasn't mean about candles—and Mrs Cook, Annie being an orphan, was better to her than some would have been to a kitchen-maid who was a bastard; and she had her good print dresses for summer and warm ones for winter, and later on, when she had been at Newton House five years, she was promoted to housemaid; another five, and she had her starched embroidered aprons and her frilled caps for her dark red hair and was handing cakes and tea at the fortnightly 'at homes'.

Annie . . . she had been with the family for more than fifty years . . . she had certainly been the 'good servant' named by Jesus; she had, if anything, been *too* 'faithful', thought Marcia. (Old servants were apt to develop into tyrants; it was the price that had to be paid for their service.)

There had never really been any question of Annie leaving the Furnivalls. She had always been a quiet girl, neither animated nor pretty—although Marcia could remember a young man, one of Daisy's odd acquaintances who called himself an artist, telling Annie to her face when she carried in the tea to which he had been unexpectedly brought along by Daisy that she was *beautiful*.

"Has she ever had a lover?" he demanded fiercely, after Annie had gone scowling back to her kitchen. "I really don't know; I've never thought about the matter," had been Marcia's answer, "but in her youth, of course, unmarried lower-class young women were always afraid of having babies," and the young man, a defender of sexual promiscuity, homosexuality, and experiments with drug-taking, had been so shocked by her 'lower-class', that he had said no more.

Secret lovers or not, there had been at least one suitor who had openly offered for Annie.

Marcia had forgotten his name, but he had been very respectable, she recalled, and had taken to hanging about the kitchen premises on summer evenings *(oh, the river shining in the afterglow! and the birds calling in the willows)* and they had all been amused, upstairs, because Annie had suddenly taken to wearing her 'front hair' in a high pompadour. Mrs Furnivall, who strongly objected to anything exaggerated or vulgar in dress, had had to speak to her about it.

She had spoken to Annie's suitor, too; quite firmly. She had no wish to lose a good servant, and there was no reason for Annie to marry; the girl had an excellent home, she explained, and—always providing that she continued to give satisfaction—she need never want for anything or leave it. Then Mrs Furnivall had strongly advised Annie, for her own good, to send the young man about his business.

Annie had obeyed. A little kindly teasing from the family, a little firmness with a few sulky moods, and the affair was ended. Annie was twenty-eight years old; with her red hair and her large features and her quiet ways the Furnivalls were all rather surprised that she had succeeded in attracting even one follower.

She did not attract another. Later, she had gone into the service of Ella's mother.

Poor Annie and her young man! It had been a family joke for a week or so.

Marcia gathered up her parcels and her books in a net bag as the bus approached the stopping place.

Annie could be—more than just spiteful. Marcia remembered with unpleasant clearness the state of affairs she had discovered on her return to Newtown House, after she got back from Serbia in 1920.

It had been really ugly: Annie domineering and insolently 'kind', Ella cowed and grubby and wretched. Marcia had lost no time in taking things into her own hands; and if Annie had not made such an astonishing *fuss*—tears and sobs and hysterics; Marcia had never suspected that she had it in her under that quiet manner, but of course that class had no self-control—she would have been dismissed there and then.

But Marcia had also discerned, beneath the distasteful scenes, a true remorse and a genuine loyalty to the family. (It was, after all, the only family that Annie had ever known.)

She had allowed her to stay on, and of course, as soon as Annie found herself under a firm hand again, she had settled down perfectly—except for those occasional sulky moods which she had had from childhood and which just had to be ignored— and there had been no more trouble.

She had gone with Marcia and Ella to the house in King Edward's Road when they bought it in 1925, and there she had been ever since . . . and tea, perfectly prepared, elegantly served, would be waiting when Marcia got in. Yes, she supposed she must say, 'Thank goodness for Annie'.

Swaying easily on the platform with the conductor's hand at her elbow, a sudden swerve of the bus all but sent her into the road rushing by below. "Hey!" said he, "hold up! Don't want to lose you before your time, do we?" Marcia said, no, we didn't, and smiled while he carefully helped her down at the stop.

As she walked with unlessened lightness and speed up King Edward's Road she was wondering where the Marcia she had known for longer than half a century, the thing that sometimes banged about like an angry fly in the rickety old box that was her body, when 'her time' came to go, where would that thing be?—the thing that had loved Ella ever since the day, more than sixty years ago, when she had rescued her from a group of teasing children at a party. Where would it be? Where? Or . . . would there be any 'thing' to 'be' anywhere?

Ella was sitting at the window that overlooked the garden, watching the shadows gathering in the railway cutting. She lifted her hand, smiling, as Marcia came up the path.

And Ella? The beautiful, funny spirit whose smallest harmless thought and secret Marcia knew and loved, where would Ella be?

With an effort of the will that was not slight, she exorcised both questions.

"I went past Minta Cavendish's house today," she said to her cousin at tea, "it looks very shabby. And she has lost her char-woman." She repeated the overheard conversation.

"She'll be very angry," said Ella. "Were there still marigolds in the garden?"

"I didn't notice. It all looked very shabby."

"Daisy telephoned while you were out. A friend of hers is coming to live at Mrs Cavendish's, she said, and she thinks you would be interested in her."

"Oh, does she? What kind of a friend?"

"Daisy only *thinks* she *may* be coming. Her name is Mrs Hulton and she's *very* clever. She has," Ella's face was sad, "a Degree in Chemistry."

Marcia smiled at her. "Never mind . . . it's a long, long time ago. It really doesn't matter any more, darling, not one bit . . . she's married, is she?"

"Yes. Daisy says she has two children and a baby."

"And a Degree . . . is she working, did Daisy say?"

"No. She can't, because of the two children and the baby."

"Silly girl," said Marcia. "What else did she expect . . . What does Daisy want *us* to do about her?"

"Daisy said, if she does come, could we have her to tea. She said—you might like to talk to her."

"I don't suppose I should, if she married too young . . . If a girl takes a Degree, she should use it. However, we shall see. Would you like some more tea?"

CHAPTER IX
Old Cavendish . . .

THE letter said:

"Can't imagine what you can have to say to me that's so important after all this long time, but do come in to coffee on Wednesday evening about half past eight—Anthea will be there—she's longing to see you again. So nice to hear from your father again too. Looking forward to seeing you—" and she was Daisy's always affectionate M.A.V. Cavendish, in a large, splashy Edwardian hand.

Daisy glanced across the breakfast table at James and *The Times*.

"Darling, do you very much mind if we don't go on Wednesday evening after all?"

"Yes, I do. I've been looking forward to it. What's up now?"

"It's Old Cavendish—you know—I told you. I've got to go and see her about these rooms for the Hultons on Wednesday."

"Put her off. Telephone her."

"I can't." Daisy consulted the letter. "Yes, she says, *'No telephone now, alas'* (two exclamation marks. I'm blowed if I'd think it was 'alas', would you?). I *must* get it all fixed up by Friday because the Hultons' in-laws can only have them until Friday week and—"

"All right, so you aren't coming. That's what it boils down to." He returned to his paper.

"Can't you go alone?"

"Certainly. Probably shall." He did not look up.

"I'm frightfully sorry, darling. But you do see, don't you, that it's more important my finding somewhere for five people to live than just going to see a movie with you that we can see *any* time? I did promise that little Katy."

James did not answer.

"Can't we go on Friday?" Daisy said reasonably.

"We've got the Beresfords on Friday."

"Oh damn, so we have (and Delia will be so full of herself after that fish-poisoning or whatever it was). Friday's out then. Saturday—no, Janine's mother will be over from Toulon."

James was folding up *The Times*. "That's settled, then. We wash the film out."

"You *can* go *alone*, lovey."

"I shan't enjoy it alone. I want to take you."

Daisy, at this, got up and went across and put her arms round him. Very durable, irritated, and different from herself he felt, too. But he kissed her sweetly enough, with a satisfactory hug, and when he went out of the house a moment later, he was whistling.

Bless him, thought Daisy, forgetting him as she went back to her coffee and making plans for the Hultons.

James, running down the thirty steps, was thinking how nice it would be to live in Canada, where none of Daisy's friends lived.

As she approached Mrs Cavendish's house through the damp and chilly darkness some evenings later, Daisy was feeling less confident than usual, and she had been going over the sentences of the letter in search of reassurance. She had not derived any. She had been rapped over the knuckles for her long neglectful silence and there had been a glancing sideways dig at her father. Well, Old Cavendish always had been rather sharp and sour. It might safely be assumed that advancing years and (presumed) increasing poverty had not sweetened her.

It did seem low, when you faced it squarely, to practically drop someone because they were a snob and a bore and then pick them up again because they might have a couple of rooms to let . . . but then Daisy remembered the Hultons. Heavens, Old Cavendish had had her life, hadn't she, and not too bad a life either, with a house and a prosperous husband and a pretty daughter . . . ? 'The older generation may take such blessings for granted, but *our* generation,' thought Daisy, 'the generation that has grown up alongside refugee camps and the bomb and overcrowding—we know just how lucky Old Cavendish's generation was. Why *shouldn't* they "do their bit", as they would say, towards helping ours?'

Reinforced, she marched up to the house on the corner.

She glanced up, through the one tall leafless tree growing in its front garden, at the highest windows. No lights; she almost thought that there were no curtains either. Was that a sign that the rooms were still empty? Or just that Old Cavendish couldn't afford curtains? She pushed open the graceful old gate of rusted iron.

The garden was wet, silent and dim. No lights shone in the lower windows either, but then she remembered that the drawing-room used to have shutters. Yes, they were still there, and behind the delicious little bulbous iron balcony they were closed. The steps leading up to the front door were faintly visible in the light of the nearest street lamp. Cautiously—for she could just see that the lowest one was broken away—she went slowly up them.

Two pulls at the shining bell-handle—someone had been at work there—having produced not even a remote tinkle in the basement, she attacked the glittering knocker. It made an alarmingly hollow reverberation within.

'No carpets?' wondered Daisy. 'But if Old C. has had to sell her carpets she may be glad of lodgers.' She waited a moment, looking absently down into the garden. Some last tall pale flowers glimmered near the gate; a bus rumbled by; there was a smell of soot and wet old earth and just the faintest breath of fog . . . Daisy shivered and thought angrily, 'How I do hate cold dark dreary places. If I were Old C. I would sell every stick I owned and retire to Butlin's . . .'

The spider's-web fanlight sprang into delicate shape against a faint glow; a beam shone out weakly above her head and the front door opened.

"Daisy!" said Mrs Cavendish's thin, gushing, remembered voice, "how *nice* to see you again! It's such a *long* time. It must be—why, it must be *four years*!"

H'm . . . Daisy, accepting the little tap, replied with her ringing voice and her wide smile. But the cold in the hall was so intense that she almost cried out. It struck against her face; it was like pain. The light was dim; she could barely make out her surroundings, but how clearly she remembered it all now—the gleaming black boards, the old wallpaper with its Chinamen in wide hats, the curve of the staircase. She had only forgotten how really charming was the hall, with its vaulted ceiling decorated with plaster mouldings. It was the prettiest place; prettier, really, than the square shape and the old, painted panelling of the hall at home.

But surely there used to be a long rich-coloured runner on the floor, and where was the silver bowl filled with rose-leaves that had always stood on the gate-legged table? The freezing air smelled slightly of coffee.

"We've only just taken to fires, it's been such a wonderful autumn, hasn't it?" Mrs Cavendish was saying, as she opened a white door. "Anthea dearest, here's Daisy!"

The girl crouching over the tiny fire looked up with a pretty smile.

"Hullo. How nice to see you again," she said softly.

"Nice to see you," smiled Daisy, trying not to shiver.

"Do sit down, my dear . . . Anthea, must you hug the fire like that? She's just back from Italy," turning to Daisy, "well, she got back about a month ago . . . she's been staying with the Seymours and she says she *can't* get warm. (Get the coffee, will you, dearest.) Do you know the Seymours, Daisy? They're well-known Hampstead people."

Daisy shook her head. She was divided between delight at her hostess's beginning, straight away, to behave in character, and that glassy-eyed inability to comment suitably upon Old Cavendish's remarks which had afflicted her as a schoolgirl.

"They've got one of those beautiful houses in Church Row . . . he's a big man in shipping. Well, Daisy, how are you? You look very well . . . do you know we haven't met since your wedding? I hope the little Spode dish has been useful?"

"Oh yes, thank you." Daisy guiltily recalled its present humble employment as ash-tray to the bathroom. "Are you both well?"

"Oh, we're all right . . . don't you think Anthea looks brown? She was motoring, most of the time, in Italy. There was a young man, a friend of the Seymours (a Roman, of very good family), and he simply put his Mercedes at her disposal—didn't he, Anthea? Oh, thank you, darling," as a small white hand put down a cup on the brass-rimmed table at Daisy's elbow.

Daisy's first cautious sip at the fluid it contained caused the word 'foul' to flit bat-like through her mind.

She put it down, thinking that Mrs Cavendish had changed hardly at all; the neutral twin-set, the tweed skirt, the tiny brooch with that uncopyable flash of true diamonds, the brown hair that looked like some wig made in the twenties above the skeletally thin face where fixed colour glowed—Daisy had known them, it seemed to her, ever since she could remember, and, suddenly and quite unexpectedly she felt fond of Old Cavendish just for having remained the same.

Daisy did not know, yet, how strongly and deeply she cared for old friends, familiar places, family traditions. In twenty years' time, a group of young relatives was to say of her: Daisy's a great *family* girl.

This feeling, however, was going to make it even more difficult to ask about those rooms. However was she going to get around to it? 'I'll probably have to be brutally frank,' she thought. 'But that's just what Old C. hates.'

There were things lacking, too, from the drawing-room, she was certain. Where was the Bechstein piano? Surely there used to be a procession of enchanting china figures along the mantel-shelf? Old Cavendish must be in a bad way . . . unless, of course, the things had been stored away because she had no one to keep them clean. The round carpet with its circle of flowers, that Daisy used to call 'Ring-o-Roses' still occupied the place of honour in the middle of the gleaming black floor, but it did so unsupported; William Morris's bright little fruits and narrow green leaves still covered the walls but they were almost indistinguishable beneath a film of age and soot. The ceiling was frankly black. And there was something desperate, secret, starving, in the cold air. Daisy suddenly longed for the house with the pink front door.

Her hostess's voice ran on. Mrs Cavendish always did have the most unfailing flow of small change . . . the weather, the fashions—'pretty' or 'too extreme, really bad form'—and never a reference to any human creature without its accompanying tag—'really nice people', 'not quite out of the top-drawer' (Daisy was glad that she could not see *her* top drawer in the bedroom at home), 'such nice friends for Anthea'.

Anthea dearest, sitting gracefully on a long stool and holding out her hands to the weak flames, smiled whenever her mother spoke to her and said very little. *Her* twin-set was pink; her pearls were tiny, but Daisy betted to herself that if they were not real they were as near real as Mrs Cavendish could afford: a twenty-first birthday present, probably. She certainly was pretty, pretty as a girl on a chocolate-box; but she looked curiously *out-of-date*. 'That chignon and those waves close to the head look really 1917,' thought Daisy. 'Of course, it's fashionable to look twenties-ish, but she goes back a bit too far. It's almost dowdy. And an ash-blonde should always wear her hair dead straight.'

Mutual news was exchanged, and when Mrs Cavendish enquired after James Too, she added with an arch glance at Anthea that of course *she* hoped to be a grandmother . . . one day.

Daisy, who chanced to be looking at Anthea, noticed that her colour changed. But she did not blush: she paled. Peculiar, thought Daisy—though God knows the poor little beast has enough to make her turn *green*; I should, permanently, if I lived here.

"But Anthea isn't in a hurry to settle down, are you, dearest? She loves her job."

"You teach dancing, don't you?" asked Daisy rather bluntly, speaking to Anthea directly for almost the first time. But her mother cut in—

"She's *chief assistant* at Miss Croydew's. You must know Miss Croydew's, Daisy, it's the oldest school of Dancing and Deportment in London. It's in Knightsbridge. It's mostly for small children, but there are evening classes for adults who want to learn dancing . . . and *that's* where," a significant smile towards the fireplace, "Anthea met Michael."

"Oh? Is he the one—?" Daisy felt that this teasing tone was expected of her; it made Anthea sound as if she were sixteen and having her first date. 'But how else,' thought Daisy savagely, 'could I have said it? As if I hoped he'd got his divorce, and lots of money? She treats her as if she were in ankle-socks.'

"Michael Devon, yes. Yes, he's definitely the favoured one, isn't he, Anthea dearest?" An indistinguishable murmur and a smile. "They aren't exactly . . . there's nothing *definite* yet," Mrs Cavendish went on, "but, oh, he is a charming boy, Daisy! A real 'heart-throb'. Not conventionally good-looking . . . but a fine profile . . . He's a connection of the Earl of Devonhurst."

Daisy tried to look pleased.

"Of course, there is very little chance of his ever succeeding . . . there are—how many lives is it, Anthea dearest—three?— yes, the Earl's nephew and his two little boys—between him and the *title*, but he sees a great deal of them. He's often down at their place in Berkshire."

"Herons," murmured Anthea, for whom Daisy was feeling increasingly sorry; she had kept her eyes fixed on the fire through-out her mother's remarks, with a pensive smile.

"Yes . . . Herons . . . it's a beautiful old place, I hear, but of course—death duties—and this *awful, crippling taxation*—I believe the National Trust is responsible for one wing of it and the Earl may have to let visitors in to the other part, *paying*, you know—the papers seem to think it's *funny* to have stran-gers tramping all over these beautiful old places and gaping at them—*I* think it's *tragic*."

Daisy thought it as well to steer the conversation into other channels; these remarks did not bode well for the introduction of *lodgers*.

"What does he do?" she enquired.

"Michael? He's with that big West End firm of estate agents, George Mansfield and Company, and there's talk of his getting a partnership later on. Of course, he has private means, and his *connections* are very useful to them; he can drive people all over the place in his car, looking at houses and that sort of thing; it's so much more interesting than a mere office job."

"There's still a great shortage of places to live, isn't there?" Daisy had almost interrupted her hostess, but she felt that she was unlikely to get a better opening. "Actually . . ." and as she spoke she put her hand lightly on Mrs Cavendish's, "please don't think me an appalling nuisance . . . but that's what I want to talk to you about . . . Daddy's letter, I mean."

"Oh?" Mrs Cavendish's eyes softened, a very little.

She had been so pleased—and relieved too—to hear from Godfrey Furnivall again *(we're dropping out of things because we're poor, it isn't decent how poor we are now, and where is it all going to end?)* that she had not really paid much attention to the sentence: *'Daisy has something important that she wants to talk to you about'*; so long as she could receive Claire Furnivall's daughter, and, through her, keep up her acquaintance with the family, she did not care what it was that Daisy had to say.

And as she looked now at the gay, delicate, confident face, she felt a stirring of affection towards her, and an actual gratitude to Daisy for her impeccable voice and manner, even for the aristocratic length of her legs. While this type of young woman came to sit in her drawing-room, thought Mrs Cavendish, she and Anthea were still 'inside'.

"What is it my dear?" she asked, with less than her usual gush.

"Well"—Daisy hesitated, then went boldly in—"I was wondering if you still have those empty rooms at the top of the house. Because I want you to let them to some friends of mine."

Again Mrs Cavendish's expression changed slightly. She said without hesitation:

"Are they nice people, Daisy?"

"Very nice," said Daisy promptly. It was the expected question, and she had answered quickly only so that Mrs Cavendish should not have time, even at this early stage, to feel any doubts.

She knew that the Hultons were not 'nice', in Old Cavendish's sense, at all. However, it was something that she had not shrieked with horror at the mere idea of letting her rooms. And now for the really bad news.

"They've got three small children," she said blithely.

"Oh." Mrs Cavendish 'pulled a face'. "Children . . . of course, I've never seriously thought about letting rooms at all"—Anthea just stirred in her seat and looked down at the floor—"but if you had said that they were old friends of your father's . . . I know, from experience, how difficult life can be in these days for those of us with gentle blood in our veins."

"I was up at Oxford with them. They're about my age," Daisy said, thinking that her hostess's veins were more probably full of bits of Spode and tiny Regency commodes.

"Oh, were you?" This was better; Mrs Cavendish's disappointment at not having some reference to a really good family or a title was slightly assuaged; at least they were educated.

"He's a chemist and—"

"Do you mean that he keeps a *shop*?"

"No, he doesn't keep a shop." Daisy found *herself* keeping her temper; the room was so cold, and she was desperately tired. "He's with the biggest of the electricity corporations, Eastern Electric."

"I have always wondered how anyone can *bear* having their beautiful possessions exposed to *children*—how *do* they stand it? I can't imagine," said Mrs Cavendish.

The remark sounded irrelevant, and while Daisy (wishing to stall off the inevitable question about 'his background') was rapidly explaining the Hultons' situation in detail, it became obvious to her that Mrs Cavendish's thoughts were elsewhere.

Indeed they were. She was suffering the last, the final, the decisive struggle about the letting of those rooms, and the pain of it drew the blood from her face beneath its out-moded coating of powder and rouge.

It had begun years and years ago, before the war, as a kind of proud little whim, the keeping of them empty and unused until she found exactly the right, the perfect, pieces to furnish them. And after Francis's death (in the prime of life! in his prime!! who could have dreamt of it happening?) they had remained empty from necessity. Years had passed; Anthea had grown up, and always there had been less and less money. The proud little whim had ended up as an ever-present, gnawing anxiety: the knowledge that the rooms were there, empty except for a few frail old pieces, and that people were willing to pay fantastic rents nowadays for unfurnished accommodation. Piece after beloved antique piece she had been compelled to let go to the dealers . . . and Anthea would be twenty-eight in January and she had not had a satisfactory proposal yet. Mrs Cavendish herself was sometimes faint with actual hunger.

She looked up at the mirror above the mantelshelf, in its frame of gilt *gesso* with the pretty shells, and experienced a familiar sensation of comfort and pride.

"Have you any idea what they were—how much—I mean, do you know what are the usual terms in such a case?" she asked, sitting upright, and forcing back the deep recurring sigh of the chronically anxious woman.

Now Daisy had been dreading this question. Either Old Cavendish would demand ten guineas a week for her rooms, or she would let them go for twenty-five shillings and blame Daisy ever afterwards. Inexperienced landladies always did one or the other, in Daisy's experience. But best to get it said and done with.

"They couldn't pay much. They're hard up," she said firmly. "They won't be, when once he's qualified to get a really good job, but just now they are. Very."

"It was only idle curiosity; I wasn't serious. I could never face the thought of sticky little fingers all over my furniture," Mrs Cavendish said with a small laugh. "Especially as I shall have to look after my things myself now. My *daily help* has been pleased to give *notice*."

Her voice was very bitter. So they were poor, of course, these people, like everybody else. She was a fool to have imagined it would be otherwise. But at least she had made up her mind: the rooms would have to go.

'She always did have a thing about servants,' mused Daisy, who was herself gifted with the power of 'managing' such specimens of that almost extinct race which are still in circulation. 'Bang goes Katy's chance, I suppose. She wanted someone rich.'

Anthea said, in her little, deb's voice: "Poor Mums. She was a disrespectful old thing, that Mrs Crossley. Does your friend like housework, Daisy? Perhaps she could help Mummy, and we could charge her less for the rooms."

Mrs Cavendish, who had been staring into the fire, glanced up.

"Oh do you think she would, Daisy? Is she strong?"

Daisy was exceedingly surprised. She had thought that the discussion was over. She did not know how low Mrs Cavendish's heart had sunk at the prospect of the advertising, the interviewing, the arranging, and bargaining. It would all be simplified, if she let to Daisy's friends. Nor did Daisy know how exhausted her hostess became, nowadays, after doing even the lightest forms of housework. The idea of having a strong young woman (who was probably not quite a lady and could therefore be ordered about) *living in*, even paying something, although it might not be much, and washing paint, polishing silver, and scrubbing the kitchen floor, was as irresistibly alluring to Mrs Cavendish as any prospect of speedy relief is to someone approaching the limit of their endurance.

"She's as strong as most people, I suppose," Daisy said.

"She didn't take her Diploma in Domestic Science at Oxford, I suppose?" eagerly.

"She took an Honours Degree in Chemistry." Daisy was feeling rather as if a horse had run away with her. "I don't really—"

"Because, as Anthea says, if she were prepared to give me an hour or so's help in the house every day—I'm so desperate to find someone who will really care for my beautiful things and take a pride in keeping them nice—and if your friend is so desperate for somewhere to live—I might let her have the rooms at a ridiculously low rent—in exchange for housework."

"That's very good of you but—"

"The children, of course, I forgot the children." Mrs Cavendish's manner was growing excited, and Daisy felt rather uncomfortable. "I don't think I could face the worry of wondering if they were breaking things and leaving dirty marks everywhere—"

"They're unusually good children. Or so their father says." Daisy was advancing cautiously, because she did not like the sound of all this: she might, if she entered into any definite arrangement, be letting Katy in for something that she would heartily dislike.

"'Good', are they? What a wonder, for nowadays!" Mrs Cavendish's dentures showed sourly for an instant. "But what do you think of the idea, Daisy? Would she do it?"

"I simply don't know, Mrs Cavendish. The youngest child is only three months—"

"A baby!" It was a faint shriek. "Oh, that really *does* settle it! Nappies in the garden!"

"You could make her hang them at the top of the house," Anthea said, with a trace of impatience, "you needn't ever see them, or the children either. You'll have to be firm with these people if you're going to be a landlady, you know." She smiled quickly, secretively, at Daisy.

"A 'landlady'! Doesn't it sound dreadful! They would drip all over my floors, dearest."

"How much do you think they could pay?" asked Anthea, turning to Daisy, and, with the latter's firm announcement that she was certain it wouldn't be more than thirty-five shillings a week *(Katy can always offer more)* which brought a cry of protest from Mrs Cavendish, there followed ten minutes of discussion and argument; with the mother quoting the sums generally asked by the owners of unfurnished rooms (it was plain to Daisy that she had been studying the advertisements in the press—a good sign) and the daughter quoting 'Michael' on the extreme difficulty of getting unfurnished flats without paying a large premium or buying numerous expensive 'fittings'.

"Well, may I see the rooms?" Daisy asked at last, perceiving that nothing definite seemed likely to emerge. "Then I can at least tell Katy what they're like."

"Yes; I think perhaps you had better," Mrs Cavendish said. She was looking extremely tired. She glanced hesitatingly at Anthea, then continued, "And I think, Daisy, that you can write to your friend—Mrs Hulton, is it?—if you will be so kind, and say that I am willing to let her have them."

Daisy exclaimed in surprise and relief:

"But that's wonderful! When do you think they could come? Next week?"

"Next *week*? You *are* in a hurry, aren't you? I don't think I could possibly manage next week. There will be paint to clean— and I must see about some sort of a carpet for the back room—you will make them understand, won't you, that I'm *strictly* letting them *furnished*?"

"Oh, they want them furnished, they haven't—"

"Because I gather that if you let *furnished*, you can always turn them out if they are troublesome."

"Yes, but they won't be, I'm sure." (Daisy just prevented herself from adding the rash 'you'll love them'.) "And they haven't a thing of their own. They'll want every bit of furniture you can give them."

"Coming?" Anthea said.

They went up the stairs, through an increasing chilliness and silence. Daisy glanced at the signs of privation as they went: the carpetless landings, the brocade curtains, clean but almost in shreds, the paint worn away by continual scrubbing, the deadly, insinuating cold of a house that had not for years known any central core of lavish heat; and thought, 'It's like a museum that's gone bankrupt.' But everywhere there was something to delight the eye: a graceful chair, a long window whose narrow panes revealed the dim face of the rising moon. In spite of her exhaustion and chill, Daisy began to feel calmed, and the confusion of plans, which had rushed into her head on hearing Mrs Cavendish's decision, gradually receded. There was so much to be done; but, meanwhile, it was refreshing to move amidst this chill, spare, fragile beauty in silence.

But Anthea soon began to whisper.

"You know," she began confidentially as they reached the first landing, "it would be a very good thing if Mummy could get this girl to help her."

"She doesn't look at all well," Daisy retorted; it wasn't kind, but she thought that Anthea could take it.

"Oh, I know. But she *will* wear herself out polishing and washing paint; the whole house has to be washed down every three months. And she hates doing it."

"I'm not really surprised your char gave notice."

"Oh, she was the usual Bolshy type. Mummy was always kind to her and gave her elevenses and that kind of thing—she ate like a horse, too. But then, of course, that class always does. They're all spoilt nowadays. Michael says it's just the same even in the country."

Daisy, who accepted the alleged spoiling as a fact which she wasted no time in lamenting, did not answer. She was trembling with the cold.

"Let's go on, shall we? By the way, can your friend cook?" Anthea asked casually.

"She has to. But she hates it and she's not good," Daisy improvised. She was beginning to feel slightly uneasy. Just how much housework did they mean Katy to do?

"Here we are," said Anthea. "Fearful climb, isn't it . . . just a jiffy, until I find the light."

A jiffy! What peculiar world, frozen into the present century's teens, did Miss Cavendish inhabit?

A weak glow suddenly shone down on the usual gleaming boards. Daisy stood, frankly shivering now, at the top of a noticeably steep flight of stairs. She could just discern four white doors, grouped about a landing which retained graceful proportions although reduced to the smallest possible size. Somewhere a cistern dripped quietly, and she could hear the wind whining overhead around the roof. She was so cold that she ached.

"There are some things in here," Anthea carelessly opened a door; "but there isn't much, I'm afraid."

"No, there isn't." Daisy's righteous indignation rose at the understatement: the room was almost filled by a solitary Empire sofa. "Your mother will have to find quite a lot of stuff."

"Haven't they *anything* of their own?"

"Not much." *(And what they have will be provided by Mrs James Muir, the well-known Angel of Mercy.)* Daisy was now so cross that she was beginning to feel warmer; she ran rapidly through a list of people who could profitably be raided for bed-linen, saucepans and old carpets.

"Perhaps one of the children could sleep on the sofa," Anthea suggested in a kind voice. "It could be made really cosy up here . . ."

"They haven't a thousand pounds to spare."

There was a rather conscious pause while Anthea opened another door. Daisy saw that she must not give way to her feelings; Anthea might inhabit an extraordinary private world in which she called working-class people 'Bolshy', but she was quite capable of making some petulant objection to her mother that would threaten the whole plan. She must be kept sweet . . . and keeping people sweet was one of the tasks which, when she was engaged in one of her campaigns for helping her friends, Daisy really disliked. She was by nature both honest and brave, and she liked to speak her mind.

"I shan't mind them coming, actually," Anthea said suddenly, keeping her eyes fixed on the couple of delicate old chairs that were the sole occupants of the next room, "the house feels awfully spooky sometimes with just Mummy and me."

If it was a plea of *some* kind, for *something*, Daisy was too occupied with her own plans to hear it. She was also deciding that she knew nothing about Anthea, except that she did not much like her.

"How will they heat the place?" she demanded forthrightly.

"Oh, coal fires." The big blue eyes now rested innocently on her face. "Don't you love these pretty old grates?"

"They're absolutely charming . . . aren't you wired for power up here, or isn't there a gas pipe?" She peered keenly at the floor near the fireplace.

Anthea shook her head.

"It'll have to be coal, I suppose, unless they can run to oil heating."

"Mummy could never stand the smell, Daisy."

"The new kind doesn't smell . . . (is this all?—let's go down, shall we?) How will they manage about water?"

"Mrs Whatsit will have to carry it up from the kitchen. I don't think Mummy will want her tramping in and out of the bathroom."

How Daisy longed to say that she had decided Mrs Whatsit wouldn't want to tramp round here at all!

But, remembering the note in Katy's voice on the telephone, she had a conviction that she would come here, *and* carry coal and water up fifty stairs *and* polish Old Cavendish's furniture, and be glad of the chance.

"I say, I'll have to warn Katy about these," she remarked, as they cautiously descended, "the children might break their necks . . . do you think your mother can find enough stuff to furnish four rooms?"

Anthea shook her head. "Then she'll have to let me help," said Daisy. "I'll have a whip-round . . . if I get on to it first thing tomorrow I think we could be ready by tomorrow week. I'll make a list tonight . . ."

"Come into my room a minute," Anthea said. "The only really important thing, Daisy," she began when they were in that pink apartment furnished with a few fine old pieces, "is to get your friend to help Mummy in the house. That matters much more than the money—though that will be useful too. (It's shockingly little; we ought to be getting quite six guineas. Perhaps Mummy could put the rent up later.) If she'll only agree to do some housework, Mummy will put up with the tiny rent and the children." She paused. "Perhaps you could get your friend to sign a paper," she said.

Sign a paper! Daisy was speechless. "You see," Anthea went on, "Mummy really does have this sort of 'thing' about servants. It's—it's kind of her 'thing'. And she really is doing too much. She knows she is, but she can't stop herself. It's a sort-of what-do-you-call-it."

"Yes." Daisy was wondering just what Anthea did to relieve the sort-of what-do-you-call-it. Her hands were white and her nails rosy and smooth.

"I do what I can, of course, but I really do hate chores, and I *can't* do my kind of job with awful hands," Anthea added. She had evidently noticed the quick glance.

"*I* don't see why everything need be kept so immaculate. It really is dotty, Anthea. It's keeping up a—a pre-1939 standard in the *Atomic Age*." Daisy brought out the phrase with a solemn air.

"Oh well, I know. But Mummy likes to do it, Daisy—at least, she likes the results. She would be miserable if she didn't."

And what is she now? Daisy wondered. She looked into Anthea's innocent face; if you did not study her closely she might pass for nineteen. What did she really want—care for—work for?

Or did her days pass in a kind of mocked-up upper-middle-class dream? Daisy, who had known her, off and on, almost ever since she could remember, had never thought much about Anthea Cavendish until this moment.

"Mummy's things, you know, her furniture and that, are sort-of her *life*," Anthea irrelevantly said.

Daisy continued to look at her in silence. She definitely did feel slightly uneasy. What was she letting that little Katy in for?

Suddenly, she realised that four clean rooms at thirty-five shillings a week were within her grasp. Had she actually been *hesitating*? She said quickly:

"I'm certain it will be all right about the housework. Do you think your mother would mind if I sent her a note tonight, from here, just to tell her the thing's settled?"

"I don't expect so. But do make it *clear* about the housework," Anthea laughing gently, said.

"What a delicious smell. It's 'Joy', isn't it?" asked Daisy as they were leaving the room.

"Oh no, just some stuff I bought myself; quite cheap," Anthea babbled, and rather quickly shut the door. "Have you ever had any? I've always longed to possess a bottle."

But it was 'Joy'; Daisy did happen to have owned a bottle once, and why was Anthea lying?

Mrs Cavendish's eyes fixed themselves on Daisy as the two girls came back into the room.

"Well?" she enquired with a painful playfulness, "are my poor little rooms going to be good enough for your clever friends?" She half hoped and half dreaded that they wouldn't be. Yet they were such charming rooms! Anyone ought to be grateful . . .

"I think they could fit in very well there," Daisy said firmly, smiling. Poor Old Cavendish looked worn out. "The point is this: *they* haven't any furniture, and there's next to nothing up there, is there? So I'm going to get really busy and collect some. It'll all be other people's cast-offs. You won't mind that, will you?" Her smile was as disarming as a full-blown rose.

"My dear Daisy," Mrs Cavendish said wearily, but with a smile too, "having once brought myself to let the rooms, I really don't mind what goes into them. My own things must stay up there of course."

"And I must see about a cooker of some kind . . ." Daisy's voice had taken on an absent, ruminative tone that would have been gloomily recognised by James.

"Cooker! I thought she would use the kitchen."

"And carry hot food up fifty stairs? We *can't* really ask her to do that, do you think?"

"*I* think," Mrs Cavendish pronounced, "that beggars can't be—well, I can only hope she won't set the house on fire frying—what do they call them—*chips* all day. You do what you please, Daisy." She leant back again in her chair and looked wearily at her old friend's daughter; she felt too tired to move, but there was a sense of refreshment in being thus manoeuvered and decided for and managed; a current of reviving air seemed to be sweeping through the house, such as she had not felt since her husband had been alive.

Daisy's note to Katy, which she wrote at Mrs Cavendish's desk, said simply:

'I've got you the rooms. Four of them, furnished rather tattily. No telephone, icy cold, she wants you to do a bit of housework every day. BUT v. quiet and only thirty-five shillings a week. You move in on Friday at tea-time. Aren't I clever? Will write again tomorrow. Love D.'

"Have you made it *quite* clear about the housework?" Anthea asked, putting her head round the door; she had been putting on her coat in the hall. Daisy nodded as she sealed the envelope.

"I'll come with you to the bus," Anthea said.

"Oh dearest—must you? It's such a horrid damp night," said her mother.

Anthea smilingly said that she wanted some air, and, Daisy having given Mrs Cavendish one of her hearty kisses, they went out together.

The conversation while waiting for a cruising taxi (Daisy soon disabused Anthea of any notions about the use of buses) was taken up with arrangements for the following week: Anthea would be working such and such hours if Daisy wanted to telephone her;

her mother would always be at home in the afternoons to take in parcels or receive van-men; there was a large single bed, among other things, that Anthea thought the Hultons might have; Daisy was pretty certain that next week she would be so busy collecting furniture that she could not take a job at all; and so forth.

She glanced out of the taxi window as it drove away, and Anthea, just passing a telephone box on her way home, smiled and waved to her.

"That place is a morgue," Daisy said emphatically to James, while they were sitting over the drink he had prescribed for her as a reviver, "and so *depressing*. I'm sorry for Anthea, but she's rather peculiar and *sly*, I feel. However, with a Mummy like Old Cavendish you jolly well have to be sly."

"It sounds like it," said James.

"If it was me," Daisy handsomely announced, "I should be getting all the madly expensive bottles of scent that I could get out of Michael Devon, and sleeping with him into the bargain."

"Perhaps she is," said James.

CHAPTER X
. . . *And Daughter*

ANTHEA, standing in the telephone box, pressed the button marked A and waited. Her heart was beating faster than usual, but not as it used to beat a year ago.

"Hullo?" A girl's voice, still warm with the laugh that had been broken off to answer the telephone. "Yes . . . who wants him? Miss who? All right, hold on: I'll get him."

That was all right; it was only Caroline. She had met his sister, twice, but Caroline had not remembered her name . . . or perhaps she had not troubled to listen . . . she heard a good many girls' names, Anthea knew, when she came up from Richmond to a dance and stayed the night at Michael's rooms in Green Park. She could faintly hear the gramophone playing *In the Still of the Night*. It would have to be that, wouldn't it.

"Hullo?"

"Oh—hullo—it's me. I just wanted—"

"I thought I asked you—" The voice checked itself and went on more quietly, "You knew Caro was going to be here, didn't you?"

"Yes . . . I'm sorry, but—"

"She's rather too inquisitive about my affairs, that's all. Well?"

"It's all right."

"Good girl. We'll celebrate on Friday. I'll call you. Take care of yourself. *And* I mean it."

"Are you—"

But the receiver had been replaced.

Anthea replaced her own and went out of the box into the quiet damp night. Once more the question had been asked and answered. It was the only intimacy that existed between them—that question (apart from the unbelievable, the shocking intimacy that it would kill Mummy to know about); it was never mentioned, much less discussed; it never had been, since just after the first time.

And then its inferences had only been casually referred to, as an unwanted possibility. She could see his fresh handsome face as he said the words; casually, with the smile that used to make her heart turn over lurking on his charming curly mouth.

No, her heart did not turn over any more, because she was no longer wildly in love with him. 'Wildly' came into her thoughts unexpectedly; it was not the kind of word that she used. Yet once, the sight of him, the sound of his voice, the mere sound of his name, even 'Green Park' on an Underground map, had made her heart beat as though it would break through her breast.

Funny; where had all that feeling gone? Nowadays, her only feelings were anxieties; would anything go wrong, would anyone find out, was there any chance at all of his asking her to marry him? Worry, in fact; worry about Michael added to all the other worries.

Now they began to go round in her head again: the points that were in her favour.

She was a lady . . . he thought her very pretty . . . it had been going on for more than a year and yet he still . . . he could be very kind (she tried to shut out a sudden vivid vision of his face, intent and grave, bending over her own that first time in the summer twilight; she shut her ears against the memory of his muttered words) . . . he had been so *unexpectedly* kind, that first time . . . he was never rude to her or casual, at the very worst he just didn't tell her things . . . he kept her shut out . . . and sometimes a kind of gentleness, that was very attractive, showed through the smooth, amused surface of his personality.

It was through this gentleness that she would get him, if she ever did. But it came so seldom! He was usually rather amused and cheerful, and quite ungetatable; bored by tales of hard luck (she had learned, very early, not to complain to him about anything), irritated to the point of disgust by signs of poverty, impatient of other people's muddled or painful lives. His surprise, when he had learned that she was not on the telephone at home, was another thing that she would not easily forget.

"Going far?"

It was a young policeman, standing square across the path of her leisurely progress homewards, and she did not like his expression or his smile. She swung the latchkey from one gloved finger as she answered gently: "I've just been seeing someone to the bus stop," and had the satisfaction of seeing his manner change at the sound of her voice. She looked up innocently into his youthful face.

"Not a very nice evening, is it? Good-night, miss." He walked slowly on.

They have to be careful; there are so many of these dreadful girls about, Anthea thought.

No; Michael didn't seem to want to slip out of their affair or to break it off; he didn't *seem* to, but how could she really tell? He never talked about their relationship, and she was afraid to. She coloured slightly in the darkness, as if at the memory of some social blunder, as she remembered his expression when she had called *In the Still of the Night* 'our tune'.

"Do we have to have a tune?"

"Oh . . . no . . . I only thought . . ."

"It's rather sort of corny, don't you think?"

And Anthea had answered, smiling, that she supposed it was.

She learned her lesson. She had never made that kind of blunder again, any more than she ever introduced the topic of marriage, or even that of engagements. She was not a fool, and she had quite as much pride as the next girl.

Yet her only aim in life, the one thing that she wanted, the wish that was always behind everything she thought and felt and did—was to . . . well, rather than to *marry* him, it was to get a proposal out of him.

It would be so marvellous! Good-looking, well-connected, with private means, ambitious, in the running for an old title— he was so utterly desirable in every possible way; an ambitious mother's dream.

Mummy certainly thought so—poor Mummy, who had kept such a close watch on all Anthea's not-very-numerous young men, and made her turn down two unsatisfactory offers, ever since that silly boy-and-girl affair with Jimmy Field eleven years ago (poor Jimmy too—his father had been a builder's merchant in St Albans). Mummy was so sick of scraping and pinching and going without.

She couldn't be sicker of it than Anthea was.

And if she did get a proposal out of Michael, of course she would marry him. But young men got tired of one, that was a well known fact, sooner than one got tired of them, and Anthea knew that she would have to get that proposal out of him before he began to get tired of her.

She was safe, she thought, so far. He was not getting tired.

But how much time had she? How long before he began to tire? She just did not know.

As she pushed open the garden gate, she looked about her; at the dimly-lit, dreary road, and the elegant old houses falling into dilapidation; through their windows she could see beautiful rooms filled with modern furniture or the bright colours of contemporary taste. Dirt, shoddiness, decay: the road was slipping down into slumdom as fast as it could go. Oh! to get *out* of it!

How did one make a young man propose?

The answer came back like a blow: *not by doing what you have done.*

Yes, that had been . . . silly. But she had lost her head.

It was done now and it couldn't be helped. She would not lose it again. She didn't feel like that any more.

She went up the steps and entered the quiet, cold house.

Her mother was dozing by the dying fire.

"Hullo, dearest—well, did you see her safely on to the bus?"

Mummy looked old tonight, and these fussy questions were something new . . . well, she was over sixty, poor Mummy. But she could still look elegant; she had kept her figure and she never slopped about, even when they were alone.

Daughter looked at mother with fond eyes. There was no question of sentiment, it was not in Anthea's temperament; but she felt that there was no one quite like Mummy.

They talked for a while about the letting of the rooms and Anthea soothed some doubts. The money was ridiculous, of course, but it would be useful, and it would be wonderful to have help in the house. Mrs Cavendish gradually began to feel more cheerful; Anthea was always so sensible and such a comfort. And so pretty; tonight, in her rose pink and her pearls—in her mother's eyes at least—she was perfect.

For the thousandth time Mrs Cavendish repressed an impulse, strengthened by the lateness of the hour and their intimacy and the hopeful prospect of change, to make the most delicate of tactful enquiries about Michael Devon.

She had been controlling herself thus for nearly a year; ever since the day when she had actually knelt down and thanked God, with tears running down her face, because Anthea was going out with him. She never relaxed her guard upon herself; she even avoided scanning Anthea's face when she came home from dining or driving with him, and it was an effort that needed all her considerable powers of will, because the longing to hear Anthea say, "Mummy, we're engaged—" was strong as thirst.

She had no doubt that her pretty, sensible girl would know instinctively how to bring a young man to the point (ladies always did), but time was going on, and Anthea told her nothing, and every month there seemed to be bigger bills and smaller dividends, and she felt older and more hopeless and more tired.

If Anthea were married to Michael, Mrs Cavendish could live out her days in modest comfort on the income that could not longer, in these days of inflation, be stretched—even with what Anthea contributed—adequately to support two.

There were beginning to be debts. Oh, not big ones. Just bills left owing here and there for longer than she thought dignified for herself or fair to the tradespeople. Francis had always settled all bills within ten days of their arrival: it had been a household rule, and he had always budgeted their income so that it could be carried out. Francis . . . how safe and prosperous she had felt in his care . . . with the years stretching comfortably ahead for them!

"Daisy hasn't changed a bit, has she?" observed Anthea, as they made to go up to bed.

"No, bless her." It gratified Mrs Cavendish to sound maternal towards Mrs James Muir and, indeed, this evening she did feel fond of her. "She's just as pretty . . . I never did *like* her style of dressing, of course. But she can carry it off."

"Too extreme," murmured Anthea. "Those beetle-back suits look sort of deformed, I think."

Her mother glanced at her.

"I think I'll ask Godfrey Furnivall in to coffee one evening, when once we've got these people settled upstairs . . . would you like to see him again?"

Anthea, who knew quite well what train of thought had prompted this suggestion, made an indeterminate little sound . . .

Mummy was seldom so *obvious*. It was rather maddening, really. There was quite enough going on, about Michael, without having Colonel Furnivall produced as alternative choice. As if, too—having had poor Jim Field's memory exorcized for ever by Michael's first kiss—one would want to marry an old man . . . unless, of course, one were actually desperate to marry just *anybody*. But Mummy did not know about Michael's first kiss and God forbid that she ever should, unless it could be made retrospectively respectable by an engagement.

"Let's get these creatures arranged first," she said soothingly. "It won't be too bad having them in some ways, do you think?

Company for you while I'm out daily-breading." She slipped her arm about her mother's waist.

"I don't think I shall want *their* company, dearest," Mrs Cavendish said.

CHAPTER XI
Three Little Mice

BUT the next week was one of the liveliest socially that she had spent for years, yet not exhaustingly so, for Daisy Muir, who looked in at least once every day, took most of the work on her own shoulders. Having allowed herself to be persuaded that the rooms needed no more cleaning ("God knows the walls are nearly worn through with washing now," was Daisy's private verdict to James), Mrs Cavendish had only to stay at home—and she had almost given up going out, anyway—and open the door to people carrying things.

They surprised her by possessing educated voices, in spite of wearing the most peculiar clothes and driving very odd cars (but she knew that that was fashionable). Bearing a chair or a rack for drying clothes or an old blanket, up the stairs, they would bound, deliver their burden and wave a cheerful farewell as they made off. "I'm a friend of Daisy's," they would shout.

Sometimes, alas, they were foreigners.

It was extremely sad, disgraceful, really, the way London was becoming given over to foreigners. If there was a class of person that Mrs Cavendish disliked as much as she did those of inferior birth, it was those who had been born outside England, and in these she included visitors from the Commonwealth—'Colonials'.

But even when they were foreign (alas) they were polite. There was one little man, dark and silent, who arrived bearing two gas-rings. On one visit, Daisy had joyfully announced the discovery of a gas-pipe lurking under the floor-boards in the room to be used as a kitchen. 'They belonged to Hester Bryant' was the only detail of the rings' history that Mrs Cavendish ever heard. He also had a large box tied up with rope. He vanished upstairs;

standing at the drawing-room door, she heard distant banging and clanking. After an hour or so, he descended, paused long enough in the hall to say, "I make them an oven," and departed. Mrs Cavendish tiptoed up to her little rooms, so soon to be handed over to un-nice strangers and saw in one of them a—a *contraption* arranged over the two gas-rings on a table. It all looked highly rusty, improvised and unsafe, and she was only partly reassured by the grudging verdict concerning its trust-worthiness given by a Gas Board official who arrived to inspect it some days later. He qualified his approval further by adding that no amachoor ever fixed up these things *really* correct. Mrs Cavendish began to wonder if it wouldn't have been wiser to let Daisy arrange a proper kitchen. But it was too late now.

The only room in which she herself took any interest was that overlooking the distant trees of Primrose Hill, and here, in the prettiest of the four, she insisted on arranging some charming old chairs and a faded carpet all over ribbons and roses; adding a looking-glass above the fireplace and one or two graceful oddments on the mantelshelf, she made what she was satisfied was a delightful sitting-room. She shuddered over the battered pieces collected by Daisy for the two bedrooms—"I had a job getting that out of my rich girlfriend Sue Ruddlin, she said she had been *meaning* to sell it—exactly the right word," said Daisy—but better this rubbish being bounced on and scratched by the children than her own beloved things, Mrs Cavendish thought.

On the day before the Hultons were due to arrive, Daisy, who always came and went by taxi, sailed up accompanied by a very large oil convector heater and a tin of pink paraffin. These, she explained, were a belated wedding present from herself and James to Katy and Don. She showed the taxi-driver where to put them while Mrs Cavendish stood silently watching.

"I'm *amazed* at how much I've remembered about cast-offs," confided Daisy, as they followed the man downstairs "Saucepans—old rugs—pillows—I *cast my mind back* and I remembered *masses* of people I'd heard say they were getting new things. I just asked for the old ones."

"Will it *smell*?"

"What? The oil heater? Oh no, the new kind don't." She turned back on the doorstep to smile at her mother's old friend: pretty thing, in her fluffy coat and her hat like a beehive. Mrs Cavendish had returned the smile faintly. It was hopeless to expect the young to understand how one felt, and a gentlewoman never whined, anyway.

Daisy, riding homewards in the taxi, was running over in her mind all the last details. Yes: everything was ready. She had written twice to Katy, keeping her informed about the progress of the arrangements, but not mentioning her own part in the equipping of the flat; she had from the first allowed Katy to believe that the rooms were completely furnished.

She was now so absorbed in making a home for the Hultons that she thought and talked of nothing else. In the evenings James sat with the *Evening Standard* for company while Daisy attacked the squares and avenues of Belsize Park, Primrose Hill and Hampstead in search of cast-offs. Janine took the opportunity to see her friends while James baby-sat, and three times his soup was served nearly cold. The Meissners, the Beresfords, the Lanes and Trevelyans and NacNeils also passed a lively week, thanks to Mrs James Muir.

It may have been with a subconscious wish to spike Daisy's final plans that James suggested to his mother, who lived outside London, that she should come up to spend the day with them on Saturday. She said that she would let them know.

Daisy, at the end of the week, had become extremely tired and violently irritable.

On the Friday evening before the Hultons arrived in London, she had Katy on the telephone:

"The train gets in to Paddington at two o'clock. You'll be there, won't you?"

"Oh—well—the fact is, James's *mother* is probably coming up to spend the day—it really is rather sickening, I did want to see you in, but—"

"I took it for granted you'd meet us, Daisy. It'll make things so much easier if you're there to introduce us to her." (By 'her'

Katy meant their new landlady, and Daisy, fussed and dismayed, knew that it would.)

"I'll try. If I can't be there I'll—somebody will be, anyway."

"All right." It seemed to be one of Katy's days for not saying 'thank you'. There was a pause. Daisy remembered that she had not equipped the flat with a frying pan. And if they were to ask Old Cavendish tomorrow she would scream and start talking about smells . . .

"They wrote to me, you know," said Katy abruptly.

"Old Cavendish did?"

"No—her daughter, I suppose—she referred to 'my mother'. She'd got it all worked out. No housework, no rooms."

"Katy!" said Daisy. "How—perfectly—extraordinary!"

"I thought it was, myself."

"What did she say about the housework?"

"Oh, just that she didn't know if Mrs Muir had made it perfectly clear, etc. etc."

"The little—" Daisy checked herself *(do not put the tenants against the landlady's daughter)*. "Did she say how much house-work they'll expect?"

"'A certain amount', she said."

"I don't like that," said Daisy decidedly. "It's too . . . elastic. I wish you'd consulted me before you agreed to it."

"I didn't agree to it. I didn't answer the letter."

"Good for you . . . I do hope you won't mind it too much, Katy." Daisy's voice became almost timid.

"I shan't *like* it, of course; I'll have quite enough housework of my own. But Hultons can't be choosers." Her voice had the unexpected ghost of a laugh.

"Oh Katy, I *do* hope you'll like it there!" cried Daisy, moved by memories of old jokes together, and old arguments, and a mutual disrespect for Oxford authority—unable to help wanting to hear some expression at least, of *pleasure*. "It looks . . . it's quite comfortable, really, I think," she added. "The living-room's a bit museumy, but—"

"I expect I'll like it, it'll be just too bad if I don't," Katy said dryly. "Never mind what it looks like, if we've got four rooms to ourselves and it's quiet."

There was a pause.

"All right then," said Katy, "we'll be seeing you."

James entering at that moment with a card from his mother saying that she would be with them by eleven on Saturday morning, Daisy hastily rang up Molly Raymond.

"Saturdays are very precious," was Molly's contribution to the dilemma. "I never know what may crop up of a Saturday."

"*Tibbs*, I suppose?" said Daisy fiercely, her frayed nerves crackling. "Are you seeing him again?"

"Oh no," said Molly, who had just been sitting opposite his eyelashes in a tea-shop. "Nothing *regular*. But he's always liable to call me up Saturdays. Just casually."

Daisy began to plead.

"Listen, Molly, it won't take more than a couple of hours—not that. I'd be so grateful if you would. Just meet them at the station and take them along and introduce them for me. It'll make all the difference, having them taken there by a friend of mine—I did promise Katy I'd send *someone* if I couldn't go myself."

"Is she nice, this Katy of yours?" Molly, driven towards a decision, took refuge in sentiment. "I imagine her with one of those soft Scottish voices. I'm a pushover for the Scotch."

"She has a Scottish accent. It isn't particularly soft," *('God give me patience')* Daisy answered, wondering if Molly would have refused outright if told about Katy's Glasgow tones. "Listen, I must fly. You *will* go, won't you?"

"I'll do that, Daisy. I've taken a fancy to this Katy of yours, so don't you worry—I'll see her through, and the children too."

"Thanks awfully. That'll be a weight off my mind. Good-bye . . ."

"Oh . . . er . . . er . . ."

"What?" sharply; James Too was bellowing in the distance.

"Would you terribly mind if maybe I took Tibbs along? The fact is, he's borrowed a car from a friend, and he could maybe drive us to your Mrs Cavendish's. It would save the fare."

"I don't mind. Good-bye."

She did mind. And she pitied Tibbs's car-owner sucker. But Molly's problems and moral welfare were of long standing, and Katy's troubles were new. Daisy put her irritation about Molly aside; she would concentrate on the Hultons.

She often regretfully found that working on the problems of new friends replaced working on those of the old.

Tibbs and Molly, side by side in the borrowed car, soon identified the Hultons, standing in a cross, pale, shabby group.

"Refugees," said Tibbs, in the light mocking voice that he knew how to make musical, "English refugees—from the English way of life, your housing shortage, your class system, your cost of living."

"Next you'll be saying you were better off at home."

"So I was—in some ways." Molly glanced at him, alert for a sigh. But when one came, it was from herself. He never would tell her anything about 'at home'.

"She isn't like what I'd imagined her," she said, studying Mrs Hulton, "and aren't the kiddies small, poor little mites."

Tibbs shrugged. Molly was always imagining people; she had imagined him, and a tiresome fuss she had made when he had turned out to be different. As for the children, he had seen plenty of small, pale thin Czech and German and Greek ones—what was there to say about these? Molly was annoying, with her silly chatter. But not so annoying that he had had to throw her over; she was still useful.

Molly sat for a moment longer before rousing herself to her task. How unfriendly the Hultons looked! Wrapped up in their own affairs, shut glumly inside their unattractive family circle. And *plain*! Molly did so love good looks and friendliness and a bit of glamour. Well . . .

"This won't do," she said, beginning to get out of the car. "You'd better stay here," at which he merely shrugged.

The car was parked alongside one of the platforms and the Hultons were standing some fifty feet away, motionless in the midst of the hurrying Saturday afternoon crowds. Molly made her way towards them, mentally rehearsing a welcoming speech. She was nervous, as well as disappointed in their looks, for Daisy had inadvertently let slip the fact that Mrs Hulton was clever. But Molly had said she would see the Hultons through, and she would.

"Are you Mrs Hulton?" she began cheerfully, addressing the small woman in the duffel coat. "I'm a friend of Daisy's—Molly Raymond, at your service. Daisy's awfully sorry but she couldn't make it after all. She sends her love and—will I take you to the flat—we've got a car—just over there—a friend of mine's driving— she hopes to get a peep at you this evening. She's awfully sorry but it's just one of those things." She faltered rather towards the end of her speech, because the grey eyes looking at her were so steady and so cold.

Katy Hulton slightly moved her head, as if to settle the lank red hair hanging on her shoulders, and answered in a low tone, "Oh. I see." Her lips just parted; smiling did not improve her pale, gaunt face. "She did say she mightn't be able to come. This is my husband"—indicating a large shape in the background at which Molly felt it more prudent not to glance (not just yet, anyway)— "and here are Mark and Mary. Now you know what to say," she added to them sharply.

They were dressed in faded shrunken duffel coats exactly like her own. Their small white faces were lifted to Molly's and they made a shot at 'good-afternoon', the boy bringing it out intelligibly, the girl (*oh dear, freckles and carrots and not even quaint*) following her failure with a burst of babble, which her mother checked with a look.

"This is Maggie, she doesn't say anything yet," added Katy Hulton with another faint smile, glancing down at the carry-cot at her feet.

Maggie was no beauty, either. Fast asleep, more red hair, and what a scowl!

Mark was pulling at his mother's sleeve.

"What is it? I told you to be quiet. He's all right. Father's got him. Yes, he *has* got his seed. No, his water *isn't* spilt. Oh well, we'll be there soon and you can give him some more if you're not naughty on the way . . . yes he *has* got his groundsel . . . *Don*," turning suddenly on her husband and raising her voice with a disconcerting effect of anger, "let him *see* the blasted bird, will you, and then perhaps he'll be quiet."

Mr Hulton now groped behind himself and produced to view what Molly (with the size of the car in mind) dismayedly thought of as *a regular Taj Mahal of a birdcage*; large, wide, deep, and plentifully adorned with domes, gilt, blue china, and bunches of wilting greenery. The budgerigar was clinging to the wires and chattering hysterically with every feather on end.

"There, isn't he a beauty," soothed Molly, who was rapidly getting to hate Katy Hulton. "He's only excited because of the journey, he'll be quite all right when you get home. What's his name?"

"Budgie. Original isn't it?" said Don Hulton with an awkward laugh. Molly darted a glance at him for the first time. Very *rough*. And she did like a man to be *close*-shaved. But even an unrefined type would appreciate feminine softness, and compare it with his wife's . . .

There was a rather long pause. Molly was beginning to feel as if she had been with the Hultons for three days. Why couldn't Katy H. say, "I'm simply dying to see the flat," as any other woman would have done? And a word of gratitude to herself for taking Daisy's place wouldn't have come amiss. What people! Positive savages. Say what you like about Tibbs, he could have very nice manners when he liked. If these were college-educated types, give Molly people who weren't.

She pulled herself together, in a way that was far from being natural to her, and prepared to take charge of the situation.

"Well," she was beginning, when—

"Good-afternoon," said the most charming of Tibbs' voices, "I also am a friend of Daisy's with a long foreigner name that you cannot remember. So you can call me Tibbs. It is my *petit nom*. I expect you are cold and tired and hungry after your journey, no?"

His cat's eyes dwelt with hypocritical sympathy on their unmoved faces. Journey! He could tell them something about journeys—and being cold and hungry and tired, as well as half-blinded by caked blood. He brought in his 'No?' because he knew that the interrogative intonation of this word had, for some reason, a softening effect upon the English. "I have my car here," he went on, "and I shall be glad to drive you to your flat. I shall carry this little one, no?" He tenderly lifted up Mary, looking at her freckles with distaste from under his eyelashes.

"She can walk," Katy said. "Oh, all right . . . Mark, you keep by me." She glanced keenly around, making certain that every bulging parcel and shabby case had its bearer, and, draggingly, with Molly struggling under Budgie's cage, the procession set off.

"Bloody circus, isn't it. You married?" Don Hulton grinned at Tibbs, who shook his head.

"It's got its compensations . . . I suppose," Don went on.

Tibbs was wondering just how to get the birdcage on to the car. Nowadays, when he spoke of any other problems than strictly practical ones, it was only to please some English intellectual who expected a foreigner from Mittel-Europa to be philosophical—and who might one day be good for a bed or a meal.

He managed it all, this afternoon. The car looked very small, the party and its baggage looked very large, but he got everything fitted in somehow, with smiles and jokes for the children and a gallant hand to assist Katy which brought from her the first low 'thank you' that Molly had heard. She was beginning to think she did not know the phrase. He then triumphantly produced a stout bit of rope from somewhere and lashed the birdcage in the boot.

Soon they left the traffic and the crowds behind and began to pass through a quieter district of old white houses, large blocks of new flats, and wide gardens with big trees.

"Want your tea?" Molly asked Mary, who was sitting on her lap. No one had spoken since the ride began; it was *so* unpleasant.

"Tea!" said Katy Hulton vigorously. "It's not three yet. Don't start them thinking about tea, please."

"Isn't it? It seems later than that." But Molly was not really surprised; time simply crawled while you were with these people, whereas when you were with Tibbs—she stole a glance at the intent irregular profile above the shabby muffler—it just flew.

"Here we are," she said, as they stopped outside the tall, forlorn house on the corner. Katy hardly turned her head but Don, Molly noticed with some satisfaction, was frankly staring around him. Every window of Mrs Cavendish's house was shut; dead leaves blew up and down the crumbling steps; knocker, bellpush and letter-box flashed in the fire of the declining sun.

"Pub just opposite, thank God," Don observed to his wife, and Molly was surprised to see Katy give him an answering smile.

"Like the look of it?" Molly asked out of sheer nervousness and desire that Katy should like the house, for Daisy had succeeded in transmitting some of her own interest in the Hultons to at least one other person. Katy only moved her head again, with that movement that was neither toss nor shrug but only extraordinarily offensive.

Up the steps the procession trailed; Don and Tibbs laden with the luggage, Molly and Katy managing the carry-cot with the now awakened and crying Maggie, and the children staggering with the birdcage. At the top of the steps they all halted and Don turned to Molly:

"Got a key?"

"No, Daisy didn't mention one. You'll have to knock, I'm afraid."

"Doesn't the bell ring?" asked Katy brusquely, and, taking hold of the pale brass knob, pulled hard and long.

The sound came into the silent drawing-room.

Mrs Cavendish had been sitting in the chair that was always thought of and spoken of as her own, upright, staring out at the wintry afternoon light and holding to the flames her thin hands that still showed the marks of rings sold some months ago, awaiting the summons of the bell with a stricken look on her drawn face where the fixed bloom glowed. Lodgers! To come to this.

They were not going to be nice people. She knew it. They might be nice from Daisy's point of view, but Daisy was young, and even she, Colonel Furnivall's daughter, did not seem to have escaped these extraordinary ideas that were turning the world upside down . . .

From the moment that the bell rang, she, Minta Cavendish, would be a landlady. A *landlady,* that coarse, vulgar word with its associations of rapacity and the music-hall; and she did not, for the first time in her life, know what manner to adopt towards strangers: these people, her *lodgers.* She would be taking money from them, but Mrs Hulton would be taking orders, domestically, from *her*.

Because there was not going to be any mistake or misunderstanding about it. Orders they would be. She meant to give her daily instructions very clearly, and she would be the mistress . . .

She was so tired. She began to doze a little in the growing warmth given out by the flames. *I shall want you to polish the cabinet this morning. Yes, isn't it a beautiful old piece . . . my husband bought if for our silver wedding anniversary* (because you couldn't talk to the woman exactly as if she were a servant. She couldn't be called 'Katy', or ordered about).

Or—could she? Could she—if she were young and very hard up and desperate to get somewhere cheap and quiet to live? Suppose it were made quite clear to her, from the start, that if she didn't do what she was told to do in the house, they would have to go?

That way, couldn't she be forced to do almost anything?—all the rough work, anyway, the scrubbing and the carrying of coals and the wretched, the *disgusting* washing-up? I am a lady. God help me, I have gentle blood in my veins. Why should I ever have to put my hands into washing-up water again?

Katy, I shall want a fire in the drawing-room; Mr Devon is calling for Miss Anthea . . . so pleased, my darlings, so very happy for you . . . you're going to be my son now, Michael . . . so happy . . .

Then she heard the bell.

She started up, her heart beginning to beat so heavily that it shook her side, and, summoning every ounce of self-command that she possessed, walked slowly out of the room and almost marched, so unnatural was her gait, along the hall.

"Well!" she cried, in her most gushing voice, as she flung open the front door, "safely here at last! Mrs Hulton"—seizing the hand of the dreadful little creature in the student's coat—"*pleased to meet you.* And Mr Hulton," she smiled at him but the effort was actually painful, because *he* wasn't even clean, "and these . . . are the children. Mark, isn't it, and Mary, and this is your little sister . . ." Then, with a drop into dismay as her eye travelled past them,

"Oh, a little *bird*! I don't think I really expected pets . . . but never mind . . . er . . . will your friends come in, too?"

She was overwhelmed, almost speechless, for the Hultons looked even worse than she had feared. And a common girl in an ugly great muffler, and the little dark creature who had fixed up the gas oven . . . and the bird, that dreadful little bird. Seeds all over the carpet.

"Come along; it's a long climb, I'm afraid," she said, standing aside and managing a smile, as they streamed into the hall, making footmarks all over the shining floor.

Mrs Hulton, who had made no answer beyond a nod and a careless smile, stopped at the foot of the stairs.

"Don't bother to come up, Miss Raymond," she said firmly to the girl in the muffler. "Thanks . . . *you've* been a blooming marvel," she added suddenly, with a smile to the little man now holding the birdcage, and this time it was such a dazzler of a smile, it made her look so different, so much younger, so almost like a school-girl, that both the men grinned from ear to ear.

Mrs Cavendish did not smile, and it was at this moment that Molly Raymond decided that Katy Hulton was a *man's woman*, and felt that what she herself needed was a strong coffee.

As the procession resumed its slow march to the upper regions, she sat down on the one of Mrs Cavendish's frail chairs that adorned the hall. Tibbs, taught by years of standing about in the offices of consuls and emigration officials never to lose a chance of taking the weight off his feet, sat down on the stairs. She glanced at him.

"We may as well wait . . . Daisy'll want to know how they got on. How about a coffee at Grania's afterwards? It's not late."

He did not answer.

Up, up they went, the children climbing laboriously, unaided, from stair to stair. The air was like ice. Katy looked back at Mark, who was recovering—as far as he ever did—from one of the colds that made his small life a martyrdom to paper handkerchiefs and Friar's Balsam. He looked blue already, and his mother's face set into sullen lines. It was all beautiful she supposed, but, God! it was cold . . . and now these stairs; they were really dangerous; they were frightful. She clasped Maggie tighter. Don must put a gate at the top. But Don, unlike 'the boys' at home in Glasgow, was not good with his hands. His expression, now, was getting smug. Of course, he liked the quietness and the upper-class atmosphere; presently he would be telling her that he could really get down to work in this place. She scowled, as Mrs Cavendish, with a little flourish, opened one of the doors.

"I thought perhaps a fire would . . . the afternoons are beginning to get chilly, aren't they? . . . the kettle is boiling . . . it's just next door . . ."

She was *not* going to call the room *the* kitchen.

She thought that she could never feel as bad as this again. It was the worst moment of her life.

They crowded to the door, the children peeping round their mother's skirt.

It was elegant; it was peaceful; it was even a little warm. From the rosy silk curtains to the Georgian brass fender, everything pleased the eye. The oval table was set with delicate china and a silver teapot and miniature sandwiches.

Katy cleared her throat.

"It's very pretty. Thank you very much. You've—gone to a lot of trouble," she said stiffly. She was trying to keep dismay out of her voice. This was a drawing-room, not a living-room. How was she going to keep sticky fingers and dirty shoes off all these museum pieces?

"Oh . . . I wanted you to feel welcome," Mrs Cavendish came forward. "Now, Mark, Mary, there's something here for you. I got one for your little sister, too, I didn't want her to be left out. Look, do you like them?"

Mark had gone straight across to the fire and was holding out small blue claws to the flames, while Mary had sat down on the floor and was picking industriously at a loose thread in the rug. Mrs Cavendish's eyes widened slightly.

"Mark! Mary! Come here and see what Mrs Cavendish has got for you," Katy commanded.

Mary scrambled up, and together they went to the table, which Mark was just tall enough to see over. Don lifted up Mary, whose eyes at once became fixed upon the pink cups and miniature knives with pearly handles.

"Pretty—pretty," pointing.

"Yes, aren't they? I can see you're a little girl who likes pretty things, and I'm sure you'll take care of all *my* pretty things, and not pull the poor rug to pieces with your little fingers, will you? Now here's what I've got for you and Mark and baby sister."

They were three little mice made of cloudy white sugar, with black comfits for eyes and tails of pink marzipan curled along their backs.

"Quite life-like. You make them?" Don Hulton asked.

Mrs Cavendish shook her head. "Oh no. I am a very poor cook indeed," she said clearly *(make them understand from the first that I can't do anything in the house)*. "I had them made at a place near here that specializes in sugar fancies; they do all the birthday cakes for us, locally," *(and make it clear that I have my own 'set', and my place in the neighbourhood)*. "They did my daughter's twenty-first birthday cake . . . Well, do you like your mouse?" to Mary.

Mary, who was picking at its tail, nodded.

"Mary! What do you say?"

When Mary had said it, and Mark had been sharply told to do the same, Mrs Cavendish suddenly felt that she could bear no more. She must get back to the drawing-room.

"Well, I think I will leave you to explore for yourselves," she said, with a tinkling laugh, "if you have all you want . . ."

"Yes, we'll do that," said Don easily, taking the baby from Katy and settling her into the carry-cot. "Thanks a lot but you run along now . . . oh, where's the toilet?"

"The?"

"The lavatory," Katy said distinctly, without looking up. She was kneeling beside Maggie, taking off her woollen coat.

"Oh . . . yes, of course . . . on the landing at the foot of these stairs." Mrs Cavendish crimsoned under her rouge and moved towards the door. "Well, if you want me, Mrs Hulton, I am usually to be found in the drawing-room." She paused. "I do hope you will be comfortable," she managed to make herself say.

"It's very nice. Thank you. Those mice were a brilliant idea, they're a success," Katy said. But she was too tired to smile; if only the woman would *go*.

"For God's sake," she said hardly, as soon as her landlady was safely down the stairs, "let's see if the rest of it's like this . . . Mark! Mary! You stay here. Do you understand Mother? Come right away from the fire and don't you dare move until Mother comes back."

"Please may Mark have a chair."

"What for? No, leave the things alone (and you're going to hear a lot of *that* from now on). What do you want a chair for?"

Mark looked down at the floor. "Want to look out . . ." in a whisper.

"All right, Daddy'll move it for you," said Don.

While he was doing this, Katy exhaustively tested the fastenings of the window.

"They seem all right," she said grudgingly at last, "but you dare touch them, that's all, and if you make Mrs Cavendish's chair dirty you know what you'll get." Mark did know, and he looked even more solemn than usual, for his mother's chastisements, if not frequent, were certainly not light.

"For God's sake . . . I'll put a bit of paper on it . . . what is this, the Victoria and Albert?" demanded Don. "There you are, son."

"And not one squeak out of you until we come back, mind. You can watch Maggie for me."

"Mary wash Maggie."

"Yes, Mary too. Now remember."

They left them: standing motionless side by side on the stool covered with newspaper, and looking out.

"This is better," said Katy, as they opened another door. "H'm . . . who's responsible for the heater?" She drew in the deliciously warm air of the shabby room, furnished sparsely with bed, worn carpet and chest of drawers, with a sensation of pleasure that was largely relief. "There's a label, look, down at the side."

Slowly, Don read it aloud:

"Katy and Don with love and best wishes for lifelong happiness from James and Daisy. Only five years late—you know the proverb! (Oil down in the cellar.)"

"That's nice of them," he said, in a surprised tone.

"It's just like Daisy," was all Katy said, but for some minutes afterwards her expression was softer and the set of her lips less grim.

"What do you think of it?" she demanded, when, having examined their domain and made some tea, they were sitting on two rather peculiar chairs in the kitchen (well, it had a thing you could cook on in it, didn't it?) and eating biscuits.

"It's no luxury flat but at least it's gloriously quiet. And . . . I like . . . it's . . . you feel people have lived here who at least did know how to read. I can work here. I shan't feel I'm surrounded by howling, resentful savages."

His wife looked at him sideways out of her cold, defensive eyes. But the sentence she was waiting for did not come, and she drank off her tea in silence. Then she said, "Well, you'll have to put up some kind of a gate at the top of those stairs."

"Can't you put the fear of God into Mark?"

"Into him, yes, but not into Mary. (We're going to have trouble with that young lady later, if I don't get to work on her now.) I'll get some wood and nails on Monday, if you can start it in the evening."

"I've got to work, Katy," he grumbled; "this is my third try, you know. It can't go on much longer."

"It won't have to," she said, putting her arm for an instant around his flabby shoulders. "This time, you're going to pass."

"I may too, at that, with a place as quiet as this to work in." He got up from the table. "Come on, let's unpack."

. . . Side by side they stood on the long stool where there was just room for the four little American-style boots on the newspaper covering the rose silk seat. The sky was red, the lights were shining in the houses, far below in the clear dusk the buses ran busily to and fro. The glow died away and the room became dim and silent, the bird, cheeping and ruffling in the cage, which had been set down in a corner, gradually became quiet except for a soft sound of returning content.

Mark stood with hands at his sides so that he should not, even accidentally, touch the window. In one hand he clutched his sugar mouse, now moist and sticky; Mary, having picked the tail and eyes off her own, had begun to suck it. Presently Mark put his mouse near his face and whispered, then he held it to the window pane.

"Now he can see a' things," said Mary.

"Yes, I'm showing him. Don't *scuffle*," sharply, and Mary whose pleasure and pastime it was to scuffle, stopped at once. The room became quite quiet.

Silence, stillness and instant obedience were by now almost natural to these children, whose earliest memories were of their mother's voice telling them not to make a noise. Almost: not quite; sometimes, behind their pale faces and their bright, still eyes, something stirred—an impulse to shout, to run stamping round the room—that was immediately quenched. Their father had spoken truly when he said that they had *had* to be good.

Presently Mary began to make an eerie tuneless drone.

"Shut up," said Mark vigorously, nudging her, "be quiet. If we make a noise she won't let us live here. There's an old man asleep. Mrs Cubitt's ill. You don't want us to go and live with Readinganny, do you? Do you want to go and live away from Mummy with Gasgowganny? So you be quiet."

Mary was quiet. Mark, satisfied that he had done his part towards keeping them in this place whence buses could be seen, resumed his intent watching. It was almost dark in the room. The children at the window, the child in the cradle, were as quiet as the three sugar mice.

CHAPTER XII
Thin End of a Wedge

"WELL, what do you think of her?"

"What?" But Molly knew that Tibbs meant *who*; he did still get his pronouns mixed occasionally. He was also trying to be unkind.

"Katy H., of course," she said patiently.

He shrugged. Evidently he wasn't in a cosy mood today, though when he liked he could be cosier than anyone.

"I was disappointed, I must say. I imagined her more . . . Scotch, you know, with one of those *lilting* voices and"—Molly's own voice assumed a lilt—"coming from one of those remote villages way, way up in the Hielans, with the heather, and the mountains, and perhaps an auld father in a plaidie . . ."

"She is sexually attractive," he interrupted gloomily.

"*Sexshually* attractive? Oh, Tibbs, no," said poor Molly. "That's the *last* thing I should have said about her."

"You would say! What do you know about it?"

This was a facer, and Molly took refuge in a prolonged survey of Grania's café, sunk in the languor of half past three in the afternoon. Presently Tibbs said:

"She is what a woman should be. She reminds me . . ." He paused.

"Oh, Tibbs! You are unkind. You never will tell me about anything that happened to you over there."

"Why should I? Do I want to remember it? All I care now is to make some money and be happy. I was going to say she remind me of my wife. When she smiled at me, she reminded."

"I . . . didn't . . . know you had got . . . a wife."

"Now, I haven't got her. She is killed."

"Oh Tibbs. How terrible—I'm so—"

"What does it matter what you are? She is killed and I don't want to think about it. So take away that look off your face, and drink your—it certainly isn't coffee. I don't know what Grania makes it from."

"But poor Tibbs, you're so brave. If you would only let yourself talk about it, I'm sure you would feel better. It's all this bottling things up that's so bad for you. *Repressions* . . . and I would understand, truly I would."

"You're English. How can you understand? And now we don't speak any more about this woman, but remember, please, that I admire her." He bit energetically into an oozing cake for which Molly would pay.

"But she's *plain*, Tibbs. Sexshually—"

"English people always think of the face. We are different. A woman can be plain in the face and yet all that a man wants."

Molly felt that she simply must change the subject.

"Well, what did you think of Daisy's other friend, Mrs Cavendish?"

"The *bourgeoisie* in decay. It is a sight typical of the present."

This, Molly felt, didn't really help when you wanted cheering up. She herself saw Mrs Cavendish, in spite of Daisy's irreverent comments, as a great lady: one struggling to keep her beautiful home going in painfully reduced circumstances. Molly would have liked to drop a cheery word to help her along life's highway, but Mrs Cavendish's manner earlier that afternoon had not been encouraging . . . not that Molly seriously minded being discouraged by a proud aristocrat. She rather liked it. She tried again.

"And Mr Hulton. What of him?" she enquired, elegantly moving her spoon round in her cup. "Did you like him?"

"Do you say that he is a chemist?" Tibbs asked, his bored expression changing a little.

"Daisy said so. Not in a shop. But he's some kind of a chemist . . . research or something. He might be company for you, were you thinking?" One of the few *facts* she knew about Tibbs was that he had held a post as a chemist, in a firm which had made patent medicines, in the capital city of his own land.

"Perhaps, yes." He pushed aside his cup. "I am going now, Molly. I have to be to my job."

She did not answer. It was too bad that he had to earn his living by washing-up, evenings, in that café near Sadler's Wells, but if he *would* be so difficult . . . the job with Foyle's, that Daisy had got him, had lasted exactly three weeks. An educated man . . . but it was his own fault. He just couldn't take orders.

She watched him pause, on his way out, to exchange remarks (he seemed cheerful enough, now), with the friend who had lent him the car, and which was now returned and parked in the side street nearest to Grania's; and she felt depressed.

It had been a day of small disappointments and one biggish shock: Tibbs was a widower. Funny to think of him as one: it was such a respectable, elderly sort of word.

Molly did not demand much from life, only that people and situations should resemble those of the stories in the women's magazines. Real life: that was what she liked, only . . . just not *quite* real; she did not want rubbish about dukes or that kind of thing, but she did like beautiful thoughts and a haze of starshine . . . and people were so disappointing . . . even Colonel Furnivall had been disappointing, in a way, not behaving *like* a Colonel . . . polite enough, if they happened to meet in the hall, but so *distant*! That dream of having coffee and seeing his Indian Treasures was just a Might-Have-Been now. And Katy Hulton—where was the bonny, cheery, plucky Scots lassie Molly had expected? Glum looks, and a sharp way with her poor mites of children, and you could see that she was clever. (Much good *cleverness* did anyone.)

But Katy had remembered her name. That gave her a faint feeling of comfort. She could not know that Katy, a minister's daughter, had been trained from childhood at church, and on church social occasions, and at Sunday School outings, to remember everyone's name and to use it, even that of the quietest, most retiring elderly body present. The habit, with its touch of Christian courtesy, had persisted as a merely social one never would have done with Katy. She had picked up much of her husband's surly impatience with gracious living but she still remembered people's names.

Molly pushed aside her cup, and picked up the bill. Four and ninepence for two coffees and three cakes. Whoever died poor, thought Molly, Grania wouldn't. She paid it, and went out into the quiet, wide, darkening roads of Belsize Park.

She wandered on, up Fitzjohn's Avenue, beneath its leafless trees, intending to look in on Daisy and tell her how the Hultons had got on. The broad pavements were dark with damp and almost deserted, the broad road was one unbroken stream of big cars heading out of town. Lights glittering early, bare trees, the faint smell of fog. Winter. What would she be doing this time next year?

Molly did not often think about her future. She drifted on, living from day to day, keeping casually in touch with the men she knew, and occasionally ignoring a sketchy suggestion about marriage, and doggedly, almost unconsciously, seeking what she wanted most from life: The Real Thing.

It was Love, of course. She had not had it in the two or three affairs that had culminated in a weekend and ended in a gradual and mutual cooling-off, but she would know it when it came because it would be a flash of light, a burst of song, a rose scented more deliciously than all the bottles on her dressing table. She did not often think what would be the feelings of the other person involved in The Real Thing; her thoughts were all of what *she* would feel, how *she* would know that she possessed it at last, and so forth.

The dim gardens looked chilly and quiet, the big trees were black against the fading light. She had saved a hundred pounds and Mum had told her that they were leaving her the house at Harrow . . . she wasn't afraid of being poor, because she would always have the house; she could not imagine what it would be like to be past the age for attracting a man and therefore growing old had no fears for her; but she was afraid of living her life through without ever having had The Real Thing.

Daisy, now. (Molly came out into the narrow, noisy picturesque High Street of Hampstead Village.) Had she got it? She became all haughty, Daisy did, if you spoke about love-making. Sexshually, perhaps, she was cold: she never spoke tenderly about James, except for a rare 'bless him'; more often she said 'curse that boy', which made Molly feel sad although she knew it was a joke, and she often made a mock of Romance in a way that brought on Molly's wistful smile.

Molly had never met 'James', but her thoughts were playing about him as she slowly ascended the thirty eighteenth-century steps leading to Bottle Court.

(She had started by thinking about Tibbs and his being a widower but it was no use doing that.) James had always been out on the few occasions that Molly had been to the house with the pink front door, but she was bound to meet him some day, of course—and she went on to imagine Daisy dying, and herself, pale as death and very slim and smelling irresistibly of some brand-new scent, being caught up into his arms as he muttered shakenly:

"We can't fight this, Molly . . . and, after all, it's what *she* would have wanted."

At this point she reached the last step and saw, across the intervening road, the house with the pink front door and its quiet little street. Low grey clouds keeping as still as if they were asleep, delicate black trees against red streaks fading in the west, the lights of London glittering far below, and a view, through a window, into a brightly-lit room.

That must be him. That must be James. And he was bending over the pram. How sweet.

And how good-looking. Daisy had never mentioned it.

It looked like an illustration to one of her favourite stories; the one about the helpless young man left alone to manage the crying baby. The tale went on about a girl coming in, unexpectedly, and them managing the baby together. Molly's head tilted gently on one side. She crossed the road, and, going up to the house with the pink front door, tapped softly at the window.

James looked up quickly. Damn, who was that, muffled up like Dracula? One of Daisy's, of course. He sighed; it was too late to pretend he had not seen her, so he went out into the hall.

"Oh, good evening," said Molly, at the front door now, "I just popped in to tell Daisy how her friends—you know, the Hultons— got on."

"Oh . . . yes . . . she's out, at the moment."

('*How* good looking!' she thought. 'Nice voice; nice old clothes, not arty and corduroyish, but grey-"bagged" and tweedy.')

"Will she be long?" she asked, dreamily staring.

"I don't know," lied James, "she's gone out with my mother." So she had; three hundred yards down the hill to the Underground. At this moment, James Too took up his crying again.

"Are you left in charge?" asked Molly, and went on, in response to a fleeting smile that might have meant anything, "I expect he's playing up. Babies always seem to know, don't they?"

James said he supposed they did. He was now thinking that if she had not got that fatal manner she would be attractive; the combination of fair hair, grey eyes and clear sallow skin was unusual.

"Like me to give you a hand?" she asked.

It sounded extraordinarily pert and intimate; it was almost as if she had guessed what he was thinking. He said hastily and firmly:

"Very kind of you but he's only sleepy and won't give way. He's as obstinate as a mule. His mother will be back any minute now. I'll tell her you looked in—er—"

"I'm Molly. Molly Raymond."

"Oh yes. All right, then—" He was beginning to shut the door.

"Will you tell her I got them settled in all right?"

"I will. Thank you."

"I may give her a ring later. Thanks a lot. God be with you." She turned away.

James, much struck by this mode of farewell, returned to the sitting-room and vigorously pushed James Too's pram to and fro. It must be the seduced character; she always, so Daisy said, said that. What an ass of a girl. God be with you!

"Go on, now, you know you'll have to give way in the end," he observed to his son. James Too, concealed behind an apron of Daisy's which James had flung in despair over the hood of the chariot, was making what he supposed to be a loud and terrible roar rather like those threats uttered in extremity by King Lear, but which was in fact a kind of hollow, diminishing murmur, which now abruptly ceased. James One drew the window curtains: no more tappers this evening if he could help it.

"We nearly got landed with one of yours," he said, when Daisy came in some ten minutes later, her face cool and rose red from the evening winds. "Molly Raymond, 'God-be-with-you'." He gave her the message about the Hultons, then added, "Isn't she the seduced one?"

"I do wish you wouldn't, James."

"*I'm* not doing anything."

"How do you mean, *you* aren't?"

"'God-be-with-you' has a rather forthcoming manner. She offered to come in and help me rock James Too."

"She is very helpful," said Daisy primly.

"I should call it a bit more than that."

"You imagine things . . . Can you get out the sherry while I do his supper?"

"Have we got to wake him up, after all that?"

"You know we have. He'll just have time for a nice little sleep and he'll be like an *angel*."

"He'd better," James said.

Molly kept to her threat of ringing later, and about nine o'clock she gave Daisy a detailed account of the arrival, and settling-in of the Hultons, followed by her own verdict upon their appearances and personalities and that of Mrs Cavendish. Then she added:

"I was sorry to miss you, but I did get a peep at your James."

"Gorgeous, isn't he?" said Daisy absently. She was used to the fact that he was; it still pleased her, but she was a very busy girl with a great many people to do things for and think about.

"I thought so. Aren't you lucky!"

Daisy said, 'so was he', and rang off.

'Just what I thought', mused Molly, slowly mounting the staircase to her quiet room; 'she doesn't appreciate him. And a man doesn't want to be left alone to rock a baby to sleep; it's humiliating and it doesn't seem right, somehow. A man wants all a woman's attention when he comes in of an evening.'

Before she settled down with her magazine in front of the gas fire, she not only passed some moments in imagining James Muir seated beside it with her, but decided that in future she would not hesitate to offer her services as babysitter etc. at the house with the pink front door. She could, she thought, perhaps make things a bit more comfortable there—for him.

Katy Hulton had been surprised and slightly touched by Mrs Cavendish's offering of the sugar mice: the new landlady looked so unlike that kind of thing. Katy hoped it did not mean that she was going to be 'all over them', popping up and down with cups of coffee and gossip, for she herself was not a sociable woman and God knew she would have plenty to fill her days. However, it was kind of her.

But after twenty-four hours in the flat, the slight prejudice in favour of Mrs Cavendish had vanished.

The place was quiet and clean, and that was all.

The inconvenience was beyond belief. Already she had a pile of dirty napkins, and others waiting to be boiled, stowed away in the least furnished room of the four; her back and legs ached from climbing up and down fifty-odd stairs with water and coal (for Don, full of satisfaction with the new home, had at once settled down to work, and had also expressed the hope that she would keep the living-room fire in so that they could have a cup of coffee in front of it before going to bed, and she had not wanted to disturb him with requests for help); and she seemed never to cease telling the children 'don't touch'. And the bed was just not quite big enough for two.

Nor, to Katy, did the elegance of some of the furniture and the graceful proportions of the rooms help to diminish the inconvenience. Beauty of line and colour meant almost nothing to her, brought up as she had been in a tall ugly house of grey granite in a poor district of Glasgow where the only beauty recognized or admired had been moral, or that of Nature. She had of course come across pictures and music at Oxford, but they had only made her feel disapproving and impatient, and now she heartily wished that Mrs Cavendish had put the same kind of shabby nondescript furniture into all her rooms. The preservation of all that stuff in the sitting-room was going to be a nightmare. (Daisy had closely kept the secret of the rooms' furnishing and it never occurred to Katy that their contents did not belong to Mrs Cavendish.)

Something had got to be done about those napkins, and soon. She granted herself the indulgence of a night's sleep, such as it was, and, soon after breakfast, went downstairs in search of Mrs C.

The quiet of a London Sunday in winter lay over the house and in the deserted roads. There was a thin fog veiling the trees in the garden at the back. 'They can perfectly well hang out there,' thought Katy fiercely, her mind on the napkins, as she saw this promised land through a staircase window.

Mrs Cavendish was alone by the drawing-room fire—if you could call it a fire; Katy was domestically lavish by inclination, and dearly loved a laden board and a blazing grate. In response to her smile and "Hullo," her landlady favoured her with an unsmiling inclination of the head—neither bend nor nod and very slow—which caused her to stare. Had the woman a chronic stiff neck?

"Good morning," Mrs Cavendish said. "I expect you have come to ask about the housework." Her tone was even, but she was rather flushed, and Katy saw with surprise, that she was trembling. She became annoyed.

"No," she said distinctly, "I thought we could fix that up later on, when I'm straight upstairs. It's about the napkins. They can go out in the garden, I suppose, and I'll boil them in the kitchen. I can't get lunch for five on that—contraption—upstairs and boil them all the morning as well—and I must wash them in the bathroom, I think. I can't get enough water up for all the rinsing."

Mrs Cavendish gave a small laugh. "Oh dear. I'm afraid I hadn't thought about the napkins. I'm not used, yet, you see, to the idea that I'm a *landlady*. Now . . ."—she looked at Katy quickly, then away again—"suppose we—we make it a fair arrangement? You will clean the silver for me this morning and I shall allow you to use the bathroom this morning and hang the napkins in the garden? How will that be?"

Katy stared at her. She was speechless. Then she decided that the woman was deranged; the children must never be left alone in the house with her even for a moment.

A lot of thoughts went through her head: *'This is going to get worse. I can feel it is. Is it worth it? Don's exam is so near; he's simply got to pass this time. At least we've got the place to ourselves. I wonder if I can stick it? I'm so damned tired all the time and I'm getting into nothing but a drudge.'*

Mrs Cavendish was looking steadily at her. Her expression was dignified, composed and rather severe.

"All right," said Katy at last. "Where is it?"

"I have it here . . ." She got up gracefully and went across the room, to a table near the window. "It's all ready. You had better do it in the kitchen . . . hadn't you?"

"I'll take it upstairs," Katy said firmly (at least it would be warm up there, and she would be surrounded by sane children). "Whew! There's plenty of it, isn't there?" The big papier-mâché tray was covered with tiny sweet-baskets, miniature boxes, bowls, photograph frames, forks and spoons, and containers for salt, mustard and pepper.

"I have been collecting it all my life," her landlady said. "There is a very great deal more packed away downstairs." The tone was complacent, a little absent, as she stood gazing down at the blackened treasures. "I like them cleaned with Goddard's Plate Powder, of course. My mother-in-law's butler always used it, and I mistrust these new preparations. Now here is the brush, and some cloths, and you can get to work! Oh, Mrs Hulton," she added, as Katy, resting the tray against the edge of an occasional table, struggled to open the door, "you won't permit the children to play with the silver, will you? There are some miniature chairs and animals that are just the thing to attract little fingers."

"Little fingers will get a good crack if they do," Katy assured her, and got herself out of the room.

She managed to toil up to the top of the house without calling to Don for help. If he was working well—and he did seem to be—for heaven's sake leave him alone. She did not want his help, and she would not ask for it. She would get through this by herself; the difficulties of keeping house here, the drudgery, the cease-less care of the children, and the tyranny—because she guessed that that was what it was going to be—of a landlady who would demand housework from her in return for the right to remain here at all—she would take it all on. And when it was over and Don had passed, and a better life was possible for the Hultons (he *must* pass, this time; she would will him to pass with every ounce of determination she had), then she would have the secret satisfaction of knowing that *she* had done it all.

When she was a very little girl, set on by schoolfellows because of her stubbornness, she would mutter, over and over again, in the midst of the pinching and pulling and scratching: "You can't make me—you can't make me."

She said it again to herself now, as she climbed the last stair with the heavy tray balanced against her body. Hard work, endless tiredness, resentment, long hours, no fun (fun! she had almost forgotten what that was) she would fight them all and she would win. 'It takes a lot,' she thought grimly, as she dumped the tray on the landing table, 'to get Katy MacRae down.'

It took a lot to get Minta Cavendish down, too. They at least had that in common.

CHAPTER XIII
Merry Christmas

THE presence of lodgers made less difference to Mrs Cavendish's life than she had feared.

Her day, with its small rituals, its tiny meals and the familiar changes of light or shadow in the bare rooms, passed as usual— but in a week or so she did notice that it passed a little quicker; and she noticed, too, that the house seemed warmer; the heating of the attics must make a slight difference, she supposed.

The Hultons were very quiet. Sometimes she caught herself listening for the children's voices, but she seldom heard more than a distant subdued piping; their mother certainly kept them in order. Nor did she see much of the woman herself; sometimes the only sign that Mrs Cavendish saw, all day, of another person's presence in the house were the small black footprints on the news-papers she had put down to protect the kitchen floor, showing that Katy had been out to get coal. There was plenty of coal in the cellar now; the man, Hulton, had come down to tell her that he had ordered some and she had told him he *must* have it put quite separately from hers. She was not going to have them stealing her coal. Fortunately the cellar was a good deep one. Mrs Hulton had to grope right at the back when she wanted to fill her bucket. Well, it wouldn't hurt her; she was young and strong.

And life was certainly a little, just a little, easier since they came. The money, small sum though it was, helped; and the floors were swept, the rooms dusted and the brass fenders cleaned once a week. Later on she meant to have the fires laid, and cleared away, and the stone floor of the kitchen scrubbed. But all in good time. She must not work Mrs Hulton so hard that she began to rebel; lower class people were always so lazy.

Mrs Cavendish had enjoyed that first interview no more than Katy. She always had disliked dealing with untrained domestic workers. So, to avoid further unpleasantness, she took to putting her requirements on paper and stealing upstairs to leave a note on the landing table, while Katy had taken the children out shopping. She made no further references to any 'concessions' or 'arrangements', having been, in fact, slightly scared by Katy's expression when she had used the word 'allow' about the napkins, but let it be taken for granted that she would say nothing, if the stairs had been swept down, when Katy occupied the bathroom for a morning's washing, and so on. It was, she thought bitterly, a one-sided gentlewoman's agreement.

The napkins fluttered in the garden on every fine day. On wet days they hung on a line across the Hultons' landing; Mrs Cavendish shrank from the thought and shuddered when she came face to face with them on one of her periodical spying visits to the top floor, but she said nothing.

Katy's days, which began at six in the morning with Maggie's first hungry cry in the dark, were seventeen hours long. She washed, she cleaned, she sewed and shopped and cooked for her own family, and in the intervals of doing that she did the work required by Mrs Cavendish. Don settled to his studies every evening after supper and she sat opposite to him by the fire, nodding over the evening paper, silent and sleepy, with her head and every bone in her body aching.

Daisy soon got in touch with her by means of one of her characteristic imperious postcards, issuing an invitation to tea. A taxi would call for them at an appointed hour.

Katy accepted, by telephone, with that mixture of comfort, affection and envy which she had always felt when allowing herself to be managed by Daisy Muir; and on one dull, lowering afternoon some weeks before Christmas she and the children, with Maggie wrapped in an old shawl and Mark burdened with a bag containing his sister's paraphernalia, were whirled away to the house with the pink front door.

"Now," began Daisy at once, when the visitors had been arranged round a roaring fire and were smelling a heartening odour of toasted buns while listening to the trilling of the canary, "*is* Old Cavendish sticking it on with you about the housework? I've been worrying."

"I scrubbed the kitchen before I came out," and Katy held out both small, ruined hands with a mocking smile.

"Katy! I'm so *sorry*. I didn't think she'd really dare."

"There's quite a bit of rough work, anyway," Katy went on, "carrying up all the coal and water, before I start on what she wants done."

"I am so *awfully* sorry—"

"It's all right, Daisy, really it is."

The tone was very decided; the spectacle of Daisy, sitting there all good-nature and willingness to go to any trouble, and now full of dismay, had brought to a head all the feelings of gratitude which had been struggling for some time now with Katy's pride. "I don't really mind. It's grand to have a place to ourselves, and it's so quiet there that Don's working better than he has for months. You've taken no end of trouble for the Hultons, and—and thank you very much. Thank you."

The deep colour that rises to certain faces as an accompaniment to strong feeling was in hers. Embarrassment is contagious. Daisy coloured too.

"I'm so glad . . . it wasn't anything," she babbled.

"And Mark and Mary do what Mother tells them and don't touch Mrs Cavendish's things," Katy added, and just brushed with her roughened finger the soft cheek of Mary, who had come to lean against her. "They're both good little things," in a lower tone.

'Too good,' Daisy thought, not for the first time. She knew that in the home of Katy's own childhood, the smallest daily duty had been performed with its moral value in mind, and thus had been weighted with an awesome responsibility. That training showed itself in Katy at every turn. She glanced at James Too, sitting on the hearthrug with his toys and occasionally casting a glance of profoundest indifference at the visitors. Later on he would have treats and fun as a matter of course and take them for granted; the six small MacRaes (she had gathered) had had enough to eat; but that was all they did have, and treats for the minister's family had been so rare, and so much enjoyed by the four boys and two girls, that a kind of halo of awed delight surrounded them in Katy's memory to this day—'the time my Uncle Angus took us all to the circus'—'my sister's twenty-first'—there never had been such enjoyment. It had set up a standard against which all future treats would unconsciously be measured.

Scholarships, prizes, bursaries and grants had showered on the clever young MacRaes, and Katy, coming up to Oxford as a serious, arrogant, nineteen-year-old, absorbed in her studies and excessively ambitious, had been the cleverest of the six. Obstinate and proud, too.

'Of course,' Daisy thought, as she studied the flinty pale face staring into the fire, 'with her background she would want her children to be *very* good. And if she's had to make them, well, *unnaturally* good, it isn't her fault.'

"And that heater—" Katy suddenly said, looking up. "I did write to you—but I—I must thank you again, Daisy. When we opened the bedroom door and felt the warmth" (her r's rolled irrepressibly) "and saw who it was from—well! It cheered me up," she ended coldly.

Daisy, glowing and beaming like a convector heater herself, studied the sleeping face of Maggie.

"Don says if there were more girls about like Daisy Muir things would be—better," Katy concluded, bringing out this tribute with such a solemn air of its being a compliment indeed that Daisy, who was no admirer of The Hulk at any time, controlled a strong impulse to laugh.

She had spent the previous day with Susan Ruddlin, behind her worst friend's smart white front door, under those glittering and envied chandeliers that adorned the great mid-Victorian house in Canonbury. "Let's hear all about your ghastly friends," Sue had said, putting up her pretty feet on her cane and bamboo Edwardian sofa, and off Daisy had gone—broken engagements, outraged feelings, personal quirks and solemnly imparted confidences going down in all directions with shouts of laughter.

It had been the greatest fun; they shared the dangerous link of an identical sense of humour, and perhaps too there was something of revenge, unconsciously taken on Daisy's part, in thus ridiculing all the people who preyed upon her time and energies and patience.

Susan was particularly interested in Molly Raymond. "And how's the one who's always being seduced and says 'God be with you'?" she had asked, her large eyes gleaming with curiosity and contempt.

"It's just lack of Buss-and-Beale," she said on this occasion, as Daisy paused for breath. "Where was she at school?"

"Oh heaven knows. Harrow Secondary Tech, probably. I don't think Buss-and-Beale comes into it."

"It does, I tell you. The number of times the Farquhar's words— her very words: 'Susan, you can do better than this and you know it'—have stopped me from leaping into bed with someone, you wouldn't believe."

"No, I wouldn't." But as Daisy looked at her, in her trapeze dress of stiff pink silk, with arms behind her chestnut head and her triangular face alight with laughter—she wondered. There were rumours . . . But Daisy, whose own code was rather that of a nice thirteen-year-old, dismissed them. Time enough to worry when the Ruddlins bought a huge dog.

This theory emanated from James, who had, he said, observed that people in matrimonial or other difficulties of ever-accelerating complexity invariably went out, when things were really serious, and bought a rampageous out-sized Airedale. The idea was that it would be so good for the children . . . and, indeed, it often did accompany them to the parent who had been awarded their custody.

When the Ruddlins bought a Borzoi, Daisy would begin to feel really concerned.

Then Susan had got out the Zephyr from the garage where a carriage and two horses had once been accommodated, and drove her friend and James Too, at a great rate and laughing all the way, through the wide, quiet roads of Highbury and over the top of Hampstead Heath between the dim woods, to as near the house with the pink front door as she could get the car. James, who disapproved of her, had been rather cross.

It had been a good day. But Daisy had not told her worst friend anything about the Hultons.

It was strange, thought Daisy, as she poured tea and put hot buns or biscuits into small hands, how the presence of Katy and her children brought back to her the happiness and gaiety that had filled her childhood, in the little house on the edge of Regent's Park named The Grove.

When she thought of that house, she still thought of *home*, and she heard the trilling and whistling of her mother's pet birds in the little aviary and with the sound the laughter and bird-sweet voices of the little girls who had been her friends. She had been so happy! Her mother had been such a darling.

Now the little house was quite gone; in order even to see what it had looked like before the bomb struck amidst its white may trees and mauve wisterias, she had to look at an old print, engraved more than a hundred years ago, of the road where it had stood. On the site there was now a block of flats seven storeys high. Yet Katy Hulton, that grim girl with her quiet children around her, could call back into Daisy's heart precisely the excited gaiety, the sense of something delightful coming at any moment to crown the happy day, that had been the characteristic mood of her childhood at The Grove.

'It's because she's good, like my mother,' Daisy was thinking, though in fact at this moment Katy, with her red locks falling around her face as she bent over Maggie, looked more like a young Lady Macbeth suckling her savage infant, and Daisy was also struck by her air of what she could only call exhausted doggedness.

"Do you ever get out at *all*?" she demanded as she at last sat down to her own bun and tea. Her tone was imperious, but she was resenting The Hulk; no doubt *he* got out all right, and some of the chivalrous wrath that occasionally overwhelmed her on behalf of Molly Raymond had come over her as she studied Katy.

"Every Wednesday. Pub," Katy answered without looking up.

"Oh good. Do you go far afield or just locally?"

"It's local, all right. Just over the road. We can see the children's bedroom window from the saloon bar and I keep an eye on them while we're drinking . . . Mark would let me know if anything went wrong," glancing towards him, where he stood in front of the canary's cage, slowly eating his bun with eyes fixed on the trilling bird. "I'll tell you who we've run into there," Katy went on, gently pushing aside Maggie's mouth and beginning to fasten her blouse: "your friend Tibbs."

"I thought around Belsize Park was his beat," surprisedly.

"He isn't there every week. But most Wednesdays he is. Don likes him. He's a chemist too, you know? They've got some scheme on together"—Katy shrugged her shoulders—"it's an idea for making a wind-bringer-up."

"A *wind-bringer-up?* Do you mean for babies?"

"Yes. Tibbs came back for another drink with us after closing-time one evening (I say, he can put it away, can't he?) and I was having trouble with Maggie . . . well, she's always a windy girl, aren't you?" softly to the replete and peacefully staring creature extended in her lap, "and he and Don started saying what a lot of money was lying about waiting to be made by people who could invent something universally wanted—like a real cure for the common cold or something to do away for good with washing-up—and I cut in (they annoyed me, rather) and asked why someone didn't invent something that really would bring up all of a baby's wind. Well, you know yourself—"

Daisy, with an eye on James Too, agreed that she did indeed, and after some minutes' technical discussion, Katy went on:

"They said it was a very good idea, in fact, but then they started talking world affairs . . ." She paused, pushing her hand through her hair. "When they get started—well, we didn't get to bed until one, and Maggie has me up at six—" She broke off.

Daisy said nothing. She remembered the endless talk at Oxford over the cocoa or coffee cups; talk about everything in this world and the next; luxurious, lavish, ranging, expansive talk, with no rules and no holds barred, and Katy the most idealistic, the most ardent talker of their group.

"I hate talking," said Katy in a low tone, suddenly. "If I never had to open my mouth again or hear anyone else open theirs, I'd be glad."

"I do think a wind-bringer-up is a first-class idea," Daisy said, after a rather long pause. "Are they really going to do it seriously, do you know?"

"I think so. Don's enthusiastic. But I'm not having him doing anything about any schemes until he's passed his finals. I told him so. Rather firmly." She laughed an unamused laugh.

"I suppose it'll be easy enough getting a good job once he is qualified?"

"It ought to be."

"When will you know if he's passed?"

"End of February."

"Three months."

"Yes. It's . . . just a question of hanging on till he does."

Daisy wondered quite what this meant; putting up with old Cavendish's demands for house-cleaning, or being condemned to a strictly domestic existence? She had not liked to ask Katy anything about her own career. An impenetrable barrier of prickly reserve on Katy's part seemed, to Daisy, to surround that subject.

"What are you doing for Christmas?" she asked next. "Going to your people or to Don's?"

"Staying where we are. They don't want us at Reading and the fare to Glasgow's quite beyond us—with the children. What are you doing?"

"Having our usual family gathering. My father and his sister and the old cousin she lives with always come to us, and then I usually ask someone in who wouldn't have much of a Christmas otherwise, and this year I'll probably have to ask Molly Raymond to help, because my French girl has suddenly decided to go back to France. Molly's making herself quite useful here, lately."

"She's in our pub sometimes, with Tibbs."

"Molly? I'm not surprised. I do try to keep her off him, but she's *besotted* with him," Daisy said vigorously, and Katy gave an irrepressible laugh.

"Are you still managing other people's love lives?"

"Used I to?" Daisy was really surprised.

"You know you did; we used to call you Cupid."

"So you did . . . tsk, I'd *forgotten*. Oh Katy, doesn't it seem ages ago! Another world . . . another *life*."

"It was another life," Katy said, but her laughter had died, and soon after this she looked at the clock and said that they must go.

"Good-bye, and mind you keep those men up to the wind-bring-er-up." Daisy, standing on the corner of the little street, waved them off in a taxi. "What are you going to call it? Names are very important."

"Oh, I don't know. 'Wind-Up,' Don thought." The taxi moved forward.

"You'll be able to buy a swimming pool," Daisy called. "See you again soon," and tucking both chilly hands into the sleeves of her jersey, she ran back on her high heels to the shelter of the pink front door.

I don't want a swimming pool. And Daisy's house is too . . . I don't really like it. But a small house in the country would be nice, thought Katy, leaning back in the taxi with Maggie on her lap and the staring, absorbed children sitting on either side. Red-brick, with white woodwork, and a kitchen garden. Yes . . . Meanwhile, was Mrs Cavendish going to make her scrub the kitchen floor every week?

She ached.

Anthea heartily disliked Christmas. It reminded her, bitterly, of what fun life could be if one had money. Sharing her mother's contempt for Oxford Street, she usually put off the spending of a few necessary pounds until just before the 25th, and then went out to buy soap and bath salts in the local shops, accompanied by a strong sense of being put upon.

She was absently studying the garish windows one afternoon some three days before Christmas, surrounded by cheerful crowds and holding an umbrella against the thin rain, while thinking about the news that Michael had broken to her yesterday as they lunched. He was taking his holiday in January, and going for three weeks to Bermuda with the Devonhursts.

Short of his announcing his engagement, no news could have depressed her more. He would meet rich and glamorous girls, he would be enjoying blue sky and sunlight while she was going off to work in cold drizzling fog, and he would not be in London for her birthday.

She saw again the slightly embarrassed expression on his high-nosed, clear-skinned face. "I thought I'd better accept. They're always so decent—and besides, I'm damn glad of the chance. Who wouldn't be!" There had been no wishing that she could come too; no apologies for being unable to celebrate her birthday; no sign of any remorse or regret beyond a rather better wine than usual at luncheon and an exotic little posy from a florist's for herself on their way back to work.

It was all too sickening . . . and Mummy was so fussed about the Hulton lout having the cheek to put up a gate at the top of the stairs—hammering and banging half last night—that Anthea had not dared to break this latest piece of bad news.

. . . She became aware of bustle and exclamations around her; someone gasped, parcels were scattering over the pavement together with drawing paper or something, and suddenly a small stout old woman was sprawling at her feet.

Violently irritated at having to be the sweet helpful girl on this, of all other, days, Anthea nevertheless stooped down to the sufferer, with her pretty smile.

She found herself looking into the round pale eyes of the dotty Miss Furnivall. She was now sitting on the pavement with both legs straight out in front of her and her extraordinary hat on one side.

"Poor old dear!" said a kind voice.

"Here you are . . ." an extended hand, offering papers.

"It *is* slippery, isn't it . . ."

"And all her Christmas cards too . . . what a shame . . ."

"I'm all right. I'm perfectly all right, thank you. Thank you . . . thank you very much . . . *thank* you."

Rebuffed by the soft cold voice and impatient manner, the Good Samaritans in headscarves drifted away, leaving Anthea and the victim in the middle of the pavement.

"It's Miss Furnivall, isn't it? I don't expect you remember me. Anthea Cavendish."

Crossly, Ella scooped up her sketches and glared at her. "I remember you perfectly," she snapped. *('I'm not old, I'm not poor, I was only walking down the hill, I tripped, I'm always tripping, now it's smudged, and I'd just got that rainy light on the Whitestone Pond properly.')* She struggled to her feet, trembling helplessly, and glad, in spite of her irritation, of the help of a young arm.

When she had straightened her hat and jerked it down so far over her eyes that she had to tilt her head back in order to see Anthea at all, she said in a different voice:

"I was rude to you. I beg your pardon."

Anthea's tactful murmur was followed by, "May I walk a little way with you? It is so very slippery, isn't it?"

Poor Mummy would be pleased to hear of this encounter with one of the Furnivalls, whom she was always so keen to 'keep in with'; Anthea must make the most of it.

"I suppose you may—if you want to." It was a return to the rude manner, but Ella was frightened to find that she literally could not take a step forward without the aid of this girl's arm. She took a disconcertingly prolonged, sideways and back-tilted glance at her, rather like a tortoise studying some intruder from the safety of its shell. Anthea Cavendish was pretty: she made you think of those flowers people always had at weddings. Ella said, in a conspirator's lowered tone: "Shall we go in a taxi? I've got some money, it's my day for having it; and will you come and have tea with me?" Anthea was pleased to say 'thank you' and yes. At least it would be better than buying cheap presents while brooding sorely about Michael; and Mummy would be pleased. In a very short time, they were sitting side by side in a taxi and on their way to King Edward's Road.

But although she summoned all her social resources, Anthea was beginning to feel steadily worse. The broad crowded road and its hurrying shoppers, the familiar dull shops temporarily brightened for the season, the grotesque appearance of her companion, and the sickly colourless evening coming down over all . . . and Michael going off to warmth, colour, luxury, fun . . . oh, it was too much! By the time she was following Miss Furnivall up the stairs, in the wake of a tall, neat, elderly maid whose presence strangely and suddenly made her feel much worse, she was dangerously close to crying.

A maid—she and Mummy used to have maids once. What chance had she got of ever having one again, of ever having anything like a decent sort of life, if Michael didn't ask her to marry him?

Ella, coming back into the drawing-room after taking off her outdoor clothes, just as Annie, having put down the tea-tray in front of the fire went quietly out—Ella saw her guest's fair head turned quickly towards the fire and caught the unmistakable sound of an angry sob.

She was angry and dismayed, herself. People . . . what a nuisance, and how strange, they were . . . crying, worrying, wanting things done for them . . . she had had the idea of asking this Anthea-girl to tea because Marcie was out, and Annie wouldn't dare to say rude things to her while there was a visitor . . . such a good idea, so clever . . . and now it was going to be a bother. But she must keep Anthea here . . . she remembered the day at Newton House when Annie had hit her . . . and actually gave a small start.

"You're crying," she said accusingly, as she sat down opposite Anthea and stared at her.

"Yes, I know. I can't help it. You'll have to excuse me." Anthea dabbed weakly at herself with her handkerchief. "It's this dreary weather, I expect, it sort of gets on my nerves and"—tears came on again—"I'm worried about something."

She felt recklessly that she must pour it all out to someone—anyone—and this old thing was half-dotty, she probably wouldn't take it in properly, anyway.

"I was worried about something once," Miss Furnivall said, not confidentially but in a detached voice, after she had supplied her guest with tea and bread-and-butter. "If I tell you what it was, will you tell me?" She was not really interested, but she must keep the girl here until Marcie came back. She looked like a flower out in the rain, now.

Anthea smiled but did not answer. The tea was restoring her self-command.

"I used to cry all night. It was because I couldn't do my Chemistry," pursued her hostess. "Now," she took a good bite of bread-and-butter, "you must tell me."

The last light was fading from the window, where the curtains remained undrawn. Ella's face suggested that of some ageless goblin—on its best behaviour, certainly, but also quite determined to have its own way about some secret desire of its own.

Anthea roused herself. Deeply conventional, she was beginning to feel the lack of ordinary conversation. She needed it; it would get her back to normal.

"Oh . . . I'm just being silly," she began briskly, but Miss Furnivall interrupted her, so loudly that Anthea stared:

"You *must* tell me. It's only *fair*."

'Oh, very well,' Anthea thought tiredly. 'Let's see what you make of it. You might even say something helpful . . . after all, you do belong to Michael's world.' (She sometimes had to tell herself, rather firmly, that so did she.)

So, in the simplest words, with lifted head and her blue, still-wet eyes fixed upon her old hostess's face—now half in shadow and half illuminated by the rosy glare of a side-table lamp, and looking odder than ever—she related how sad she felt because a young man friend was going to Bermuda after Christmas and wouldn't be here for her birthday. The story did not take long.

Miss Furnivall reflected—or appeared to do so; in fact, she was wondering just when Marcie would be in, and if she could safely and politely take the last slice of cake while her visitor was talking. Then, entirely in order to keep the talk going, she said:

"I suppose you would like to marry him?"

"Well, yes," with a self-conscious little laugh, "I suppose I should. But I don't think that's very likely. He doesn't like people being poor, and besides—"

"Are you poor?" In Miss Furnivall's voice sounded a sudden note of interest. "You can't be. Your house is so big."

"Oh, but we are, Miss Furnivall. Most people of our class are, nowadays, don't you think?" She was relieved that at least the extraordinary old thing hadn't asked anything about *love*; if she had, Anthea wouldn't have known how to answer.

"I don't know," said Ella, sounding as if she didn't. Then, while Anthea had returned to a depressed study of the dying fire and was not really listening to her, she added suddenly, "What's his name?" and before Anthea could check herself she had told her.

Miss Furnivall stirred and sat upright, a dumpy figure, in her small square chair.

"Devon? Oh, one of the Devonhurst Devons? I was at a ghastly party once with Basil Devonhurst. He brought me a water ice, and some jelly, and some trifle with five almonds on it."

Her 'ghastly' had had a relishing small-boyish ring, and Anthea, very annoyed with herself at having let slip Michael's name, stared at her.

"But . . . that must be Michael's father's cousin, the present Earl, he's well over seventy," she exclaimed.

"I expect he is; I am speaking of sixty-three years ago," Miss Furnivall said. "At the time of the party he would have been twelve. (Yes, twelve, I remember Marcie telling me so, on the way home in the carriage. That was the time she fought a little girl for making fun of my hair.) Basil was an unusually *honourable* boy. He promised not to kiss me if we should happen to be sent out together for 'Postman's Knock', and he kept his word. Have you ever played at 'Postman's Knock'?"

Anthea could only shake her head. She was beginning to tire of this Mad-Hatter's tea-party—and Mummy would ask her if Colonel Furnivall had been there.

"Oh, you have been lucky; it is such a *vulgar* game; I used to dread it . . . and so you really would like to be married to this young man?" surveying her with wonder that anyone could prefer the state of marriage to that of celibacy, which offered one so many more opportunities for solitude. But she knew that people did like to get married. If Randolph had not been killed in Africa, Marcie would have been married, and Ella never ceased to be wickedly grateful that God *had* wanted him, and had taken him.

"Yes, I do," Anthea retorted, really tartly; she was still shaken, not yet quite herself. "There's nothing peculiar about that, is there?" she added. "Girls do."

Yes; they did: other girls. And so frequently, and often so *well*. The papers were full of their sickening smiling faces.

Ella, on whom the tartness had been lost, continued to look at her unseeingly.

"He's sure to be an honourable young man, as he's a Devonhurst," she said at last. "I should count on that, if I were you. I feel certain he will ask you to marry him, in the end."

Count on it! As she got up to go, and prettily thanked her hostess with murmurs of apology for having been a nuisance, Anthea was thinking scornfully that she could 'just see herself'—on the strength of a plate of trifle with five almonds on it and a promise that had been kept at a children's party, sixty-three years ago.

Nevertheless, as she walked away from the house—and just in time, for there was the other Miss Furnivall, the feminist one of whom she had always been rather scared, getting out of a small ancient car at the corner—she did admit that she was feeling less depressed.

There had been something in the atmosphere of that room, with its flowery carpet and its pale walls where quiet mirrors and delicate water colours in gilt frames caught the gleam of the firelight, that was exceedingly calming; it seemed to set the stresses and frustrations of the present at a distance by interposing, between them and oneself, the peace of the not very distant past. Something of safety, of certainty and order, lingered there. She had not felt it as emanating from the presence of Miss Furnivall herself, but she had felt it; and she was more cheerful.

After all, Michael *was* very kind . . . and while there was life, there was hope.

"Have you been having that silly little Anthea Cavendish to tea?" enquired Marcia, coming in with her fur coat and a cap with a jewel in it, both of which she threw into a chair. "Is there any left? No, I'll ring—why not? Oh, sulking again, is she? Well, well. I won't be a minute." She went through to the kitchen, which she found empty but with a kettle dutifully boiling, and returned with it to the drawing-room.

"What did you find to talk about?" she asked curiously, as she sat down, and when Ella had repeated the events and conversation of the afternoon (leaving out only her own fall in the street for fear that Marcia might at last forbid these winter walks in search of places to paint), she said:

"That's what comes of not training a girl; all she thinks about, naturally, is marriage. Did you gather that she cares for him?"

Ella shook her head. "She sounded cross when she talked about him. I was wondering," Ella did not hesitate, "if she had been like a real wife to him—you know. I don't know why I wondered that," she added.

"It had occurred to me, too, while you were talking." Marcia lit one of her strong cigarettes. "You remember Grace, that very flighty housemaid we had? She had just Anthea's air of super-innocence. Really innocent people," she smiled at her, "seldom look so convincing."

Ella said nothing.

"Very silly of her, if she has," Marcia went on, "but nothing like so serious, of course, as it was in our day. Then, you really were finished—and as for anybody marrying you—! Today, so I understand, thousands of girls do it, all the time, and many of them make good marriages—good in every sense. But I shall never be able to accept it, now. Something in me says *no* to a girl's doing it . . . though as for virginity, it seems to have become a joke. But I don't know why we're gossiping like this; poor Anthea may be as good as gold."

She picked up her coat and went to her room. Ella sat still, looking into the now replenished and cheerful fire.

CHAPTER XIV
Flashback to Switzerland

REALLY innocent people. Marcia had meant her.

But she was not innocent.

. . . It was quite early in the morning. How hot it had been, so hot. The air was silvery and dazzling except where, beyond the

edge of this narrow path winding round the outskirts of the hotel
gardens, there was the cool dark greenness of the pinewoods
coming down—

'Round about, solemn and slow,
One by one, row after row,
Up and up the pine trees go
So, like black priests up, and so
Down the other side again.'

She had murmured the words to herself as she walked. Her
heavy linen skirt just cleared the path, white with the dust of the
long summer that was ending, the high collar of her blouse rubbed
her soft young neck, a big hat of Tuscan straw balanced on the
slipping coils of her hair. She was eighteen years old.

There was all the day spreading out before her in lonely peace,
for Mamma and the others had driven off to see a waterfall at
many miles distance and would not be home until the evening.
She need not even go back to the hotel for luncheon. She carried
hers with her, packed away with the water jar and brushes and
paint-box in her haversack. She was alone, and she was free, and
she was happy.

She was eager to begin painting the light, turned by the sunrays
to that molten silver, as it streamed between the trunks of the
pines. As she walked quickly on—even in youth her walk had
been clumsy—the air began to grow quieter; the voices of visitors
gossiping on the hotel verandah died away, and the roofs of chalets
in the village disappeared behind a curve of Alpine meadow. When
I get there, Ella promised herself guiltily, I'll take off my shoes.

But when she did get to the favourite glade, where the great
white and violet face of a distant mountain looked in at her through
the quiet, dusky trees, it was so hot and silent and sweet-scented
that she did more: soon she was sitting before her blank paper,
staring at the untouched whiteness, with both small feet—already
a little less than shapely because of her mother's insistence on
her wearing a two when she took a three—naked on the warm dry
ground. She took off her hat and shook down her hair to protect

her nape from an errant sun ray, then gently touched the paper with her pencil's point and forgot everything else.

Some time, certainly, had gone by. The picture grew; Ella pulled her sleeves above her sallow wrists, and her ankles were smarting from the kisses of the sun, for the ray had travelled downwards.

"May I look?"

Exceedingly startled, she glanced up. It was a young man's voice, and he stood a little way off from her, with bared head, wearing with some grace a clergyman's dark grey summer dress of markedly good cut. Another sunbeam, penetrating the canopy of branches, touched his hair to a bright gold.

She remembered that she had immediately thought of her mother's repeated warnings about the removal of gloves or hat—shoes, much less *stockings*, of course, she had never dreamed of including in her list—when alone. It was to prevent just such an embarrassment as this.

Confused and irritated, she rose, and stood in silence while he came slowly forward. Oh . . . she had forgotten her hair—trembling with annoyance, she lifted her arms and hastily twisted it into a knot on the top of her head and pinned it. Slowly, without hurrying itself, it slid down again, and pins and combs showered on the ground at her feet.

"Please leave it," he said, keeping his eyes fixed on the little picture, "it's so beautiful."

So Ella, already comforted by his calm tone, thankfully left it. They stood silently in the quiet glade, where the only sound was the occasional faint movement of the wind in the high branches, and he studied her picture of black boughs and blinding light. She felt nothing but peace.

"That's beautiful, too," he said at last, sighing, and turned to her. "May I stay and talk to you? My name is Currey—the Reverend Arthur Currey. I am taking the services at the English church here."

"We don't go to church," Ella had said, and he had answered, "Yes, I noticed that none of you were there, last Sunday. Shall we sit down?"

There were some rocks in the bed of a dry stream near by, and here they had seated themselves.

How she had disliked the company of young men when she was a girl!—their silly jokes, their stares when she said what was really in her mind, instead of something about the weather, their scarcely concealed wonder at her appearance and manner. She had neither liked, nor wanted to please, them; they seemed stranger to her than any casually encountered animal, and she had been content to watch the triumphs over them of Marcie.

But this one—how often she had thought of it during the last half-century—this young man had not been like the others.

For at once, without hesitation or preliminaries, they had begun to talk together; not about those things which Ella had often to pretend an interest in, such as politics or the new King or the social life of the neighbourhood, nor yet even about those 'deeper' subjects which her family ('rationalist' and 'liberal', as she now knew them to have been) sometimes discussed, while she sat silent: she and the Reverend Arthur Currey had talked of what truly and secretly interested her.

Odd indeed, by commonplace standards, were the things they spoke of: the personalities dwelling in inanimate things; communing with animals; Time; the light of the stars; sounds; and, at last, love.

He had said that he supposed she was not engaged to be married, and she (ignoring, because she did not perceive, what would in those days have been thought an almost unbelievable piece of rudeness) has answered earnestly that she wasn't, indeed, and didn't want to be.

No, he answered, nor was he. As for wanting to be—for the first time he looked away from her as he spoke.

"You see, Miss Furnivall, there isn't only one kind of love, the kind between men and women. There are many different kinds— so many! And unless you can find the kind that you were created for, you won't be satisfied here below. You *will not*."

"Have you found the kind you were created for, Mr Currey?" she had asked, looking curiously at his downcast, almost femin-inely beautiful, face.

"I? Oh no. God forbid . . . I am never going to find it *here*, if He is merciful to me. But I have made up my mind to that, so it isn't so bad, you know."

But she had thought, with a wondering pity, that if his expression showed his feelings it probably was rather bad.

Perhaps, like that poor friend of Marcie's, he was in love with someone already married—though why one shouldn't be, Ella had never been able really to imagine.

Then he had told her, as they strolled homewards together through the lengthening shadows, about Christian love. She must become a Christian, he said.

"Because, you see, you aren't at home here, are you?" and when, after some thought, she had realized that she never had been, and had told him so, he had cried—his first calm manner had vanished some time ago—"Then you're just the kind of spirit that Christianity was made for . . . it's full of cool crevices and crannies for people like you and me . . . of course, we have to be out in the world as well—though I'm not much good at that, I'm afraid—but we can always stretch out and rest in those places. You *must* be one, Miss Furnivall."

And when she had explained to him that her family would strongly object, he had charmed her by saying that she must become like those people who were secret Christians in the persecuting world of Diocletian and Nero, worshipping by night in the catacombs, drawing the Fish that was their symbol in wine on a table or hastily in the dust of a roadside, to reveal themselves to a fellow believer.

She answered that she liked that thought very much, and would try to do what he had said.

They said good-bye, happily, in the woods where the path to the hotel began. He said nothing more about another meeting, he took both her hands and actually kissed her cheek, and strode away, hatless, with the evening light on his bright hair.

She never saw him again. But two days later there came a note for her to the hotel: 'I am in terrible shame and trouble. Remember what I said. Christ bless you. A.C.' And from the shocked conversation in undertones that went on between the older people around her, and ceased when any younger ones approached, she understood that he had done something dreadful.

"Ella, what *was* in that letter from Mr Currey—from the parson at the English church?" her mother had abruptly asked her later that morning in the empty public room of the hotel. "Our waiter tells me a boy delivered it to you this morning." She kept her eyes fixed on her daughter as she spoke; she was pale and rigid with distaste.

"I tore it up," was the answer, after reflection.

"What—how did it come that he was writing to you? What could he possibly have to say to you?—a man we have never met. Have you been getting to know him on the sly?"

"He came up and looked at my picture in the woods, and we had a long talk."

"In the woods! A long talk! What *can* you have been thinking of?"

"It was ripping," said Ella, feeling vaguely that a note of commonplace enthusiasm might not come amiss.

"'Ripping'! Really, Ella—and you know how your father dislikes these meaningless expressions—how—" She broke off, muttered something about *innocence*, and went on severely: "But why was he writing to you at all? What was in the letter?"

"I don't know why he did. It said, 'I am in terrible shame and trouble. Christ bless you.'" She kept her round pale eyes, clear as dew-ponds at dawn, fixed on her mother's face.

She seldom lied outright, having found that half-truths and suppressions better served a protective purpose.

"Hypocrisy, too! That makes it all the more—"

"Is he in love with someone who's married?" interrupted Ella, but when the only answer was an impatient shake of the head, she asked no more questions; she was not really curious. "He was very—pleasant," she added. "And—and polite."

"Yes, well, I daresay—he is a gentleman, too, that makes it even more inexplicable. The best thing you can do is to put the whole thing out of your mind, and—understand me, Ella—you are *not* to discuss it with your cousins."

"Not with anyone?" She was thinking of Marcie.

"Not with *anyone*. You are to forget it, at once and completely. Now that's enough. It's all most extraordinary—his writing to you, of all people—but we'll forget it."

She swept with her stately walk from the room, her expression betraying bewilderment at having discovered the difference between reading about these people in Plato and Virgil and having one of them talk to her own daughter. But, of course, the wretched man was mad, that explained it all.

Ella did not discuss the mystery with her cousins. But neither did she put the whole thing out of her mind.

God had evidently not been merciful to Mr Currey. But the word 'Christian', the name 'Christ', were now interesting to her because of what Mr Currey had said. She learned one more fact: he had been hastily sent away from Adlerwald. And that was all. She felt extremely sorry for him; he had been so nice, so interesting to talk with; the only likable young man she had ever known.

She never did find out what his crime had been.

The years passed; for her they were like quiet dreams. Gradually, very gradually, as a gentle wild animal is drawn, first to graze on the fresh herbage surrounding a certain tree and then, at long last, to couching beneath its scented shade, she began to read the New Testament, and also to search for, and ponder on, the rare references to Christ in poetry. When she began upon *The Divine Comedy*, in the thirtieth year of her life, it did seem to her that she took a great step forward—in *something*, if not quite in intellectual understanding.

Later, when her family was scattered abroad or dead, and she was living alone with Annie in the house at Oxford, she began one spring to creep out in vague search of comfort, to church; any church, any service, but always at some distance from home, lest Annie should find out and bully her. Irresistibly attracted by certain phrases—'These Thy creatures of bread and wine' foremost among them—she went, unchristened and unconfirmed, to Communion, merely one amongst Christianity's many odd children.

If the worst had happened, if someone whom she knew had recognized her as she knelt in church at prayer or went awkwardly up to the altar rail, and afterwards approached her and spoken to her, she would have said only, "I like being a Christian, so why shouldn't I?"

And surely it said much for the strength, if not for the orthodoxy, of her Christianity that never once had her great fear—that Marcia would find out—caused her to consider a secret apostasy. But it made it all 'so awkward', when one of her first prayers had been that she might be rescued from Annie—and God had sent Marcia, some months later, to do it. That was exceedingly puzzling. Rescued by the one she loved best, and that one a heathen, to whom she was afraid of revealing her faith!

For of course Marcie, so brave, beautiful and clever, *was* a heathen, and, Ella much feared, would have to go to Purgatory for a bit, with Virgil and others.

Marcie would be . . . so cross. Ella had never once kept anything from her, in all their lives long, except this, and now the sole deception had been going on for more than forty years.

It was sly; it was cowardly; it was deceitful; it was enough to make *anyone* cross. It might even make the heathen whom Ella loved best in all the world—despise her.

CHAPTER XV
Merry Christmas (continued)

"THEY'RE keeping Tibbs very late, aren't they?"

"He may have gone to pick up Molly—oh, there he is."

'They' was the General Post Office, which for the last few days had employed Tibbs—among others—to sort and deliver parcels and shuttle five hundred and fifty million Christmas cards to and fro. As Katy spoke, the swing doors of the 'Queen Charlotte's Arms' closed after him and Molly, and they came towards the Hultons' corner, across the cheerful, smoky old room whose high ceiling was almost hidden in bright paper-chains. It was full of noise and people and the tang of fresh beer.

Don brightened; he always preferred a man's company, and Katy was very down this evening. Tibb's views on the contemporary struggle for existence in North London were as entertaining as they were shameless, and Don was delighted to see him. He was a very grown-up man, in Don's opinion, was Tibbs, perhaps that was due to all the things he had seen at home and abroad.

"Hullo—hullo—how many turkeys have you sent astray—the usual for me—oh, will you—thanks—I've spent all my money on Molly—Oh, Tibbs! We're going to Daisy's—Tibbs too?—Yes, I am so honoured. To you, Katee!"

Tibbs drank off most of his beer, his cat's eyes half closed in pleasure above the glass's rim. Katy sat still, thinking that he never looked more foreign than when he was lowering a glass of 'Brown'.

He admired her; she knew that. But Katy was accustomed to men admiring, and desiring her. Tibbs's admiration would have made small difference to her at any time, and this evening she was as 'off' the other sex as she well could be.

Once she had lived in their world of light-heartedness and endless talk and intellectual play . . . because it had been play, having nothing to do, as she could see now, with life as it is lived in this world.

How they had theorised! Every contemporary problem and every timeless one had been brought out, dissected and prescribed for by herself and the young men whom she had known.

Yes, every problem except one—What does a young woman with brains do when she gets caught in a trap?

Katy, sitting so still in the old Windsor chair, could almost feel the bitter bite of the gyves on her ankles. She drank some beer and tried to control this despairing desire for revenge on something or someone.

It was the eve of God's birthday; they had a flat to themselves, Don was working well, there was a feast for tomorrow that would have seemed to her, as a child, luxurious beyond deserving; there was a box for her own children filled with cheap exciting toys . . . she ought to be heartily thankful.

She *was* thankful . . . only, she didn't feel it.

She only felt the unceasing aching in her limbs and the unending procession through her tired mind of minute domestic details, and she thirsted for solitude and the pleasures of the intellect. Her seamed, red hands and her savage ignoring of what Don and

Tibbs were discussing showed what had happened to the girl who five years ago had been the most promising student of her year; that girl who, when the lilac was flowering in the Oxford gardens, had caught love as if it were some dangerous fever, so that she had been unable to work and had not cared; living only to see one other person and to touch him and feel his touch; thinking only of Don by day and by night; and going at last with him, blind and drunk with love, to the marriage bed.

Then the children had started . . . and sickness . . . and the endless washing and feeding and wiping . . . broken sleep, for months on end, no time to open a book, no desire or energy to read even if there had been . . .

She sat up quickly, draining her glass. This evening she hated Don for being unchanged. He laughed as easily, he played as comfortably with theories and words, as he had done five years ago.

That little ass, Molly, now.

"You must have an *attractive* name for your product," she was saying. "I've been working for an advert agency this last week, and, believe you me, I *know*."

"Let us first invent the tablet, please," said Tibbs, gaily, for he was now sure of his Christmas dinner. "We have not even got the formula worked out yet. And then we must test it."

"Well, I don't like 'Wind-Out', it sounds like something for cleaning windows. Have *you* got any ideas on the subject?" turning graciously to Katy, whom, she thought, the men were rather neglecting this evening.

Katy shook her head. Don glanced at her, then leant forward.

"Cheer up!" he advised loudly. "You're the skeleton at the feast! How about another—?" He held up her glass, and she nodded.

"Ah, Christmas is no 'festive season' for Mother, is it?" Molly said sympathetically. "I expect Daisy's run off her feet, too . . . I saw Colonel Furnivall just outside home this evening," to Tibbs, "and told him I hoped to have the pleasure of seeing him tomorrow . . . he looked so nice! He was just off somewhere—white scarf, black Anthony Eden and all—I do think it's grand to see one of the Old School in full rig, and such a treat to see a man wearing a hat, too."

"Good God, Molly, are you such a fool as you seem to be?" Tibbs demanded, in a reasonable tone. "A treat! To see an old man wearing a hat! If that is your idea of a treat I am sorry for you, I certainly am."

"Well, it is a treat! I get sick of seeing all you boys going about bareheaded."

"'Boys'!"

"Well, men, then."

During this exchange, Don had been making his way back from the bar with the new round of drinks. As he came up to the table he said in a casual aside to Katy: "Keep calm, but you'd better pop over the road. Mark's at the window." Before he had finished speaking she was out of her chair. Heads turned to watch her darting between the tables, and her hasty exit between the doors that swung violently behind her.

"What is it?" Tibbs demanded, while Molly stared with saucer eyes. Don shrugged. But he had not sat down again, and suddenly he muttered something and followed his wife.

Outside, there was a freezing drizzle. Through it, across the road, Katy saw the front door standing open and Mrs Cavendish on the steps, peering this way and that under her hand. Childhood habits of thought came back to Katy as she raced recklessly across the road, to the screech of more than one set of brakes hastily applied: *'Oh God, please let it be all right I was ungrateful, I was wicked, please, please.'* She reached the pavement and ran through the gate, and stumbled, slipping, up the greasy steps.

"Oh, Mrs Hulton, there you are," Mrs Cavendish exclaimed, with a kind of cold excitement, "I thought you must have gone on to another public house—"

"You know we never do that," Katy said, loudly and very angrily. "Are the children all right?"

"I believe so. Mark came down. It's that wretched oil-stove of yours—" She continued her remarks to Don, as he hurried up the steps, for Katy was already half-way up the stairs. "I never *do* trust them; if only you knew the number of times I've known this happen—"

"What's up now?" he coolly asked. The enquiring faces of Tibbs and Molly could dimly be seen down at the garden gate.

"Mark came down and fetched me. Poor little fellow, the wretched stuff was all over him, he looked like a little—" She was beginning to follow him up the stairs, as the others came into the hall. There was a strong reek of burning soot.

"I say," Don turned on her suddenly, "just let us manage this alone, will you? I don't think you can be of any use—oh all right, all right, I'll let you know the damage as soon as I know it myself," in response to her cry of "My things! But my things!"

"Tibbs, come and give us a hand, will you? No, Molly, you stay where you are. Coming!" as there was a call from above, and he ran up two at a time, followed by Tibbs wearing a highly unsuitable expression of excitement and glee.

"Always happens at Christmas, doesn't it?" smiled Molly, left standing in the hall with the Hultons' landlady. "Like railway crashes." She was really shocked when Mrs Cavendish, her face red with rage and misery, actually beat with both clenched fists on the balusters.

"The curtains!" she burst out. "My beautiful rug! Oh, how could I have been such a fool . . . ever to have them in the house . . . barbarians, louts, *Bolshies* . . . but I ought to have known. Haven't I seen it? Over and over and over again. *Blood* will tell . . ." She did not look at Molly as she spoke; she seemed to think herself alone.

There had been tramplings and voices sounding upstairs during this; now, all was quiet except that one of the children seemed to be crying. Molly's sympathetic gaze at Mrs Cavendish was interrupted by the appearance of Anthea, who came slowly and tiredly up the steps, carrying a small suitcase and a coloured dance-favour.

"Mummy! What on earth's the matter?" She looked inimically at Molly. "Is the house on fire?"

"Those *miserable* people . . ." and Mrs Cavendish rapidly explained.

"Well, do let's shut the door, I'm freezing."

She looked again pointedly at Molly, who smiled *(this must be the snooty daughter. Was that complexion Rubenstein or Max Factor?)* and said simply, "I'm Molly Raymond—at your service."

"She's a friend of the Hultons, dearest," said Mrs Cavendish hastily.

"And of Daisy's," Molly added sweetly.

"How do you do," Anthea said coldly. The pause was threatening to become awkward when Don came running down the stairs.

"Cheer up!" and Mrs Cavendish started indignantly. "None of your stuff's even touched—the stove was in the bedroom. It only needs a bit of a wipe round—Katy'll see to it after the holiday."

"After the holiday! But surely, Mr Hulton—"

"Oh forget it," he said easily. "Sorry I got a bit excited myself—I was afraid the kids' things for tomorrow might have got spoilt, but they're all right; Tibbs got them out. Molly," turning to her, "Tibbs is just coming. He's going to buy you a drink. Merry Christmas—so long."

"God be with you," Molly said. "And a merrie, *merrie* Christmas."

Don ran grinning upstairs again and into the living-room, where he had already thrown half a bucket of the coal, with which Katy had toiled up that morning from the basement, on to the fire.

He had put her into a chair with her feet up on another, and wrapped her in his shocking old duffel coat, and forbidden her to move. The rosy lights were burning, the astonished fire danced, the children were back in their sooty bed, from the public house opposite came shouts and song. They heard the front door slam, as Tibbs and Molly left, and then Anthea Cavendish's tired voice: "Mummy darling, I've bought us some sherry. Come along."

Katy stirred, on her uncomfortable perch, within his arms.

"Didn't you think Mark seemed very worked up, almost *frightened*, Don?"

"Damn the kids," said their father. "For once, there's just going to be you and me."

The damned ones, meanwhile, lying in bed in the dark, were asleep except for Mark. He was biting the sheet. Some ten days ago he had discovered his teeth.

They were still so new that he could dimly remember the discomfort associated with their arrival, and until a certain day when he had chanced to put the blunt end of a pencil into his mouth while meditating what to draw next, he had regarded them as rather a menacing bore. But suddenly, charmed by the aromatic flavour and smoothness of the pencil, he bit hard on to the wood.

Instantly, he had enjoyed a strong sensation which he did not know was the release of pent-up energy. It was as if he had done what he had always longed to do and never been allowed to, and *shouted*. From that moment, biting had become all his delight. The edges of his toys, the window-sill, the upholstery—even wretched Mary's fingers—were all experimentally tested by his teeth, and if anyone at this stage in his life had been able to extract from him a truthful answer to the question: "What do you like best in the world?" it would unhesitatingly have been: "Biting."

And what gave him the strongest pleasure, the liveliest sensation of relief, was a smooth piece of pleasant-tasting shiny wood.

"Daisy?" said a cross voice on the telephone some days after Christmas.

"Oh hullo, *Sue*—I thought you were going to be away. What happened?"

"The usual thing. Chris turned bloody-minded at the last minute. He had work to do, we should drink too much, he needs a rest, the usual blah. So we wired them we had 'flu, and stayed at home."

Susan's tone was so charged with resentment that 'no comment' seemed indicated. Her worst friend's voice went on, "What did you do?"

"Oh . . ." Daisy let out a sighing giggle, "the usual family thing. But this year it really *was*—"

"How do you mean?" The sulky tone brightened, a very little, in hope of entertainment.

"You know Janine went back to France? Well, I asked Molly Raymond, yes, 'God-be-with-you', that one, to stay over the holiday, to help, and she asked could she bring Tibbs because she dotes on him, and James hates his guts . . ."

"Then why did you let her bring him? Really, you are *bright*. If I had the luck to be married to a sweetie like James, I would at least try to *keep* him sweet."

"Well you know I always do ask someone who wouldn't have a Christmas, otherwise, and this year it was Tibbs. I can't help James's troubles, he mustn't be selfish."

"Oh . . . *self*ish . . . well, go on." Susan settled herself more comfortably in her chair.

"I told him to make an effort and try to remember the spirit of Christmas, and he did, bless him, and things were going quite well when—you remember Delia Huxtable?"

"Didn't someone try to poison her?"

"*No*, Sue, you really must *not*; that's just her story; you can't blame Jennifer Beresford for being a bit careless when Delia was making Bill as hard as she could make . . . well, *Delia* arrived on the doorstep on Christmas morning, in riding breeches and a sweater down to her knees and that poor little Evelyn with her . . . Jennifer'd *turned her out*. I always thought that was invented by Victorian novelists, didn't you?"

"It's Bill's child, isn't it?"

"Delia never will be *definite* . . . So, of course, she came round to us. I really was rather taken aback, because I don't have much use for Delia's type, and she does embarrass poor James so. And Molly, of course, went all pop-eyed over Evelyn and we had showers of Middle-European wisdom about sex from Tibbs . . . and in the middle of all this, my old cousins and my father arrived."

"'The more the merrier'."

"That's what Molly said when Delia blew in, but I said it depended."

"I suppose," Susan's voice was bored now, "they were shocked to the core?"

"Not *shocked*."

Daisy sometimes found that the entertainment provided by her worst friend had to be paid for; one payment was the disapproval of James, and the other was a certain obviousness, a hardness and a shallowness, in Susan's views of people. To her, for example, anyone over fifty was automatically 'square', outmoded, narrow, shockable and very, very dim.

"But I did find it difficult," Daisy confessed. "You see, Delia always *will* introduce that poor little Evelyn as 'my illegit'. I think they found her showing-off manner impossible to understand. My father said to me afterwards that the poor creature was defiant because she was surrounded by a domestic happiness which she would never possess—"

"How sweet."

"Wasn't it?" (But Daisy wished that she had kept that kind little comment to herself.) "At dinner I made the excuse of there not being enough room for us all to sit together, and put the elders of the tribe into one room and the Outcasts (as James *would* call them) into another, and Mrs Hill and I shuffled between with the food. We could all hear everything everybody else was saying—I *had* to have the double doors open—and there were the elders talking about old friends at Oxford and the disadvantages and advantages of this new caper about not endorsing cheques and so on, and Delia and Tibbs talking about people not understanding their own impulses, and frigid wives, and Molly putting in a 'sexshually' every now and then—I cannot *tell* you," concluded Daisy, signing off this painfully vivid sketch, "what it was like."

"Were there any rows?" Susan luxuriously asked.

"Oh no. I kept on catching James's eye and trying not to laugh. Poor James," her voice sobered, "I think he really was rather fed up, though."

Susan made a harmless murmur. What a fool Daisy was—but only about James.

In the afternoon he and Molly took James Too and my father for a walk on the Heath. Molly loved that, of course—out with two men—three, if you count James Too."

This time Susan's murmur was even more harmless. If Daisy could not *see* that James was attractive to women, why warn her?—until some amusement might be got out of doing so.

Soon afterwards, they rang off. Daisy said that she had some people coming to spend the day.

The 'people' were the little Hultons, while Katy and Don went off for a grimmish walk through the frosty beechwoods of Buckinghamshire, looking, with their rucksacks and their duffel coats and scarves and sticks and maps, like the pair of students which, in Daisy's opinion, they had never ceased to be.

Molly was left in charge (with a typed sheet of instructions about feeding Maggie, who was just beginning to be weaned), for it was now early in the New Year and Daisy—but not Molly—had an all-day job.

The temporary nurse and her charges were sitting in the warm kitchen, late in the afternoon, when Daisy got home. Smeared with dripping toast, rosy and timidly lively—Maggie, replete, was exercising her legs on the floor—they greeted their hostess with bright, silent stares.

"Katy and Don should be here any minute," Daisy said, "and all you've got to do is to dress the children and get them a taxi," and she gave the number of the rank. "I'm sorry to leave you to it again but I must fly and change."

"James not coming home first?" Molly asked casually.

"No . . . we're having something in town."

Molly 'stifled a sigh'. "They've all been *so* good," she said, "especially Mark," with a smile at him, "haven't you?"

"Splendid," shouted Mrs Muir cheerfully, halfway up the stairs.

So that was that, thought Molly. He wouldn't be in. The kitchen looked less cosy and cheerful, the children less endearing now that she was not going to see James—Jim—Jimmy . . . the diminutive suited him so much better than that stately 'James'. He was so sweet! But his wife didn't appreciate him. She was always doing things for other people . . . Oh, kind enough, Daisy was. But she ought to have enough to do being kind to James. He was one lucky woman's job in himself.

Well, if *one* woman didn't appreciate him . . .

She became aware that Mark was crying.

"Here, here, this won't do, so early in the new year!" she said, putting an arm around his unresponsive person as he leaned against the table. "What's it all about? You tell Auntie Molly."

Children usually suffered Molly's advances, feeling in her an absence of the desire to improve their characters, and Mark was soon stammering, between dripping tears (watched immovably from the floor by Maggie and from the corner where she sat picking the label off a jam-jar by Mary) that he had *bitten the oil stove.*

"*Bitten* it?" His small wet face and Molly's small one shrouded in fluffy hair, stared at each other. "With your teeth, do you mean?"

A wretched nod.

"Well," Molly said helplessly, "that was a queer thing to do, wasn't it? Did you think it was a sweetie?"

A shake of the head and a watery smile.

"Didn't it burn you?"

There was a fresh outburst, from which she managed to make out that it was 'all cold' when he bit it, but in the night there had been 'lot of black smoke'.

"Oh—that was the time it went wrong—nearly spoiled all your Christmas presents, didn't it? But Uncle Tibbs got them away from the nasty smoke in time—kind Uncle Tibbs—well, you were a silly boy but it wasn't *naughty*—Mark wasn't a *naughty* boy to bite it—biting isn't naughty so long as you don't bite *people*. I expect you thought it was liquorice, didn't you?"

And she was well away into a description of this fascinating substance, which her hearer had so far never come across, brightened by references to Bertie Bassett and the hope that Mark might one day see his picture in the tube, when a knock at the pink front door announced the arrival—chilled, rosy, and carrying a large bunch of beech leaves and bryony—of his parents.

Molly stood on the doorstep and watched them drive away at last. She did not envy the Hultons their absorption in one another and their family. She went, cheerfully enough, back to the kitchen and made everything straight there, and put the pound note which Daisy had given her into her purse, and when Mrs Hill had arrived to sit with the sleeping James Too, she shut the pink front door—on the rooms that enshrined James Muir, on the household whose mutual absorption she did envy—and went out into the cold, high streets of Hampstead.

The flower shop windows were full of violets; the far off stars glittered hopefully as if they too knew that this was a New Year.

The last thing she was thinking about, now, was Mark and his troubles. And he was riding home in the taxi, firmly convinced that, so long as you didn't bite people, it didn't matter what you did bite.

CHAPTER XVI
Unprovoked Attack on an Heirloom

'MY DEAR Godfrey' (read Colonel Furnivall, seated at breakfast one morning towards the middle of January) 'don't you think you could spare the time to come and see an old friend? I have most afternoons free now, thanks to the help I have from Daisy's little protégée; so won't you look in one day about four o'clock? I should so enjoy seeing you again and talking over old times. It must be quite four years since we met, and although of course I have news from time to time from Daisy, I should like to see *you*. So do try to come.

'Always yours,
'M.A.V. Cavendish.

'P.S. I know I'm a tiresome old woman.
'P.P.S. No telephone now, alas!'

Tiresome was the word—but stronger condemnation was checked by the recollection that old Minta had been one on whom his wife had always felt it her duty to 'keep an eye'—as if Minta, at that time so rich in this world's goods, had been in some kind of need . . .

Well, he supposed that he must go. Minta's story—prosperity, unanticipated widowhood, dwindling income, cruelly high cost of living—was a commonplace one in the middle classes nowadays. That did not make it any less sad. And he still felt slightly guilty for writing to her about those rooms. Daisy seemed to think the arrangement wasn't working out so well as it might have.

He would go at the beginning of next week, and he sat down at his desk, with the brass godlings from India, and wrote to old Minta and told her when he would come.

Mrs Cavendish, on the particular day that he had chosen, had been trying to calm a heavy attack of depression by a prowl around her house and a secret inspection of the cleaning done by the Hulton girl. The remedy had failed; she now felt worse. There was not the final gleam and gloss on things that a trained worker could bestow. The Hultons were all out—shopping, she supposed, for these interminable packets of cereals and detergents which they seemed to consume by the *ton* . . . she went noiselessly up to the top floor in her thin kid shoes, casting a bitter glance as she mounted at the napkins hanging above the blackened plants in the freezing garden, and ran her finger over tables and chairs, and feebly shook the cushions in the hope of dislodging dust . . . no, the place just didn't look as it should.

On the narrow marble mantelshelf, incongruous beside the tiny china boy with his basket of grapes and the little silver-gilt clock, there was a gaudy postcard from somewhere sunny and abroad; another dull stab; it reminded her of Michael Devon and his contempt for Anthea—well, wasn't it contempt, going off to Bermuda without a word of apology or regret? . . . she would have to speak to Katy about these stairs again.

Katy would listen in silence; her white face would betray neither resentment nor apology, but her few casual words in answer would leave Mrs Cavendish with the infuriating conviction that the reproof had had no effect. And her manner was never *respectful* . . .

The front door bell. That would be Godfrey. She began to go slowly down the stairs.

On the doorstep, Colonel Furnivall had been thinking, half about the probable state of Minta's income (for the place, he was pleased to see, looked less run down than he had feared; well, stories either of people's cash or of their lack of it always tended to exaggeration) and half about Daisy's habit of always running after these extraordinary down-on-their-luck people.

He thought that the specimens he had seen on Christmas Day were most unlikely to repay her efforts on their behalf by any return, either gradual or sudden, to normal behaviour, and James—good boy, James—was getting worried about it.

During the private talk they had had on the afternoon walk, while Miss What's-her-name showed James Too the ducks, the Colonel had been surprised by the energy and bitterness of his son-in-law's comments: "Spongers . . . loafers . . . Daisy worn out . . . never in . . . always out chasing after some Afghan in a hole or, if she's in, listening to someone screeching for sympathy on the telephone . . . He liked Daisy to be at home when *he* got in: it might be silly, it might be unreasonable, he didn't want his dinner thrust down his throat the instant he set foot in the hall, he just *liked her to be there* . . ."

Perfectly natural, thought Colonel Furnivall, remembering. Silly Daisy. She would have to be careful. Where did she get 'all this' *from*?

And then, as he stood in the still winter afternoon on the wide stone of Minta's doorstep, in front of her heavy old door with its pale and glittering brass, there suddenly rose before his mind's eye, complete in full panoply of detailed colour, sound, feelings, scents—the memory of himself, aged twenty-three, sitting in the tent at Peshawur with Owen Holroyd, poor Holroyd, until four in the morning with the noise of the torrential rain ceaselessly drumming, drumming, on the canvas overhead. How he had argued, advised, threatened . . . and none of it had really been remotely *his* business . . . and Holroyd hadn't been the last acquaintance who had unexpectedly come to him for advice, money or help.

Perhaps Daisy 'got it' from him?

He had no time to pursue this disconcerting supposition any further, because the door opened.

The warmth of Minta's welcome made him feel guilty, her emaciation and the way that she had aged shocked him, and when, following her through the hall, he felt the desolate cold of the house and saw the carpetless stairs, and missed the remembered old pieces of fine furniture, he told himself, like Edward

the Eighth amongst the workless miners, that *something* must
be done.

Conversation, over the black papier-mâché tray inlaid with
mother-o'-pearl, the silver teapot, and the sandwiches so tiny as
to suggest that they had been cut by elves, went on fairly easily,
although there was a bitter undertone to Minta's flow of small
talk that disturbed him: she supposed he had noticed the washing
in the garden? The woman, her lodger, *would* put it out today, of
course. No, they hadn't been away; she herself had had no holiday for five years—and then it had been *such* a disappointment.
Did he know Clackwell on the east coast? Well, she had gone, so
looking forward to it, to stay with a friend who had a house there.

. . . One of those pretty white Victorian houses, rose-clad and
bay-windowed, and hedged about with thick barriers of tamar-
isk that had looked out on to the tumbling grey waves since
long before Mrs Cavendish's childhood; with the bright sea-light
striking in through its windows and the fresh salt airs blowing
through its gay little garden full of roses—Clackwell had always
been proud of its roses.

The miniature sea-front was lined by such sturdy small places,
interposed with one or two comfortable elderly red-brick hotels
that overlooked the plain stone promenade immediately above
the sea; there was a little gilt bandstand banked around with
pink geraniums and marguerites, and here a visiting military
band would play sweet or martial tunes, during the long summer
afternoons of the season, to the visitors dozing over their novels
in the deck chairs.

She had promised herself, Mrs Cavendish told him, a stroll
along the bleached boards of the old Pier, and perhaps even a visit
with her friend to one of the concert parties; they were sometimes
quite good. Oh, she *had* so looked forward to it. It was years since
she had been to Clackwell.

. . . By the long, low white hotel opposite the Pier, which had
once been the little town's grandest, the fronts of the villas were
slashed with notices advertising fish and chips. The iron balcony
of the place, formerly wreathed with a splendid fig-vine, had been
replaced by forty feet or so of plate glass and indoor plants. The

woodwork of the small white houses was picked out in blue or scarlet. When the wirelesses were accidentally silent for half an hour, the amplified voices of those taking part in the Personality Contest on the Pier could be heard half a mile away, drowning the soft rustling of the sea. The air reeked, everywhere, of fried fish.

On the horizon, a holiday camp painted blue, green and red, and extending beneath a slowly-turning Giant Wheel, replaced the former faint outlines of hazy blue, then broken only by the grim Martello tower once built to defy Napoleon.

A bungalow town, its cement walls cracking and the paint blistering from its warping boards, had grown up in the dunes where once were only pure white sand, beds of harsh reeds, and drifts of pink, white and lilac shells. At evening, when a livid light lay over the darkening sea and hundreds of television masts marred the sad sky, and the wirelesses throbbed and twanged across the silent marshes, this place resembled a contemporary version of Hell.

. . . Very sad, observed Colonel Furnivall, a resort going down like that.

But, not having known honest Clackwell before its debauching, he could not feel as his hostess did, and he thought it best to turn the conversation again to Anthea, a subject to which, he had noticed, she herself continually reverted.

But even here—and it soon became plain to him that her girl was the apple of her eye—there was cause for bitterness. She didn't speak out clearly, poor Minta never had been able to do that, but she hinted that Anthea was going about with some young man who wouldn't come up to scratch and wasn't likely to; very well-connected, apparently, rather a 'catch'—and that, of course, would appeal so strongly to Minta and make her feel it all the more . . .

Women . . . what a time they did have of it, to be sure. Colonel Furnivall began to wonder at what time he could decently take his leave. Minta had now unfortunately got on to the cessation of Presentations at Court.

"There wasn't so much to it nowadays, you know, as there was in our time," he soothed her.

"There's always the honour, Godfrey, and the *cachet*, even if a girl does have to share it with hundreds of lumpy Colonials," she retorted spitefully. Then, after a brooding pause, she burst out: "I shall regret it that Anthea was never presented until my *dying day*."

He had been about to say that he supposed he really must be going. But he could not leave her here, like this, on such a note.

Recalling his impression on first entering the house that 'something must be done', he threw all his energy, natural kindness and real pity for her into a little valedictory talk in which he assured her that now they had met again, they must keep the old friendship going; she must dine with his sister and cousin and himself; Ella had been full of Anthea's prettiness and grace (some editing here); perhaps she would be willing later on to let his own man advise her on her investments, he had a very good man, he thought. As for the chap who was—er—hanging fire—

Mrs Cavendish, who had throughout his remark kept her eyes fixed, with an absent yet eager look, on his face, only shook her head, and he was relieved. It had just run through his mind to say that what she really needed was a man to take this chap out to lunch and ask him his intentions, but it got no further than his mind, and he hoped the notion would not get through to hers. He did not wish to become too closely involved with the Cavendishes. Those thoughts which he had once dismissed as 'old man's vanity' recurred. He realised that the girl now had a young man, of a kind, but they would recur . . . together with others, even less palatable and seeming to him vulgar, about *second strings*.

While he was speaking there had been the sound of the front door opening and voices in the hall, one of which—he was almost sure—was Daisy's. Well, she could give him a lift back in her taxi; it was time he went, anyway. He glanced at the clock, and got up, with the traditional observations.

Mrs Cavendish made no attempt to persuade him to stay, but she certainly looked more cheerful than when he had arrived, and as he followed her out of the room he was congratulating himself that the visit had undoubtedly done poor Minta good.

It was Daisy in the hall, with a pale young woman with red hair, and some children. They exchanged pleased, surprised greetings and then she introduced the young woman, and the Colonel said something playful to the children, and then, suddenly, while this was going on with Mrs Cavendish keeping rather markedly in the background, they heard her utter a loud, angry exclamation.

"Good gracious! Oh dear! Just look at this!"

Everyone turned round.

The Colonel had been aware, out of the corner of his eye, that she was occupying the moment's pause by bending intently over a table standing against the wall, which he recognised as one always described as having belonged to her mother. He now saw that she was bent almost double over it and pointing with one trembling finger at a spot on its surface.

"What's the matter, Minta?" he enquired, and something warned him to make his voice unnaturally jovial. "Dust?"

"Dust!" lifting a face suddenly drenched with dull red colour. "No, it isn't dust—though there's plenty of that about, too. Come here, Godfrey, just come here a minute, will you, and look at this."

Reluctantly, conscious that Daisy was pulling a face and that one of the children (and he didn't blame it) was beginning to sidle off up the stairs, he went forward.

"That wasn't there this morning . . . I *know* it wasn't . . . I looked there myself to see if it had been dusted properly," with an angry glance at the pale young woman. "It's been done since you came in," accusingly. Her voice went up. "It's one of those—those *wretched* children. Oh," suddenly she crushed her hands together, "I *knew* something like this would happen—I knew it—my mother's table. My beautiful table that's been in the family for so many years—*ruined*! It's never come out—*never*."

For the moment Colonel Furnivall found nothing to say. Because it was true. Near the table's edge, deep in the old soft wood red and shining as a rose-hip, was a perfect half-circle made by baby teeth.

"This," pronounced Mrs Cavendish, glaring at Mrs Hulton, "is what happens when you let people out of the *gutter* come into your home. Biting the furniture, like some wild beast out of the woods—"

Here Mary, who had been watching her landlady with an air of the liveliest entertainment, struck in with a cheerful laugh and the announcement that they had seen a lion.

"Yes—we've all been to the Zoo," said Daisy hastily, hoping to reduce the rising temperature. "We've only just come in—I'm sure no one *could* have—"

"I blame the parents," said Mrs Cavendish stonily, ignoring her and keeping her eyes fixed on Mrs Hulton. "If a child *is* capable of such unspeakable vandalism, I blame the parents."

Colonel Furnivall saw Mrs Hulton moisten her lips before she began to speak.

"I'm sorry," she said quietly, " . . . I'm sorry. I'll . . . whichever of them did it shall be punished, of course. Mary!" wheeling round, "did you bite the table?"

Mary, who had been encouraged by the lack of concentration upon herself to perform a short, subdued dance, stopped in mid-hop and blithely shook her head.

"She may be lying," suggested Mrs Cavendish, who was far from satisfied with the suspect's dégagée manner.

"My children don't lie," Katy said. She looked fiercely round the hall, where the light of the brief afternoon was beginning to fade. "Mark!"

There was a scuffle and a distant wail.

"That's the guilty party," said Colonel Furnivall, and set off up the stairs. There were cries of protest and sounds of struggle, and Katy started forward, exclaiming, "Oh, thank you, but I'll manage him—" as the Colonel reappeared at the head of the stairs with Suspect Number Two kicking under one arm.

"I don't see how he can have," said Daisy in undertones to Katy as the two began to descend. "We never took our eyes off them, did we?"

"Except when we went back for the carry-cot."

"Oh God yes," in a stricken tone: "he must have done it then."

As if aroused by the word, Maggie suddenly began to wriggle and roar where she had been set down in a corner.

"She's thirsty," Katy muttered, "she'll have to wait . . . Mark," looking very severely at him where he stood weeping before her, "did you bite the table? Look here . . ." gripping his arm and dragging him across to it, "you're a *naughty* boy—here—*look*."

Wriggles, shakings of the head, roars of "No, no!"

"*Your* children don't lie, I think you said, Mrs Hulton?" Katy did not look at Mrs Cavendish as she said, impatiently, "He doesn't mean he didn't do it, he means no, no, don't make him tell. Mark!" shaking him so vigorously that Colonel Furnivall made a small movement. "Stop it! Stop it at once, or mother will whip you . . . you *did* bite the table, didn't you?"

A pause. Then the loudest roar yet, "Mark did bite! Mark did, he did . . ."

Katy stood up.

"Now say you're sorry to Mrs Cavendish," she commanded. "Go on, now. 'I'm very sorry I was a naughty boy.'"

"I–I–ah–m–ah–I–Mark—"

But Mrs Cavendish, with pursed lips and lowered lids, held up a forbidding hand.

"Mrs Cavendish doesn't accept Mark's apology. She is too hurt and grieved about her beautiful table that her mother gave her, which Mark has spoilt *for ever*. Mark should have thought how sorry he would be *before* he bit the table."

This lofty translation into the third person had the effect of alienating public sympathy. It was generally felt that Mrs Cavendish, an instant ago regarded with sympathy, was a pompous ass.

"He's said he's sorry, Minta," observed the Colonel, "and you must admit he looks it."

"Let's see if we can get it out with a hot iron?" suggested Daisy, but was checked by Katy's dejected mutter: "That's for grease-spots."

Mrs Cavendish felt the change in the wind. She drew herself up, determined to maintain her rôle, and said:

"Well, you may all think that this can be settled by an apology— which I do *not* think that he really means—from the child, but I *don't* think so. A very valuable piece of furniture—valuable to me both as an heirloom and from a monetary point of view—has been ruined. *Ruined.* I don't think I am being unreasonable in expecting something more than—I was so *fond* of it," she burst out suddenly, the colour rushing up again into her face. "I've known it ever since I can remember . . . taken such care of it . . . polishing it . . . wouldn't *dream* of . . . kept it long after I had to let other things go . . ." Tears.

Daisy and her father were patting and stroking her, Mary Hulton was jerking with the best intentions at her hand, Colonel Furnivall was saying that he would get on to the Army and Navy Stores first thing in the morning and see if they could get the marks out. Only Mrs Hulton, white and silent, kept herself in the background with Mark sniffling by her side. And Mrs Cavendish knew why. She was afraid of what was coming next.

Well, she had reason to be.

Mrs Cavendish finished with her handkerchief at last and, gently and coldly withdrawing herself from the ministrations of the Furnivalls, turned to confront, in her dark corner, the lodger. This was going to be the moment of punishment for those vulgar creatures, she with her housemaid's looks and he with his back-street accent, and she made her own voice sound exceptionally clear and soft as she delivered the blow.

"Of course, Mrs Hulton, I am sure you will have realised that after this I can't continue to let you live in my house. Oh—" as Daisy uttered a gasp, "*indeed* I can't. I should never know an easy moment now, about all my beautiful things—I should be imagining your children kicking holes through the glass cabinet."

"That's not fair," said Katy quickly. "This is the first time anything of yours has been damaged."

"And *what* a first time! An *excellent* beginning! Only a two-hundred-year old piece of furniture, valued at a hundred and fifty guineas"—Daisy caught her father's eye and looked quickly away—"completely *ruined*. No, Mrs Hulton, there can be no discussion about it. You must go."

She ceased, and, with lowered eyes, carefully tucked her handkerchief away in her sleeve. *Having the time of her life*, thought Daisy furiously.

"Don's exams started yesterday. I'm not getting out of here until they're over. And I'm not telling him about all this, either," said Katy.

"As you please," shrugging. "At your request, you may remember, you entered on your tenancy on a weekly basis. So you will leave here on Thursday next. Godfrey," turning to Colonel Furnivall, "please witness that I have given Mrs Hulton notice to leave here on," a rapid but dignified calculation with the eyes shut and the head thrown back, "the twenty-fifth of January."

Colonel Furnivall gave an uncomfortable nod. He wished that Minta would at least behave more *like* a lady, he wished the little thing in the corner would stop sniffling (been too much cooped up, no doubt, nothing like cooping up for getting boys into mischief), he wished that Daisy had been born with a smaller bump of philoprogenitiveness, and he wished himself well out of it all. However, he nodded.

"Very well, then." Mrs Cavendish's tone was still dignified, though now slightly hollow for lack of real matter; all seemed to have been said. "Very well," she repeated.

"We'd better go upstairs," muttered Katy. "Mary!" She began to struggle with the carry-cot.

But this seemed to arouse her landlady. She began slowly to shake her head again, with half-closed eyes—while Daisy watched with growing apprehension. What was coming now?

"Oh no," intoned Mrs Cavendish. "Oh no. His mother may take Mary and Baby Sister (poor Baby Sister, to have such a naughty big brother!)—Mother may take *them* upstairs if she likes. But Mark is not to go with them. Mrs Cavendish doesn't want such a naughty boy in her house. Mark—"

"Oh, don't be so bloody silly!" shouted Katy suddenly in broadest Scots. "He's said he's sorry, hasn't he? What do you mean—isn't to go upstairs? Have you gone mad?"

"I'm not surprised to hear gutter language. Breeding will out." Mrs Cavendish's eyes were glittering with satisfaction; now perhaps the Furnivalls could see what she had had to put up with. "I mean, Mrs Hulton, that I am not allowing Mark to stay under my roof tonight."

Katy glared, biting her lip. Then she said reasonably, "But what am I—what are we to do? Please," she swallowed, "can't you—it really is making rather a mountain out of a—"

"I'm glad you think so!" Mrs Cavendish cried, beginning to crush her hands together again. " . . . my beautiful table . . . a mountain out of a molehill. No," recovering herself slightly, "I'm sorry, but there it is. I *cannot*, *will not* have that child in my house for another minute."

Mark burst out roaring afresh. But even as Colonel Furnivall (his patience now in that condition so frequently described to us by the late Adolf Hitler) stepped authoritatively forward, Katy had sent an imploring glance at Daisy.

The instant response was cheerful and loud. It suggested, pictorially, a lifeboat full of bronzed rescuers approaching through a thunderous sea.

"We'd love to have him for a day or two, if you can spare him," Daisy said. Swiftly she kneeled down in front of the bellowing prospective guest. "Mark will come with Mrs Muir and see Lanza" (the canary). "Yes"—rather louder—"and ride in one of Mrs Muir's nice taxis . . . come along."

During the next ten minutes Mrs Cavendish began to feel that she was declining from the position of Chief Sufferer. No one took much notice of her, as they hurried up and down stairs with the carry-cot and a case for Mark's things, or hastened out into the gathering fog to find a taxi . . . she finally went back to the drawing-room, to crouch over the fire and try to console herself with thoughts of pouring it all out later to Anthea. Well, she had been completely in the right . . .

The house was beginning to grow quiet. She could hear the taxi's engine throbbing at the gate, and good-byes being shouted. But the child upstairs was crying . . . it was enough to split one's head . . .

Godfrey Furnivall came into the room.

"Good-bye, Minta, my dear. Cheer up . . . I do hope you will forgive me for having rather taken everything into my own hands, but I wanted to get everybody off so that you could have a little peace . . . now promise me to rest, and try not to worry. It will all seem less tragic tomorrow—"

"It was the last straw, somehow, Godfrey." She looked up at him out of desolate eyes.

"I know, I know." He patted her. "But I will telephone the Stores first thing tomorrow, and we'll see what they can do."

"It's very kind of you. I'm so sorry that your visit, the first for so long, should have—"

"Oh, that's all right—I've enjoyed it, and remember you're coming to us . . ."

With assurances, with pats and quiverings and gulps and mutters, they parted. In a moment she heard the front door shut and the taxi drive away.

She went back to the fire. Now, the house was really quiet. She had time to realise how she felt, and to think. Her nerves were vibrating painfully, her eyes stung, she was angry and miserable and—at last she had to confront the fact—she was also a little ashamed.

She sat on, staring with a rigid, set, stony face into the flames.

Colonel Furnivall said nothing to his daughter in the taxi, but Daisy was occupied with soothing Mark, who was convinced that he would never see his mother or sisters again, and although she never felt comfortable under her father's displeasure, she was relieved to be able to keep silent.

It was nearly six; she hoped that James would not be in; her late arrival, accompanied by a crying child guest, would not please him. As she saw out of the corner of her eye her father's severe expression, and imagined James's when she did turn up, she felt a moment's fury with men. Hang them, they expected the universe to revolve around them. No one must ever have any troubles but them, everybody must keep up a perpetual song and dance around *them* . . .

"Aren't you going to tell him to stop?" she asked, as they drew near to Laurel House.

"No, I'll come on with you: I should like to see James and the boy."

"Oh good; Jamesey is going to be in." But she wondered if he were going to gang up with James, if they would compare notes, warn each other . . . how sickening if they were. They were as thick as thieves already. Well, she was *not* going to let down the Hultons.

She braced herself, tired as she was, to meet opposition and criticism and argument. She sat with one arm around Mark, staring defiantly at the ill-lit roads of Belsize Park gliding by. They looked old and heavy and gloomy in the chill of the January evening.

But when at last they reached the house with the pink front door, James opened the latter to them with a smile and his mouth full of toast.

Yes, he had been in about half an hour, yes, Mrs Hill was just getting restive when he arrived. But it had been quite all right, Molly had happened to drop in, and she had made him some tea and the toast. She had only just gone. How nice to see Godfrey . . . and who was this? (It was Mark.) Oh, and he had a bit of news . . . he *must* tell Daisy . . .

"Molly?" asked Colonel Furnivall, as they all stood in the hall taking off hats and coats.

"Yes—Molly Raymond, she lives here nowadays," said Daisy. "Quick, Jamesey, tell me."

"The Ruddlins have bought an Alsatian!" he announced solemnly, and Daisy shook her head. Then James said to his father-in-law, "You remember Molly; we went for a walk with her on Christmas Day" as Daisy began to explain about Mark.

The Colonel looked quite expressionless as he followed his children into the living-room. He had once or twice thought recently that James, rightly incensed as he was by Daisy's behaviour, had the air of one shortly about to blow his top.

But this—toast-making, and sloping off before Daisy appeared—this was much more serious.

CHAPTER XVII
In The Still of The Night

LATE that same night, Anthea came slowly up the steps and put her key into the front door.

The car that had brought her home, belonging to an elderly career girl who was taking up dancing late in life to repair the omissions of an over-ambitious youth, moved slowly off, and silence fell. The black trees glistened in the drizzle where they caught the light of the lamps, the fog was in Anthea's throat and eyes, the deadly chill ached through her bones. The coming year, long and black and empty as the night, stretched before her.

The house was dark and quiet. Good; she did not want to talk. There would be a Thermos and biscuits in the drawing-room; there might even be another postcard from Michael (three of them, all blue sky and coral-red flowers and cheery greetings, were already in her bag. They had done nothing to soften her resentment against him).

There was no postcard, and she barely glanced at a note from her mother, gathering at a glance that the Hultons had been up to something again . . . *boring, boring, God, how deadly boring it all was* . . . she pulled her fur coat closer as she knelt shivering beside the fire.

The soup in the Thermos was really hot, and already her small porcelain face was losing its cold pink for a warmer tint, but just for a moment—in the quiet and hush of the fog-shrouded night, in the silent room surrounded by the things that spoke of a happier past and a future that seemed to have no chance of becoming anything but ever more impoverished, straitened, hopeless and sad—the thought of suicide touched her mind.

Funny to think that there was absolutely nothing and no one at this particular moment to stop her going downstairs and turning on the gas oven and putting her head into it . . . No more having to be always graceful and gay, no more tiredness, no more hateful thoughts about losing one's head and one's chances . . . just a few minutes' sickness and terror, and then eternity.

The word, with its vast and mysterious echoes, brushed against her mind and hung there vibrating for an instant of time. Then—because Anthea, for all her delicacies and discontents, was no death-wisher—it vanished. She wearily told herself not to be an utter fool, and got up, cramped but warmer, from her crouching position and put the Thermos and plate back on their tray.

As she set them down, she heard through the deathly quiet of the fog-bound midnight a car furiously approaching. 'Either it's lifted very suddenly or that driver's mad,' she thought. The brakes went on—she heard the horrifying noise as the wheels skidded across the greasy road—and then the car door slammed. Someone came running—running?—across the pavement. Then there was the familiar click of the gate, and they ran up the steps.

She knew at once that this had something to do with Michael.

There was a ring on the bell; long but not loud.

She went out of the room and through the hall, with her heart beginning to beat faster, and opened the door.

The cold fog came swirling in, with its acrid breath. And there stood he, himself, hatless, smelling of brandy, his short pale coat open, staring at her. Her first thought was, 'How brown he is,' and then, how white he was beneath it. She thought, too, that he had been crying.

"Hullo," he said, making a kind of smile.

"Hullo," she answered, and her heart was hammering now in her side. The black night and its mists came stealthily nearer.

"I say, can I come in for a bit? I'm awfully sorry to turn up so late, but, the fact is, there's been—I've had the—most ghastly shock, and I'm sort of—I thought I'd come and see you. Don't mind, do you?"

"Of course not. Do come in." She thought about nothing at all. But she began to be frightened. As they went through the hall, he following her, she heard him mutter something.

"What?" she said, half turning her head.

"I only said, I hope I haven't disturbed your mother."

"I don't think so; she went to bed early."

The drawing-room looked extraordinarily desolate, like a stage set when the play is over, all shadows and dimly burning pale lamps, and the furniture seemed to be staring forlornly. She heard Michael's teeth chattering, and she pulled up the biggest of the old chairs and put him into it.

"Here, sit down. Would you—will you have sherry? Or shall I make you some hot chocolate—you're so *cold*."

"I don't want anything—I've had enough already at the airport—*and* I needed it."

She was standing before him now, looking down at him, and suddenly, with a contortion of feeling that changed all the clear, high-bred look of his face, he reached out and caught her by the waist and pulled her down until she was kneeling beside him.

"They're all *burnt*," he said. "All of them. I saw it. But I can't believe it." He quickly put his face against her shoulder, hiding it, and she could feel how he shook and trembled. "*All* of them," he whispered. "Merciful Christ."

She was stunned into a cessation of all feeling. She kneeled, with her arms around him now, and on her face, as she stared at his shaking shoulders, even the faint traces left by twenty-eight years of her not particularly satisfying life were swept away. It was the solemn face of a pitying child. She said not a word, but held him close and presently, with her white hand, she just stroked his cheek.

At last he looked up.

"I'd gone down to meet them. (I got back three days ago, you see—thought I'd better.) You see—you see, what's so awful is that they were so nearly *down*. They don't know, now, exactly what happened . . . it was so quick. One minute we were watching the lights of the thing coming nearer and then . . . he tried to land, I think . . . it wasn't even foggy . . ."

"It wasn't foggy down there?"

"No, just a bit of mist, and then suddenly I just knew something'd gone wrong." He shook his head, blindly, with shut eyes. "The crash—I wonder you didn't hear it all over London. But I can't, I *can't* sort of realise it's happened."

"I did hear something, I think." She tried to remember the earlier part of the evening: and did vaguely recall a far-away heavy sound. "About nine, it would have been."

"That was it." He was sitting back in the chair, gazing at her apathetically.

"I do wish you would let me get you something."

"Don't want it, thanks. Couldn't. I vomited, you know," he said suddenly. "At the place. I expect I'm a filthy mess . . ." He glanced down at his clothes.

Anthea said very cautiously,

"Michael, isn't there any hope at *all*—are they absolutely certain that *everyone*—?"

"Not a hope, I tell you," angrily, "not a single bloody ghost of a hope in hell. Be different, you see, if this had happened somewhere miles out—but the thing came down whole and *crashed*. I saw it, I tell you."

They were both quiet for a moment. Then the small old gilt clock struck the half hour, and he glanced at it.

"I suppose," said Anthea, "you wouldn't stay? It won't take a minute to get the spare room ready."

She couldn't let him go away, out into the fog and the night, looking like that, feeling like that.

He shook his head.

"Awfully sweet of you. But I'll get back. There'll be—a lot to see to, tomorrow, you know. (That's what's so awful.) They were always so bloody decent to me—all of them. I'll miss them all like hell. And if I hadn't gone sort-of high-minded about work, and come home three days earlier . . . they didn't want me to, you know. Old Basil wanted us to go out after tuna—he was a great fisherman, you know . . . it's so *awful* to have to say . . ." He broke off. He was absently holding her hand, staring down at it as if he didn't see the slim fingers and rose-painted nails. Then he looked up. His reddened eyes met hers.

"Sorry I didn't let you know I was back," he said. "It was a dirty trick."

Anthea shook her head. But she felt a sick pang.

"Yes it was," he insisted. "I'm sorry, dear one."

"It's all right, Michael."

"No, it isn't. (I can be pretty nasty, you know. Or if you don't know now, you ought to.)"

He began to work off the thick gold signet on his right hand.

"I say, I've been meaning to get around to this for the last few months, and then you were so decent about my going off with them, never saying a word, it was that that really made up my mind for me—only I thought I'd have a last fling, kind of thing, you know, and now this has—the fact is," he had the ring off now, and was poising it between finger and thumb, not looking at her as he spoke, "I've got to have someone fixed up absolutely definitely from now on—they'll all be round me, you see, now—I know it sounds pretty crude, put like that, but I always did sort of mean it to be you. (If you'd have me.) So will you, Anthea?" He lifted her hand in his, looking at her, with a shamefaced and anxious expression.

Anthea nodded. She felt nothing at all except that this could not be happening.

Yes, she nodded, and he put the signet on to her finger.

"It's too big," he said, beginning to get up from the chair, and he gave a desolate great sigh.

"Yes. Never mind. Are you sure you feel all right?"

"I feel bloody."

"I meant, all right to go home?"

"I must, dear. There'll be so much to do tomorrow—and it wouldn't look awfully good, if someone gets on to me early in the morning and it came out I'd spent the night here . . . You're blushing. It's awfully pretty—but I did know you've got a lovely skin. The only new thing between us'll be the children. I never wanted them before but now it will be different, won't it . . . Oh Anthea," he turned suddenly and wrung the hand he was holding, "I've lost my family, sort-of. Let's have another, quick, shall we? Little boys."

"We will, darling." She was following him out into the hall, and now she gently buttoned his coat.

Standing obediently still while she did it, and staring away desolately up the curve of the stairs, he said, "I'll ring you tomorrow and we'll go out and buy you one that fits. What do you like?"

"Emeralds," said she, dismissing an impulse to say 'Anything', partly because it wasn't true and partly because she knew that he would not like to hear her say it. It sounded slavish and eager.

"(Whew!) All right: emeralds it shall be." She put her face up confidently to kiss him, but he looked so sad, so like a small boy in hospital whose mother hasn't come on visitor's afternoon and so like a tired man racked by grief, that she ended with the warm and hearty hug of a friend.

"We're going to be all right; thank you for being so decent," he muttered, returning it, and ran down the steps.

She stood in the open door, watching as he drove away, hatless, with a wave, into the still, fog-shrouded night. Then, softly, she shut the door.

Holding her hand out in front of her, so that she could see the solid old ring on her fourth finger, thinking of nothing but how wretched he would be, alone in bed with the flames and the noises of the past hours rushing through his mind, Anthea crept up to her room.

At the airport, in the small hours, the fog came down. The flares burned on, the red-hot metal smouldered and glowed, and the pitiful stench blew away, towards the late and weeping dawn, on a faint wind.

CHAPTER XVIII
"A Perfectly Enormous Bunch of Carnations"

THE next morning at the house with the pink front door began unpropitiously, with lingering fog, Mark Hulton refusing breakfast, James Too fiddling with his own—though whether following an example or from sheer malice was not apparent—James One with so violent a head cold that he did not go to work, and, at ten o'clock, Katy Hulton and her daughters on the doorstep.

"I'm going to take Mark back," she assured Daisy, who was flying round the sitting-room with a feather duster to the strains of some Mozart, in yellow jeans, sweater, red woollen stockings and a headscarf. "Mrs C. will just have to put up with it. I'm not having us putting you out like this."

"We aren't being put out." But Daisy was conscious as she spoke, and so was her visitor, of the silent figure seated before the fire, shrouded in Vick and *The Times*. "How is the old so-and-so this morning?"

"I haven't seen her, thank heaven. I saw *Miss* Cavendish, going off to work—she was quite pleasant—for once." Katy hesitated. Daisy glanced at James's newspaper and suppressed a shudder at the thought of the holocaust that had given the title 'Earl of Devonhurst' to Anthea's young man: speak of it she could not, yet.

"As a matter of fact," Katy went on, "I'm not usually the kind that looks out of windows—but she had a visitor very late last night and I did get up and look out, because I thought it might be you bringing Mark back because he was being a nuisance—but it was a young man."

She paused again; she despised herself, but there was something about Daisy Muir that always made her want to gossip: with Daisy, you instinctively let up on your brakes.

"Oh-ho," said Mrs Muir significantly, and reached for the *Daily Express*. Life must go on, and it certainly did.

There was a flashlight photograph of Michael, dancing with last year's Deb-of-the-Year, and some details—which in a less idle age would have been presumed to be nobody's business but that of the late Earl of Devonhurst—concerning the dilapidations and rent-roll of Herons, the 'place' in Berkshire.

"I expect that was him," Daisy said quietly. "Appalling . . . but I do wonder if he'll marry her now. Perhaps it *was* only money that was keeping him back. I hope so, anyway—wretched Anthea, she's had my idea of a really grim life, so far. And just *think* of Old Cavendish's rapture! Dearest Anthea, Countess of Devonhurst! She'll probably have a stroke."

"Perhaps it might make her a bit less peculiar," said Mrs Hulton. "I hope so, anyway. But I don't expect they're engaged at all. He just came round for a bit of sympathy . . . as well he might. It's shocking . . . there were two little boys, weren't there?"

Her tone was neither gloating nor casual. But Daisy, violently starting up, was just exclaiming, "There's the telephone, excuse me . . ." when James rose leisurely and said that he would take it.

"If they are engaged, or if they do get, later," Daisy said earnestly, when he had gone out of the room, "it'll make all the difference—you'll see. She'll stop blackmailing you about the housework and have Mark back and everything—"

"I'm taking him back today, anyway," quietly. "She's probably cooled down by now. And if she hasn't I don't care. I'm not having you put out like this, Daisy. It'll only be till the end of this week when Don's exams are over and then we can start looking for somewhere else. I didn't tell him about the row, I said Mark had

gone off on a little visit. Until then she'll just have to lump us."
She glanced down at Mark, who was leaning by her side looking
up at her, and smiled at him.

The answering smile was not broad. His transportation to
the Muirs', following on the public exposure of his crime, had
filled his small soul and body with an unsettled feeling which he
wretchedly took to mean that they were going to leave the window
you could see the buses from—and that it was all his fault. Miserable and vague as a pain that has no settled point of attack but
diffuses itself throughout the entire body, this feeling had given
added heaviness and dark shadows to a face always pale from his
frequent colds, and as Katy looked down at him she wished with
passion that she could get him into country air.

"How has he been getting on?" Daisy asked.

"Don?" rousing herself. "Rather well, he says, so far."

"Does he *know*?" Daisy was remembering her own usually
erroneous conclusions about her own results in examinations
at Oxford.

"Oh yes," and Katy laughed; "we've been checking the papers—
it's not like writing essays and that sort of thing . . . he seems
rather pleased with himself."

The tone was not an affectionately amused one, and Daisy
felt a little embarrassed.

She was never quite certain that the Hultons were happy
together—at least, not as she and James were happy. The
Hulk *did* seem, well, such a hulk, and she sometimes wondered
whether Katy had not been swept away by what seemed to her,
Daisy, a first, a more than inexplicable, romantic attraction.

James now coming back into the room looking very cross, she
demanded: "Who was it? Somebody frightful?"

"Molly."

"*Molly?* What did she want at this hour in the morning—God
be with us?"

"An old man at that house is dead or something and she
thought we ought to go to the funeral." James sat down again
and inhaled from his handkerchief.

Daisy was quiet for a moment, then she said in a controlled voice, "I can see that this is going to be *one of those days* . . . I'm sorry about the old man, I expect it's Mr Plumtre, I know he hadn't been well . . . but *really* . . . she's getting delusions of grandeur . . . I only hope she won't worry Daddy to go . . . what else did she say?"

The answer was an irritable silent gesture, and she did not repeat the question.

But behind the sheets of his newspaper and the aromatic vapours of his inhalant, James was taking refuge from anger, embarrassment and guilt.

Ringing him at the office! The—the *sauce* (as his Nannie would have said), the cheek and impudence and—and—the alarming *uncontrollableness* of it! Yes, it was that that was so upsetting; you couldn't, you daren't, think what she might do next. (Fortunately, with that appalling suburban drawl of hers, the office would only think that she was someone's rather inferior secretary.) And then, having been told that he hadn't arrived yet, ringing up here in an absurd state, with some ridiculous excuse about a funeral, to know if he was ill . . . delusions of grandeur indeed . . . because why had she dared to ring him at the office in the first place?

Some babble about taking her out to lunch . . .

Well, probably he had said he would—yes, come to think of it, he had. It had been one evening last week, when Daisy was out chasing after that (James used a Biblical term) Delia Huxtable, whose child was ill, and Molly had just dropped in, as she often did nowadays about six o'clock, and had got him a meal (it hadn't been really Daisy's fault that she was late and it was only half an hour anyway. Molly had just gone . . . she usually had just gone, somehow, on these increasingly frequent occasions, when Daisy arrived home.) It had been a simple meal, just making the best of what was in the house, but it had tasted good, and he had been tired, and he was grateful.

It was then that he had lightly said—rashly now, he saw, though he had not seen it at the time because he never meant to implement his vague promise—that some day he must give her a really good lunch in town.

Fatal phrase! She was just the type that the words 'in town'—Mayfair, the Ritz, the Savoy, the Caprice—would dazzle. Trust her, he thought bitterly, not to take the remark as it was casually said, as a piece of meaningless good manners, but to stow it away, and treasure it up, even perhaps (and *that* was a pleasant thought) imagine it had meant heaven knew what, and then, five days later, trot it out and ask him for a definite date.

That girl was dangerous. She might not look it, with her slow manner and her muffled-up clothes, but she was.

And now what was he going to do? Take her out to her blasted lunch and—and somehow make 'matters' worse?

He stared resentfully over the top of his paper at Daisy, who was persuading her friend and the children to stay until the afternoon.

It was all her fault, really. If she had made a habit of always being at home when he got in, and giving him more of her time and attention, Molly (he did not always, now, think of her by her nickname) would never have had even the chance to, well, 'muscle in'.

It wasn't that he thought there was any harm in taking a girl out to lunch without Daisy knowing. And he knew now that the sensible thing to do would be to say to her, "Look here, lovey, God-be-with-you is being a bore," and explain, and then there would be gales of laughter and some indignant surprise (probably no suspicions, because of all women Daisy was the least given to that), and the thing would just be one more Muir family joke and he needn't give it another thought.

Yes . . . that was the sensible thing to do.

But he couldn't get the little ass's voice out of his ears . . . bleating away (asses didn't bleat but never mind) . . . "I was so sorry . . . I know you'll think I'm awful . . . you've been so kind . . . and I've been wondering about our lunch date . . ."

Our lunch date!

While she was bleating he had had a sudden vivid vision of her small, sallow, soft face. 'The seduced character'—that was what he used to call her. Well, a seduced character was, presumably . . . seduceable.

"You're so kind . . . I know you wouldn't want to hurt anyone by disappointing them . . ." Blah, blah. It was the corniest line.

Only, when he remembered her expression when she looked at him sometimes, it made the situation seem different. She was hurtable, all right . . .

James's reflections suddenly seemed to him exceedingly distasteful. He sat up in his chair, casting aside papers and the accompaniments to a cold, and offered to take the entire Hulton circus and his son for a walk on the Heath before lunch.

Nothing like fresh air.

After lunch, while they were drinking coffee, and laughing at James Too's latest trick of clicking his tongue as if he were saying 'tut-tut', the telephone went again. Daisy darted out of the room.

After a longish pause, they heard through the open door a hissing whisper: "Katy! Quick!"

Katy got up and went, not without reluctance, into the hall. Daisy was sitting sideways on the table with the mosaic top, her legs in their bright yellow jeans interwined, her head cocked on one side, and delighted expressions chasing themselves across her face. Without moving, murmuring "Yes—yes—I see—" she noiselessly inclined the receiver towards Katy's hesitant ear. In a moment, Katy yielded to temptation.

" . . . imagine how I felt," a faint, relaxed voice which she hardly recognised as Mrs Cavendish's was saying, "I thought it rather strange, her going off without just looking in on me to see how her old Mummy was—she always does—but I was so utterly *worn out* after yesterday's terrible scene that I was only half awake when she left the house. Oh Daisy, my dear, it seemed such a long morning!" (sympathetic murmur) "I suppose, in a way, and I must confess it, I've got used to hearing your little friend" (significant smiles between Daisy and the little friend) "bringing the children down about eleven to go shopping. I used to go out into the hall sometimes, just to tell her of anything I wanted brought in, don't you know, and that little Mary—something might be made of that poor little girl, I believe, if *I* had the bringing up of her . . . the boy of course I *never* liked, and the baby is nothing but a *pudding*" (indignant start from the pudding's mother) "well, I don't mind telling you, I missed them. I did. And I even wondered if I hadn't been rather hard on poor Mark—after all, *so much* is due to upbringing, isn't it? But you're so strong-minded, my dear!" (a tinkling laugh, and a sardonic wagging of the head from Daisy) "you whisked him off before I had time to change my mind. I did feel, after he had gone, that you acted too hastily, you know . . . but never mind that now . . . you'll learn, in time, we all have to . . . especially as I understand your little friend wanted a quiet atmosphere all this week because her husband is taking some kind of *examination* . . . a man of his age! With a young family! I must say that seems *very* strange, to me. Why did he marry if he still had examinations to pass? When I remember the years of waiting for Francis to take silk . . . young people nowadays have no more self-control than *rabbits*" (here Daisy's attempt to control a great snort of laughter while bestowing calming pats on the furious Katy caused her nearly to drop the receiver). "But where was I? Oh yes . . . Not that I wish him anything but good luck, poor man, burdened at his age with three children . . ."

"Well, I had my lunch about one, and sat down to rest afterwards, and then I couldn't find the paper. Anthea always leaves it beside my chair in the drawing-room. But it wasn't there, and I thought the boy hadn't brought it this morning—*maddening*, I thought, but what can you expect, with dockers earning twenty and thirty pounds a week? Any idea of doing one's work properly because it *is* one's work has simply vanished from England . . . dearest Anthea must have hidden it, you see, so that I shouldn't see the terrible news. She always is so thoughtful . . . Well, I sat down to rest. I was *very* tired, Daisy, and it was all going round and round in my head—the table, your father's promise about the Stores, because I thought they might be calling for it, and that poor spoiled little boy, and then the dreadful idea that one day I might perhaps have to sell this house."

Her voice had become livelier as she went on, but her hearers, both the one to whom she was talking and the eavesdropper, were no longer laughing. Daisy sat up straight with an expression growing gentler as the tale continued; Katy listened with a face of immovable Scottish gravity, incongruous with the tilt of her head.

"I hope you won't ever know what it is to have such thoughts about *your* home, Daisy. I sat there, hardly able to think clearly at all, really, and so *cold*. . . I could *not* get warm, though I went upstairs for another cardigan . . ."

"It's been bitter all day," Daisy gently said.

"Yes, hasn't it? . . . well, I suppose I must have dozed. Because I didn't hear the taxi come up to the gate or anything. I'd been dreaming, I think, because the next thing I knew was that I could smell carnations!" Pause, for effect.

"Really?" Daisy felt this to be inept, but evidently the narrator was too carried away to notice.

"Yes, wasn't it strange? (Or I thought it was.) Because they're my favourite flowers, and they were my poor Francis's favourite, too—the church was smothered in them on my wedding day, lemon and pink and white. I can see it all as if it were yesterday."

"My mother used to tell me about your wedding."

"Ah yes, it used to be one of the Hampstead legends . . . I had my bouquet of them, too. Well—are you sure I'm not keeping you, my dear?" and Daisy murmured a fervent denial.

"Next thing I knew, someone was kneeling beside my chair. I was so confused, you see, with being half-awake—I thought for the moment it was Francis. I could smell the carnations and see the church, and I remembered 'something borrowed and something blue' you know, and I said to myself, 'Yes, I had blue ribbons in my petticoat and Mother lent me her diamond bow' . . . and I just didn't want to wake up. The dream was so sweet."

"I'm sure it was." (But Katy was looking sardonic.)

"I just didn't want to open my eyes. But I heard someone call me, and I did open them. And I was looking at a perfectly enormous bunch of carnations—pink and yellow and white. (I don't mind telling you, Daisy, my very first thought was 'What they must have cost?') It was dearest Anthea kneeling there. And she was holding out her hand to me, Daisy . . . *the* most glorious emeralds you ever saw. Five of them. Of course, I had been *expecting* it for *some time*, but just for the minute I *couldn't* believe my eyes."

"Oh, but how . . ." Both listeners were laughing again, and Daisy only managed to murmur her notes of admiration.

"Yes, wasn't it? Quite like a fairy tale . . . and then she told me all about it." The far-off voice assumed an even quieter tone.

"Of course, it's perfectly dreadful . . . I am still feeling quite stunned . . ." and then there were some murmurs whose mingling of sentimentality and perfunctoriness Daisy, with screwed up eyes, shut out by covering the receiver with her palm, ". . and I don't expect the wedding will be for some time—except that I gather from Anthea he is not anxious for *too* long an engagement. That's very sweet, isn't it?"

"Yes."

"But he is sweet, a real 'charmer'—the carnations were from him, you know."

Pause. Katy sat upright, with a faint sigh.

"Well," resumed Mrs Cavendish, "I really partly rang up—chiefly to give you our news, of course—but I also wanted you to know that I've been thinking it over and I've decided that little Mark can come back."

"Oh," said Daisy, "that *is* kind."

"Well . . . he did seem sorry, poor little boy . . . and your father—he called just now, before I rang you—so kind of him—told me that the Stores may be able to do something about the table . . . so in the circumstances . . ."

"Katy's here, as a matter of fact. I'll tell her."

"Yes, I thought she might be. You may tell her the other news, too, Daisy. It will be in *The Times*, anyway, as soon as possible."

"I will . . . and thank you. Do give Anthea our very warmest congratulations, won't you?—"

"'And glory, glory, hallelujah'," ended Mrs Muir, ringing off at last. "Well!" turning to Katy. "Imagine! Do you think the Countess will let the public into her own part of the house at half a crown a time?"

"Three shillings, more likely."

"We'll take the children, won't we, and make stick-and-gom all over the furniture . . . oh, wouldn't Old Cavendish make a marvellous *guide*?"

The day drew to a close in one of Daisy's typical galas of laughter, scalding tea, and buttered buns. But although Katy was greatly relieved, and felt that she could now face the waiting for Don's results with an easier mind, she did look once or twice wonderingly at her friend's laughing face. Had she already forgotten *what* had made possible Mark's return to Charlotte Road?

It did not occur to her that there are different ways of responding to unbearable horror; and Daisy, much as she usually loved being with Katy, thought impatiently once or twice that truly good people could be damping . . . to appreciate the Cavendish-Devon engagement it *really* needed a Sue Ruddlin.

That February, for all of the circle surrounding the house with the pink front door, seemed a period of marking time.

Katy, now living under her landlady's smiling condescension, waited for Don's results to come through while she devoted herself to the children; the frighteningly outrageous demands made upon her to scrub, to polish and wash and scour, had abruptly ceased.

A few days after the announcement had appeared in *The Times*, a Mrs Watson could have been seen trudging around number forty-eight Charlotte Road, of whom Mrs Cavendish casually remarked that she had come to do the rough work, and Katy was no more than occasionally asked if she would mind bringing in a tin of polish or so forth if she happened to be going to the shops?

Anthea Cavendish—who still, to Katy's eyes, looked just a little dazed—was as distantly pleasant to the Hultons as was her mother; all, in fact, went almost literally as merrily as a marriage bell, and Katy, though she despised herself, enjoyed reading an interview with the Earl of Devonhurst's prospective bride written for a Sunday paper by the wittiest and cattiest of London's women columnists. Amusing play was made with Anthea's habit of always wearing a hat.

The Stores did their best with the table; the drawing-room, into which Katy, Don and the children were once actually invited to an elegant tea, surely seemed more full of furniture? Or was it only the flowers and the brighter lighting?

It was on this occasion that Don informed Mrs Cavendish between two gulps of tomato sandwich, that they would shortly be leaving her.

"Indeed?" (graciously, for even this boorish creature came in for a share of her personal sunshine) and when did he expect to hear the results of his examination?

At the end of this month, it seemed, and then he was going to get a job in the country. In one of the new towns. Better for the kids. Yes, the country was always so much better for children, although in the old days, before the air was poisoned with petrol fumes, Swiss Cottage had been considered one of the healthiest parts of London. As for leaving . . . when once her daughter was married, Mrs Cavendish would herself be needing the rooms; the Earl had suggested that they would make charming little *pied-à-terre* for Anthea and himself when they came up to town.

"A what?" demanded Don, assuming ignorance with a poker-faced glance at Katy.

Mrs Cavendish, not without gratification, explained, while thinking that Heaven was indeed making lavish amends; in less than three weeks she would be free of the Hultons for ever.

When they had gone upstairs (Mark glancing fearfully, as he passed through the hall, at the poor table that the gentleman from the Stores had made all better) she settled herself in front of the fire to write her monthly New Zealand letter—and this time what a glorious, what a triumphant, letter!—to Cousin Marie in Christchurch.

Perhaps only Cousin Marie, and the God Who looks after those with gentle blood in their veins, knew how Mrs Cavendish was enjoying these weeks of the engagement.

Gently receiving congratulations from the few neighbours left whom she still cared to 'know'; repressing, while relishing, the coarser, but well-meant, comments of the tradespeople with whom she had dealt for thirty years; gloating over the photographs of Anthea which appeared in the *Evening Standard* (walking arm in arm towards the camera with Michael) and *The Court* (fondling a Sealyham while staying in Italy), and even borrowing some money from dear old Godfrey Furnivall so that Anthea might have a very small, but a perfect, *trousseau*—Mrs Cavendish quietly revelled in all of it.

She believed that the Earl of Devonhurst liked her, which added to her happiness, for she found him kind as he was charming, and indeed, as Michael asked nothing more from a prospective mother-in-law than passable vowels and an address eighty miles from Herons, he did not mind her.

Anthea went through the early weeks of spring very cautiously. She was certain of Michael now; and she loved him—or, as she put it to herself, she was much fonder of him than in the days when she had lost her head, and believed that in doing so she had also lost her chances.

But there was going to be such a lot to manage: the house, and the tenants, and, when once the death duties and Income Tax had been paid, revenues of some six thousand pounds a year. It was a wide prospect, for someone who had never had to manage anything more than herself (and once she had slipped up there, badly) and an occasional tiresome man who wanted to hold her tightly while dancing. Anthea quailed sometimes, in the still of the night.

It was a conversation with Miss Croydew, at last, that had begun to make her feel she might be capable of becoming Countess of Devonhurst.

"You're going to do it most awfully well," the old creature (no one knew Diane Croydew's precise age) had said abruptly to her, in the course of their farewell interview on the last day that Anthea had spent in the fine old house in Knightsbridge. She, Anthea, had been listening with rose-fired face and surprised eyes to gruff thanks for eight years' hard, graceful, controlled application to the job.

"Oh, I daresay you feel qualmy at times. It will be such a very big change, won't it (and *so* much more difficult, of course, than when *I* was a gairl). But your paternal grandmother was a Barton, wasn't she? You need not worry, my dear; Bartons can manage *anything* . . . Now where was I? Oh yes, Elsie Hardinge . . . she was my assistant in 1910, you know, and she married into the Peerage, too . . . rather an excitable type. I always thought there was something wrong-side-of-the-blanketish there . . . and there have been three wives since her day, for all that he was so wild about her—poor Elsie, silly gairl . . . But nothing like that could possibly happen to a Barton, my dear."

Mutual laughter. And from that moment Anthea had begun to feel better.

The wedding was to be in April; a country one, at Michael's own village in Berkshire; white, with a small cousin-once-removed of Anthea's for sole bridesmaid. February blew and drizzled and sneezed on its frightful way, and Molly Raymond read of these plans in the *Evening Standard* with wistful admiration.

The house with the pink front door was not relying quite so much on her services nowadays, because Daisy had secured those of another *au pair* French girl. But the month when she had been without help had established Molly's unexpected visits as a habit, and she still dropped in whenever she felt she couldn't keep away.

And, it must be confessed, whenever she knew that Daisy would be out.

Sometimes she was there, on Denise's free evening, placidly washing up, when Daisy returned; sometimes (more often) she had already left. And James occasionally forgot to mention that she had been there at all.

No one likes to look an ass. James Muir liked it less than most men, for he was not conceited, and he knew when he was looking one. He looked it when he was bathed in the thirsty, furtive stare of Molly's great dim eyes.

Daisy was careful not to be cool to her protégée after the incident of Mr Plumtre's funeral, just because she felt that a mark had been overstepped. Stopping Daddy in the hall at Laurel House and telling him that he 'ought' to go! Delusions of grandeur, indeed. Never mind if Daddy caught a death-chill in the February wind.

Molly had explained.

Poor old gentleman . . . lying there a whole day before he was found by Miss Cazalet knocking at his door to return the corn-flakes. Heart failure . . . and no wonder, with all those stairs, Molly often felt like heart failure herself . . . nothing shocking about starvation, of course, or anything like that, always enjoyed his bit of boiled fish any of us brought in for him, lately, when he got too tired to go out . . . and such a *gentleman* (Molly's tone became mildly passionate), always pretended not to see you if he met you coming out of the toilet . . . always raised his hat to you in the street . . . stood aside to let you pass him in the corridors . . . and him nearly ninety, so white, so feeble, but always a pleasant word . . . Molly did feel it would be a shame if not a single soul from Laurel House went to see him laid to rest. She had got to work.

"Then I plucked up my courage and tackled your daddy . . . 'I think you *ought* to go, if you won't misunderstand me, Colonel,' I said" *(Colonel Furnivall's coming! Miss Raymond persuaded him! She's wonderful!)* "and he looked at me rather . . . you know . . . but then he said, 'All right, when is it, and where?' and I gave him all the details."

"I hope there were lots of flowers for the poor old thing," Daisy said, trying to suppress irritation about Daddy in that bitter wind.

Oh yes, Molly had made a collection. There had been a bit of tact needed with Miss Cazalet, she was all for carnations, nothing but show really, because they all knew she had to live mostly off bread and marge, when she'd paid her rent, and how many carnations could *she* have paid for, Molly'd like to know? But they'd settled for daffs. Molly never had been keen on Miss Cazalet . . . She was always on about her mother never liking her and her sister to use scent. Poorest of the poor, Miss Cazalet was; had to use a bit of petersham off of an old skirt that came out of the Ark for a black arm-band, asked Molly did she think it would notice . . . "And I got Tibbs to come," Molly ended, on a note of quiet triumph.

"You got *Tibbs*?" repeated Daisy, astounded.

"I had to persuade him a bit . . . I think it was mostly nosiness made him come, really, but it was one more. It all helped to make a show of respect."

"Yes . . ." Daisy felt a little remorse. Thought, tact, humiliation, time and energy had been expended by Molly on behalf of an old dead man whom she had scarcely known. Convinced afresh of the necessity for saving someone so fundamentally good from emotional shipwreck, she asked, not too sharply:

"Have you been seeing much of him lately?"

"Oh no," vaguely, "nothing regular." The conversation then turned to other matters.

It was true. Molly had recently been refusing Tibbs's sketchy invitations because she preferred to spend most of her evenings in solitary dreaming about Daisy's husband.

The dreams, certainly, were marred by the fact that the sight of Tibbs' eyelashes could still make her heart flutter, but after some serious reflections upon whether a woman could be in love with two men at once, and some unfulfilled hopes that Beverley Nichols or Monica Dickens would discuss the problem in one of their thoughtful weekly articles in *Woman's Own*, she yielded to that prejudice against foreigners first inspired in her by contrasting Tibbs with Colonel Furnivall, and began to despise Tibbs.

Her heart, however, continued to flutter over his eyelashes.

She knew, with that voice of common sense which still from time to time piped up weakly within her, that she was being a fool. Daisy was highly unlikely to succumb to some convenient epidemic, and, if she did, James would not, on returning from the funeral, seize Molly in his arms. And she meant no harm. She was fond of Daisy, and grateful to her. But gratitude is such an uncomfortable emotion—for most of us—that we resent being made to feel it, and when it comes to a tug against dreams, desire, vanity and general sloppiness, gratitude can't pull very hard.

Not that Molly thought all this out. She did what she had always done: drifted. She was the original passenger for whom dreamboats had been designed.

James was beginning to think of her as *poor little girl*; and the Ruddlins, after a rather brief period in which the Alsatian had made everyone even more uncomfortable than they were anyway, were having themselves a divorce, with a co-respondent saddled with the name of Zack Ourgler.

"It's very *bleak*, isn't it?" observed Molly, when they had been looking at the view and the long low white building that was the most conspicuous object for six miles, during some minutes. "Very exposed in the winter, I should say."

"Plenty of room and it smells grand. No stink of petrol here," and Don Hulton started up the car again and they went easily on up the wide new road that cut across the bare Essex hill and led to the plant.

The car, a shooting-brake hired by Don for the day, was full of Hultons and Molly and—sitting in the back with an air of one who was naturally urban and being martyred by exposure to fields and fresh air—Tibbs.

In the wide shallow valley below—no, it could not be said to sprawl, it was too well planned for that, and the last thing that it was doing was nestling, because it wasn't that kind of place and anyway there were no what you might call trees—they could see all of Leawood New Town: the Square, the Civic Centre, the straight pink streets lined with skinny saplings and the empty, raw little gardens. It was all salmon pink and whitey-grey; its roofs and roads had the chalky pale colours of a painting of the thirties and its weird geometric charm. The air up here, and in the town too, was biting and delicious.

"Would it be one of those?" asked Katy suddenly, pointing to a short street of small pink houses immediately below the white place that looked like a factory.

"No. Ours is one of those," and he pointed to a road directly opposite, where the houses were grouped in threes about a central plot of grass.

"Semi-detached," muttered Katy, whom five years of living in other people's furnished rooms had left with no denigrating flavour to the phrase. During those five years there had existed fully furnished in her head a house, neat and efficient as a small boat, and furnished down to the last regulating button on the electric iron. The furniture was rather vague at present; all she knew about it was that it was not old, precious or upholstered. The curtains in the living-room had roses on them—natural ones, with green leaves; not the messed-about contemporary kind; the name on the gate, fixed there by a Don who for the purpose had miraculously acquired skill with his hands, was *Shipshape*.

"What?" said Don.

"Nothing. Have you got the keys?"

"Of course I've got the keys," and he grinned at her.

She had been slightly irritated by his refusal to tell her anything about the house that 'went with' the first-class job he had almost at once secured on very successfully passing his finals, but she had felt, so strongly, that he deserved his little joke!

Let him tease her, if it gave him any pleasure . . . he was so good, so faithful and true . . . she remembered with faint retrospective pain the evenings back in the winter, when he would get up without a word of complaint and leave the warmth and cheerfulness of the 'Queen Charlotte Arms' for the hard chair too small for his bulky frame and the grind at the familiar text books.

Perhaps she had thrown away her career as a chemist, but she couldn't have thrown it away for a better husband.

Yes, *very* bleak, Molly was thinking, wedged between Mark and Mary, silent and motionless from excitement, in the back seat; and no *atmosphere*. Give her Hampstead every time, and for preference Bottle Court, so quaint and historical. She glanced, with the familiar flutter, at Tibbs; no wonder he looked bored; not but what he didn't always look half-asleep, anyway . . . he, she knew, shared her views about Leawood New Town, for he had conveyed them to her with an eloquent lift of his black eyebrows while they were driving through the place.

Molly sighed. Life itself was bleakish just now, hung up as she seemed to be halfway between her old feeling for Tibbs (and *he* seemed to feel no different) and her new one for James Muir: nothing seemed to be happening, and she did so like things to happen. Must be the time of the year.

Tibbs was pondering upon a quite new idea he had had that morning about the formula for 'Hulton's Comforter'—this was the rather dignified, old-fashioned name that he and Don had finally decided would inspire more confidence in motherly (especially young motherly) bosoms, than the more flippant 'Wind-Out' and 'Wind-Up' of the early days of the idea. They had never seriously thought of incorporating the innumerable p's and z's and y's of Tibb's name into the patent one: mere unpronounceability, as well as its *un*comforting foreignness, quite ruled it out.

What a fool Molly was, thought Tibbs, sardonically studying her small profile buried in fluffy hair. Sighing after a fellow (Tibbs's vocabulary, thanks to a perusal of old English novels during a spell of illness in a hotel-turned-refugee-hostel, was occasionally out of date) who, anyone but Molly could see, had eyes for no one but his wife, and never would have.

Well, he supposed that sooner or later he would have to do something about Molly. She had hung on—or he had hung on to her, perhaps a bit of both—longer than any of the others, and he was sick of this life: sick of discomfort and insecurity and change. Molly could earn to keep them both, or he could get himself a real job or something. Don even seemed to think there was a good chance of Hulton's Comforter making them some money . . .

But Tibbs had learned never to count on anything going right.

The car stopped at the street of square pink houses, and everybody began to get out.

"Mark! Mary! No rushing about now," was Katy's sharp command, but she hardly glanced at the thin white legs and duffel coats as she spoke. "You do what Aunty Molly tells you, and be quiet. I'm going to look at the house."

"Want them?" Don, grinning more widely than ever, was holding out to her a bunch of keys.

Up the path between yellow flowers tossing about in the cold wind marched Katy; Tibbs yawned at the view, Molly gazed at the view of Tibbs, Mark and Mary stood side by side whispering together, and Don watched his wife. She had actually set the key in the front door and begun to turn it, when she hesitated and looked round.

"Here!" she called sharply, "aren't you coming too?" and he sprang forward and sprinted up the path. He grabbed at her hand and put his arm about her shoulders and they went into the house together.

Mark, having evaded the not very vigilant eye of Aunty Molly, who was having a long talk with Uncle Tibbs, had wandered, followed by Mary, into the back garden. This went on for miles and miles until it ended in a fascinating little white gate, and after a time, slightly dazed by the boisterous wind and the big clouds running across the big sky, and having set Mary to try with a long stick to get down a yellow thing up in a tree which they both decided, unlikely though it seemed, must actually be an apple, Mark ventured to open it.

The ground was all big lumps of earth here, and far away on the other side of the great expanse was a beautiful big red and yellow thing battling its way along; Mark knew that it was a 'tractor'. It dug up the ground so that you could plant seeds.

Silent, completely entranced, he watched it work its way round the inside curve of the field until it was so near that he could see the kind red face and blowing hair of the man who was driving it. It stopped, most wonderfully, absolutely opposite the white gate where he stood.

"Hullo, sonny," said the driver, laughing. There was a lovely, bus-like smell of hot oil.

"Hullo," said Mark. The driver, high up in the red and yellow chariot with the white clouds gliding past his head, crossed his arms comfortably as he looked down.

"Like a ride?" he gloriously, incredibly, asked.

"I must ask Mummy," was the gabbled answer, even while Mark's legs, which didn't seem to have heard what he was saying, were carrying him over the grass and tiny shining yellow flowers on to the just-broken clods. The god and the car now towered above him.

"Oh, Mum won't mind. I've got dozens at home like you," said the driver, and then he let Mark scramble up on to the tractor and, when he was settled there against bundly warm clothes smelling of earth and oil, off they went.

"Where's Mark?" demanded Katy, coming down the path between the apple trees with Don and Maggie, now cheerfully awake, sitting up in her arms. Mary, like the faithful sentry at Pompeii, was still poking unsuccessfully at the last autumn's withered apple; her father reached up and guided the stick so that it fell at last to the ground, and she picked it up. As an apple, it was distinctly a disappointment.

"Where's Mark?" repeated Katy, and Mary, missing something from her voice, glanced at her wonderingly yet meekly. Maggie was twisting from side to side in her mother's arms and staring with all her eyes, for movement—blowing bushes, sailing clouds, darting birds—was all about her and she did not want to miss a thing. Her poll, grown over with red, shining down, was decently covered in a wool bonnet from which her face glowed out like that of a very young apple. Mrs Cavendish's slighting description of her as a pudding had been quite singularly inept.

"He ride with the man," explained Mary, pointing.

"He hasn't lost any time," said Don, laughing, while Katy stared away across the brown field to the delicately greening wood where the tractor was forging. Her heart was completely quiet. She felt the warmth of Maggie's little bottom resting on her arm.

They wandered down to the white gate and out into the field and stood waiting for the tractor to bring Mark round again. Soon it turned the curve and came snorting and lumbering towards them; they could see Mark's face, against the driver's brown clothes, and it was a deep pink. This, thought the father, is the beginning of it. He glanced at Katy, at Mary; all the London-pale cheeks were filled with clear blood that had danced up to meet the blowing wind.

When the tractor stopped opposite them, Mark glanced scaredly at his mother. The man smiled at them and made a friendly gesture, saying nothing as his passenger clambered and slid down from the clouds, but as he started up the engine once more he turned and called:

"Bye-bye, son."

"Bye-bye," Mark piped politely.

"Go on—shout!" said Katy suddenly, catching his hand in hers. "That's not the way—he can't hear you. Shout! go on, shout. Mary! You too."

They stood under the great spring sky, with pink faces, shouting.

At first they shouted softly and politely, as if the weight of five years of tip-toeing and whispering and creeping about were weighing upon them, but soon the sheer pleasure of bellowing at the tops of their voices gave strength to their lungs and they shouted until the welkin—that old name for the sky—cheerfully rang, while Maggie, fired by example, set up a shrill crowing that suggested nothing so much as the cries of what used to be called 'a stuck pig'. They shouted and shouted, glorying in the noise coming out of their cold pink faces, until their laughing mother, slipping her arm into that of her husband, commanded:

"That's enough. Come away to our tea. There'll be time enough to shout now, whenever you want to, later on."

CHAPTER XX
Declaration

DAISY's relief at the end of the Hulton housing problem could not express itself in helping them settle, at the end of March, in their new house, because just at this time she was occupied with the Ruddlin divorce.

Susan was so much more miserable than anyone had expected.

She talked, endlessly and bitterly, and she shamelessly demanded—insisted even, with the angry, difficult tears of a hard nature—that Daisy must be there to listen whenever she was wanted. And Daisy was there. She was out of work at the moment and on most mornings Susan would either ring her up about ten, and talk for an hour or more, or she would drive over from Highbury in the big white car and take Daisy and James Too off for the day into the country—talking, of course, all the way.

Daisy discovered, at this time, both how fond she was of this worst friend who was to her like a bossy and successful elder sister, and how deeply she shrank from Susan's outlook and habits.

Her values, to Daisy, seemed extraordinarily flimsy and shallow; she lived, it seemed for the pleasure of the hour, and her rage when she was for any reason deprived of it could be startling. Attaching an extraordinary importance to personal appearance, she was very serious about her daughter's complexion, hair and clothes, occasionally training her moral and spiritual nature by references to what the socially O.K. child did and did not do—'Vanessa, interrupting just isn't *done*.' 'Absolutely *no one* snatches.' 'Being rude to your mother is the *end*.'

Daisy became conscious how fortunate she was in having a sunny and affectionate boy, for poor Vanessa, at three, was already bad-tempered, rapacious and pert. Very, very pretty, too, to make matters worse.

James One rapidly became more than tired of the Ruddlin divorce case. He never had liked Susan and had always disapproved of her 'ways'. The fact that he had let himself be persuaded, by Daisy, into finding a home with some difficulty for the Ruddlins' beastly great dog did not sweeten his views on the situation.

Daisy filled the house with the pink front door with expensive spring flowers and was often with Susan at the pictures in the evenings. James supped off an omelette cooked by Denise (whom he frequently allowed to go out, when he knew that he was going to be at home to guard James Too), a loving note from his absent wife, or something concocted by Molly.

"Good evening, Colonel," said this friend of the family, meeting Daisy's father in the hall at Laurel House one evening early in April, when faint, fresh blue light flowed in through the high windows, "lovely to have it warmer, isn't it?" Then, as he agreed with a brief nod, she went on happily, "I'm just off to Daisy's . . . thought I'd look in, as usual, to see if I could do anything . . . she's having to spend such a lot of time with Mrs Ruddlin nowadays . . . terrible when a couple simply *cannot* get on, isn't it?"

The Colonel looked at her. The drapings of winter had been replaced by an airy affair of holes in white wool, there was much lipstick, there was a strong smell of what he did not know was 'Morning in Rome', and there was a peculiar look as if she had two black eyes or half black eyes or something of that sort . . . but here was, at last, his opportunity. He very slightly set his shoulders back, controlled a tremor of extreme distaste, and said:

"I suppose it is. In my own family and circle, I've never come across it, I'm glad to say. All our marriages have been perfectly . . . er . . . ordinary and so on . . . of course, in many cases, nowadays, I know that things do go wrong. Very much more often, I'm sorry to say, than when I was a young man."

She nodded sympathetically. Always so kind . . . always a gentleman . . . always saying the right thing. Her head was well on one side now and her eyes glistened dreamily within their little burrow of white wool and *bouffant* fair hair.

"But usually, you know," the Colonel went on steadily, recalling, to strengthen himself, the occasion when he had to tackle the parlourmaid about mild pilfering, "when things do go wrong, it's the fault of someone *outside*. Someone butts in, you know, with the best intentions, perhaps, and makes trouble. Perhaps without meaning to at all. If I had a . . . young niece, or someone of that sort, and I saw her getting into that kind of situation I should feel it my duty . . . my duty to . . . er . . . warn her to be careful. Just think a bit before she . . . er . . . butted in too much, so to speak. Besides," he ended, with a sudden emphasis caused by the double relief at both having done it, and now saying exactly what he felt, "that kind of thing's so vulgar and squalid."

Molly looked at him dimly. As usual, she was dreaming about the imaginary Colonel Furnivall who lived in her ideal world, rather than the elderly man who was talking to her. She did this with everybody. But something of warning, of condemnation and a kind of innate, detached disgust which, just for an instant, she felt turned upon her from *his* private world, did penetrate.

She began to move slowly away towards the front door, murmuring doubtfully in agreement, and he went on to his own rooms. Nasty business; embarrassing. But it had had to be done.

Molly's sensations had resentfully grouped themselves, by the time she reached the top of Fitzjohn's Avenue, about the words 'butting in', and 'vulgar and squalid'.

Vulgar. What could he have meant? She never said a word or did a thing when alone with Jamesey that Daisy mightn't have heard. (Now *she* could be vulgar, if you like . . . swear words, and always calling the toilet the lavatory.) She did so enjoy doing things for Jamesey, and it was helping Daisy as well, and what was squalid about that?

She told herself that she didn't understand. But when she rang the bell of the pink front door, she had a very large lump aching in her throat and was dangerously in need of comfort.

"Hullo," said James cheerfully, opening it. "Seen about our girl-friend's wedding?" and he flourished at her the *Evening Standard*, which carried a large front-page picture of Miss Anthea Cavendish (Prettiest Spring Bride Weds) coming out of church on the arm of the Earl of Devonhurst, with veil blowing in the April breeze. (The linen sheets in the rooms at Green Park had not, of course, blown about like that on a certain evening nearly two years ago.) The Earl and Countess are flying this evening to Majorca. That face in the background, under a model hat and looking, though composed, as if it is singing *Nunc Dimittis*, belongs to the bride's mother.

Molly had followed him into the little sitting-room that smelt of Poetaz narcissus. They were everywhere, in vases of clear glass and Chinese jars, and they drowned 'Morning in Rome', and their heavy white petals and clear, innocent, yet passionate look vaguely made her feel unhappier than ever.

James was studying the photograph.

"Done well for herself, hasn't she?" he said. "Daisy's awfully pleased . . . at least it's one of them off her shoulders. I suppose you could call Anthea C. one of Daisy's, couldn't you?"

He had sat down again (Molly was by now such a part of the family that he tended to let formal manners slip in her presence) and turned idly to the racing news.

"Ha—have you had your supper?" she muttered, not caring about Anthea C.

"Oh yes, thanks; Daisy left me one of her wonderful cold plates. Smoked salmon and so forth." He did not add that he suspected the salmon was a sop to Daisy's conscience . . . for this evening she was busy about a new protégée.

"Oh."

"Yes, I'm fine, thanks. You run along. Nice of you to look in. Daisy won't be long. She's gone charging off after some girl who makes hats or something—only lives in the High Street. At least, it isn't the girl herself—it's someone who's going to help the girl. I really don't know. But I'm all right. You," and then some of the exasperation with Daisy which underlay his breeziness just peeped forth, "buzz off," he ended, not looking at her.

'Vulgar', 'squalid', the wedding picture, the flowers whose texture and scent belonged to that half-glimpsed unfamiliar world where Colonel Furnivall's distaste dwelt with his kindness—and now: 'Buzz off'. Molly couldn't . . . she couldn't . . .

She burst into choking tears.

All tangled up in white wool and hair, she stood before him, shaking, with hands covering her face. It is to be recorded with genuine condemnation that James finished reading his paragraph about chances for the Lincoln before he looked up and asked:

"What on earth's the matter?"

Molly shook her head. "You . . . you . . . you . . ." was all that he heard.

James got up, not too speedily, from his chair and settled himself for a back-patting session. About the fourth pat he remembered all her silly little kindnesses, and she smelt very nice too, and her hair was pretty and he was deeply annoyed with Daisy, so he put his arms round her.

She subsided on to his shoulder, expecting to feel rapture but strangely enough all she could feel was that she didn't like it as much as Tibb's shoulder . . . and where, wh-where was Tibbs at this moment? Glooming in a café somewhere, no doubt, and she hadn't seen him for a week. She hugged James in despair, to his extreme dismay and not very much to his pleasure, and the key sounded in the pink front door and a moment later Daisy sailed in.

"What on earth's the matter?" she cried. "Is it James Too? What is it?" and she flung down a parcel of sample hats and two or three evening papers with pictures of Anthea and another bunch of spring flowers and tore off her coat, as if stripping the decks for action.

"It's nothing," retorted James, sullenly continuing to hold Molly. "He's all right, I mean," he added. "Molly's just upset . . . poor little . . ." But at the sight of his Daisy, so maddening and irrevocably familiar and dear, he couldn't get his tongue round another sloppy word of it.

It was hard lines. Justice and all that were entirely on his side, and domestic bliss simply hit him below the belt.

"Well, what *is* it?" Daisy demanded, and she came over and put her arms round Molly too. James, perhaps hoping to maintain a façade of shameless passion, kept a hold of her waist, but his grip was not fierce. Molly continued to gasp something into her hair.

"What?" snapped Daisy, unperturbed. "Who? What *is* it? Molly! Pull yourself together . . . please." The slightly shocked, impatient note had its effect, and Molly wriggled free and stood 'facing them both—unafraid', as she confusedly put it to herself.

"All right, I'll tell you," she said breathlessly, "if you really want to know . . . but I'm warning you . . ."

"I don't particularly want to know, because I'm tired and I want my supper," said Daisy coolly; "but we can't stand here for the rest of the evening. Let's sit down."

Molly did not want to sit down. Declarations of this kind were more fittingly made, she felt, standing up with your scarf flung back becomingly from your face. Sitting down, with both the Muirs (and she felt very strongly now that they *were* 'the Muirs') facing her, the sustaining sense of drama began to ebb. And James was looking what used to be called 'hangdog'—an outmoded, but very expressive term.

"Well, come on," said Daisy kindly, nurse, prefect and mother combining in her tone. "It's Tibbs, I suppose . . . what's he been doing now?"

"No, it isn't Tibbs," Molly cried, goaded and stung. "Why should you always think it's Tibbs?"

"Because it usually is Tibbs. Well, if it isn't Tibbs, what—who is it, then?" Daisy, between laughter and annoyance, was beginning to suspect who it was, and surprised pain mingled with the shallower emotions, but she was not going to let Molly off. If she really had this absurd disloyal bee tangled and buzzing in her scarf and hair, let her acknowledge it.

The slight, sulky jerk of the head with which Molly indicated James was far indeed from those pictures of herself swooning on his chest, with Daisy conveniently disposed of in the nearest cemetery, which had so often sweetened her working hours.

"James?" cried the only-too-much-alive wife ringingly. "*James?* Oh, for goodness' sake, Molly, don't be such an *ass* ... Why—"

"I do, I tell you." Molly began to cry again. "I tell you I *do*. And it's all your fault, too. Going off night after night and leaving him—"

Daisy looked sharply at James, who was staring righteously at the carpet.

"... neglecting him—not appreciating him—how could I help it? When I've been here most evenings ... cooking for him ... cheering him up ..."

"It was very kind of you," said Daisy gently, one glance at the recipient of this devotion having told her that his feelings about the situation accorded with her own, "and we're both grateful. But I'm perfectly sure you don't feel like that at all, really, and now what I'm going to do is to ring up Tibbs."

"I don't *want* Tibbs!"

"You will when you see him ..."

"You don't understand. You're ... you're *blind*. This is serious— it's the parting of the ways for us three—"

"Rubbish." Daisy just controlled a stronger expression. "I'm going straight to ring up Tibbs ... did you know about his job?"

"I don't care—I don't care—you don't understand. This is my *life*."

"Oh, Molly." Daisy gave a brisk sigh and got up from her chair. "Do try to be ... your age."

"And pushing me off on to *Tibbs*, now, when you've always been the one to warn me off him. I can manage my own affairs, thank you ..."

Daisy went out to the telephone, and James, after a glance at Molly, muttered that he would just see if James Too was all right and went out after her.

Molly sat quite still in the chair into which she had been pushed, feeling exhausted. At least, she told herself she was exhausted, but the more accurate word would have been deflated. She also felt distinctly, if sulkily, ashamed of herself.

She did love James, but when, while actually in his arms, she had seen Daisy come in, so kind, so cheery, as she always was, she had felt as pleased to see her as usual. She couldn't hate her or anything like that though it was a cheek always bossing one about. Tibbs' job . . . was it a *real* job or just one of the cheap make-shift kind he was always getting? Oh, his eyelashes, and his sooty stiff hair . . . she began to cry afresh. Never any luck for Molly Raymond.

"He's coming over at once," announced Daisy, returning. (James did not return.) "I was lucky, I caught him, he'd just come in from work."

Molly was slowly wiping her eyes with the handkerchief breathing 'Morning in Rome' and did not reply. *'As a matter of fact,'* she thought, *'I don't know where to look.'* Some time passed. In a minute she said slowly:

"I'm . . . I'm ever so sorry. I don't know . . . I'm sorry . . ." Daisy, answering nothing, gave her a brisk kiss.

"The fact is," Molly began, "sexshually—"

"There's the bell! It must be Tibbs! I'll go!" and Daisy flew out into the hall.

"What is the matter with her?" demanded Tibbs, very foreign on the doorstep in a belted trenchcoat and a beret. "I suppose she is going to have a baby," he went on crossly. "I am always expecting this."

"I don't imagine she is for a moment," retorted his hostess, who had not the kind of mind on which such suspicions alight. "Don't be silly. She's just got herself rather fussed . . . well, rather fussed about something and I thought you'd like to help her . . . take her out, or something."

"This day I have my money; it's always the way."

Daisy, ignoring this unpromising comment but noticing that he looked less dusty and feckless than usual, asked him how his job was going?

"It's very nice and warm in the shop," with a sudden radiant smile of recollected comfort. "My God, it's the first time I've been warm all the day for years . . . I am selling tranquillisers all the day to the ladies . . . I bring some here for Molly," feeling in his pocket.

"Don't get her started on those things, please," said Daisy. He shrugged. "Why not to be comfortable?"

"Because it's better to learn how to manage yourself."

"I do not understand you English."

"No, I daresay not . . . well, come in, won't you?"

Molly looked up waterily as they entered. She was wondering why James hadn't come back, but had reluctantly dismissed the fancy that he might be wrestling with passion upstairs in the nursery, and anyway she felt she could neither look him in the face nor particularly wanted to, and there was Tibbs, nice and tidy in a new raincoat—oo! and one of those French berets. Molly could not help beginning to feel just the least bit better.

"Hullo, Molly," said Tibbs, in his customary disapproving and teasing tone, "haven't seen you lately, no?" ('No?' came out for that pretty Daisy's benefit, though he knew that she saw through it.)

"It's just a week," said Molly—before she could stop herself.

"Yes . . . well, now I tell you. I am not seeing you purposely. I have got a new job in a chemist-shop where I am almost doing my own work. It is a surprise, no? I am making up prescriptions and selling the pills and the lozenges and the laxatives and the tranquillisers and the nerves-tonics. All of England," he turned to Daisy, "is ill. Those who you cannot see ill in the shop are ill in the mental houses."

"Do you like it?" asked both young women eagerly together, completely ignoring this alarming sketch of the Welfare State.

Tibbs shrugged. "It's warm," was all he said. "Really warm."

But presently, when Daisy had got them both out through the pink front door with brisk words and waves of the hand, and smiling smoothings-over of Molly's stuttered apologies; and they were strolling up Hampstead High Street in the clear spring twilight with the flower shops and the antique shops and the cafés glowing invitingly on either side, he admitted that he did like it.

"You see, Molly, I almost do my own work again. (And later on I shall get a better one of this kind.) This I have had the long phar—I can't say it in English—pharmacu—it is difficult—training for. (Some years, it is.) It is . . . I find I don't mind to work again like a *bourgeois*."

"I should think so . . . nice clean work, and smells nice, and using your brains for once . . . and you have *got* brains, you know."

"You think so?" Smiles, pressures of the arm, wafts of 'Morning in Rome' through the air of evening in Hampstead, and Molly's hair brushing Tibbs' swarthy cheek.

"I settle me down, perhaps," said he suddenly, "with a friend, and I am comfortable. Now you come in here with me, Molly," pushing open the door of a fiercely neo-Expresso coffee bar, "and I buy you a coffee and you may tell me why you were upset. This evening, I pay. Sometimes you pay, and sometimes I, no?"

With sensations of returning cosiness, Molly settled herself—as so often on other evenings—into the corner seat with its blown-up pictures of all the most desolate situations and alarming faces the photographers had been able to find, and unfolding her swathings of scented wool. The tide of her tears was going out very rapidly.

"Oh," she said, putting her head on one side and taking her time, "I don't know that I *shall* tell you. You might be jealous."

"No, Molly." Tibbs did not look up from the frowning survey of the tiny menu, which afforded her a good view of what had certainly proved to be the fatal eyelashes. "I shall not. Because you are my girl. You can see this. I *have* you. We find a room somewhere, and you may look after me. I shall never have the reason to be jealous, no?"

CHAPTER XXI
Second Declaration

"James!" called Daisy softly up the stairs, a moment after the front door had shut, "all clear . . . they've gone." She was ready to laugh, and indeed was laughing, as he came down from their bedroom with a book under his arm, but he was grave.

She followed him into the living-room and began to bustle about. "I'll just put these away, and then I'm going to make a toasted sandwich—I'm simply ravenous. Would you like one?" He shook his head without looking up and she, making an inward face, went downstairs.

She carried up a tray, with the tempting food and the remains of last night's bottle of wine, and settled herself into a chair opposite to the immovably-reading husband. The lamps were on, the curtains drawn, her spring flowers glowed.

Daisy munched and sipped in some content. Better not, perhaps, mention what had happened at all. He evidently didn't want to laugh about poor God-be-with-you just yet (Jamesey was the kindest person in the world); of course, he felt sorry for her. And Jamesey was a man, and he wouldn't see that Molly was the kind of girl who simply fell in love with anyone who was good-looking and kind. Also, she adored a bit of drama. She had simply dreamed up the entire thing from nothing.

Well, now that Tibbs had a proper job at last, perhaps he might settle down with her. Daisy, sipping Pouilly Fuisse, went off into complacent reflections on the happy settlement of this year's crop of protégés. The Hultons living at Leawood New Town in their own house, Tibbs rehabilitated, Mrs Cavendish basking in the glory of being mother to the Countess of Devonhurst, old Miss Parsons (of whom, for sheer lack of space, we have not previously heard but who had played a not small part in Daisy's life for the past year) settled in the Penley Home for the Aged, poor Sue off any day to America with her new husband . . . Daisy felt free to concentrate on the problems of this Mrs Davids, desperately hard up, alone, who made hats and needed clients.

"James," she began suddenly, in the tone that he knew oh, so well, "about this Mrs Davids—"

James looked up. He opened his firm and beautiful Victorian mouth.

"Blast Mrs Davids," he said, and cast his whodunit on the floor.

Daisy stared, but only a little. He was evidently crosser about that ass Molly than she had suspected. Before she could say something soothing, he had got up and was standing, half-turned away from her, by the mantelshelf.

"I'd better tell you now," he said. "I was going to leave it over until the weekend, but this business this evening has—I feel like getting it off my chest now. I'm going to Canada."

"To *Canada*?" Lips parted and eyes open wide, she gaped at him. "What—"

"The firm's asked me to go, and I'm accepting."

"But—but—" She could still only stare, but the thoughts now rushing through her head were none of them agreeable. "It's— isn't it frightfully sudden?" she said, in a shaken tone so unlike the usual one of his Daisy, that even through his chilly anger, he was hurt by it.

"Oh, not so very. I've known for some time that I had the chance but I've been making up my mind."

"How long for?" Daisy asked. She felt, she did not know why, rather frightened.

"Five years . . . or a permanency, if I like it."

"Why do you keep on saying *I*, as if James Too and I weren't going with you?" she burst out, dismay, shock, and a thousand other feelings expressing themselves in sudden irritation.

"Because I don't know that you are coming with me."

"James! What *do* you mean?"

"I mean that perhaps you'd rather stay here—with Sue Ruddlin—or Ourgler as she'll be, I suppose—it's such a *name*— and the Hulton family and Mrs Cavendish and—and Molly and Tibbs and the new Countess of Devonhurst and old Miss Parsons in the Penley Home for the Aged at Carshalton and the Huxtable tart and—and—and bloody Mrs Davids with her hats and all the other people whose comfort you seem to prefer to mine," James said, his voice shaking with anger and unhappiness.

"But, darling," Daisy began reasonably, "that's not fair. You can't say you've been *neglected*—we see each other every day at breakfast and even when I *am* racing round after other people I *always* remember to telephone you and see that you get your meals. What?"

"I said, 'I want you, not bloody telephoning and meals'," said James, and he raised his voice more than a little. "I happen to love you, and I'm damned sick of sharing you with half the hard-luck cases and neurotics in London. I married *you*—not old Miss Parsons and Susan and all the—the—the—and don't *come* at me"—twisting away from her outstretched arms—"I've had enough of it. That's why I'm accepting. I shall enjoy it—I've always felt half-stifled in London, anyway—and if you—you can come too, if you want to. But we're—we're going to have a very different way of living, if you do . . . no, I don't *want* to kiss you. I've been made to feel quite enough of a fool this evening, and I've had enough. I've had enough. That's all." He was shouting now.

Daisy sat still, gently moving her long fingers together. She felt stunned, and so dreadfully sorry for darling Jamesey, roaring at her like James Too when he wanted his lunch, that she felt she might cry. She looked up very quickly at him under her lashes and very nearly did. She was, as usual, exceedingly tired, and suddenly she felt that she *hated* Molly, Old Cavendish, Katy, Tibbs, Peter Ramsay (one more unfortunate omitted for lack of space) Delia Huxtable and—and the entire boiling of them. After all, there was really no one in the world but Jamesey.

Of course, he was being selfish. But what had she been to him? Indulging her own taste for playing God abroad, and neglecting the more familiar duties, which ministered less to her self-esteem, at home. She had often felt, Oh, if only I could just have the evening quietly with Jamesey!' when someone came round or telephoned. But when had she ever told the importunate on the wire or the doorstep simply to shut up or go away?

Marcia and her father had told her more than once that she ran around too much after people, and her eager answer had always been 'But I like it'. If she had had the honesty not to buttress her defence with remarks about lame dogs and stiles and passing through the world but once, it had only been because, to her reserved, decent sober religious sense, such phrases seemed cant, and smug.

However, in spite of these painfully honest reflections, and almost crying with love for Jamesey's cross red face, what she found herself angrily saying was:

"You don't mean to tell me we're actually *emigrating* because . . . I'm sometimes out in the evenings helping . . . my friends?"

"We aren't 'emigrating'. I'm going because they're giving to me nearly double what I'm getting now and because I want to go. I'm sick of London. I hate it. I always have. You know that. It's—a filthy great hole."

"It can be pretty awful," she admitted, more quietly, still looking down at her hands. "But up here—"

"I want to live in a place where I can ride and shoot and ski at weekends," said James. "We'll have a boat. (I'll teach James Too to sail.) I've always felt half-choked in England, anyway, where you have to be a millionaire twice over before you can get your hands on a boat or skis. As for small sailing boats, I want a lake to myself, not bumping into the chap next door round Burnham-on-Crouch—and it's all the colour of pea-soup anyway—" His tone was growing quieter. "Won't you like it?" he asked, taking care not to sound pleading or conciliating.

"It's . . . all so sudden, Jamesey," she said, thinking just how much she liked parties and people and her little house with the pink front door. In imagination, she suddenly saw mounds of raw fish, and a great many objects made of wood and leather.

"Well, we're going," was all he said, and then there was silence for a while. The flowers smelled sweet and the clock ticked and the lamps bloomed. In the quiet, a feeling of acceptance began to grow between them.

"Oh, Daddy!" Daisy suddenly cried. "I shall miss him so terribly!"

"That's the thing . . ." said James. "I thought we might ask him to come with us."

"Oh, would you? It would be wonderful . . . I shouldn't mind nearly so much . . . I mean . . ."

"I didn't think you'd be pleased about it," said James, still grimly, "but the fact is, Daisy, I think you've had your innings. You've had exactly the kind of life you've wanted and done just what you've wanted to, and I don't think I've made much fuss. Not enough, in fact. But I've been getting pretty sick of it, for some time now. It's all seemed more like some queer's life, to me, rather than a man's . . . and I hate everything being so *small*. We'll have a house three times the size of this one—we'll be able to afford it—and—there's another thing—" he hesitated.

"What?" staring, and really subdued now, "something else?"

"Just that I think you'd better make up your mind to a really big family—six or seven, if we're lucky."

"*Six or seven!!* We always said *two!*"

"That was before I knew about this job. I should like it, very much. I've always thought two was a bit on the meagre side."

"I shall be *swamped*," Daisy said faintly, but with a brightening eye. "Seven!"

"Swamped, nonsense. If you can run a family of lame ducks you can run seven children. Much better for you, too. You can see to it that *they* don't grow up into lame ducks—at least, not into the worst kind of lame duck. Don't worry. Your instinct for mothering and managing will get all the scope it needs." He moved across the room to get his tobacco pouch from the table and as he passed her he lightly drew a finger across her crimson cheek.

"Cheer up, chicken," he said, and she caught at his hand and bit it, not gently.

"All right . . . perhaps it'll be rather fun. When do we go, for heaven's sake?"

"June, they seem to think."

"Doesn't give us much time," she said, but musingly, not in a startled tone.

"Time enough. We might even start on the seven before we go?" he said.

Daisy got up from her chair. In silence she put out the lamps one by one and set the shield of delicate bronze wire to guard the fire during the night. In the dimness, the strange faces of the narcissus glimmered. As she reached the door, James came up behind her and put his arm around her waist. There was just space enough, on the narrow staircase of the house with the pink front door, for the Muirs to go up it, side by side, entwined and in silence.

CHAPTER XXII
Marcia Goes Back to College

COLONEL Furnivall, during the next few days, underwent first the disagreeable shock of hearing that his daughter and son-in-law were going to Canada, and then the surprise and pleasure of being asked to go with them.

He had scolded himself for selfishness when he found himself dismayed. The fact was, he hadn't realised how much the house with the pink front door meant in his orderly life. But that life had lately been seeming just a little pussyish, a little too regulated and unadventurous, and he welcomed the idea of accompanying Daisy and James as much for the shake-up it would give to his sedentary habits as for the happiness it would give him to share the home of his daughter.

But he did not look forward to telling Marcia and Ella. True, at their age they could be expected to have reached the period when partings are less painful, but they had also reached the period when people are most likely to die; and he had to face the fact that he might not see either of them again: they, of course, would realise it too.

They heard his news quietly but with pleasure, both taking it for granted that five years would quickly pass and that they would be there to welcome him when he returned. He could only hope that they would: both seemed well, and serene, conveying to him that blessed timeless quality which he had always associated with them because of having known them all his life.

"All those tiresome friends of Daisy's are going to miss her very much," observed Marcia, as she sat by the fireplace now filled with growing plants, pouring coffee into the familiar tiny pink and green cups. "What became of that droopy girl she brought here once—she lived in your house, didn't she? I remember hoping she wouldn't worry you."

"Miss Raymond. Yes, but she—er—she left us last week. I don't know exactly where for" (*or with whom*, he hastily suppressed) "but she seemed satisfied with her prospects."

"What were they? (I always wonder about that kind of emancipated but completely uneducated young woman.)"

"She described them to me as *not exactly getting married*." His cousin stared. "How very peculiar," she said at last, and gave a sudden, delightful laugh.

"Quite," he said, smiling too. "However, she seemed happy enough."

"Just now and then," pronounced Marcia, "I hear a phrase seeming to sum up all the changes that have taken place in our lifetime. *Not exactly getting married* would hardly have made a girl 'happy enough' when we were young."

"No, indeed . . . but she did seem happy."

He recalled a waft of richer than usual scent, the smiling eyes, the head well tilted on one side . . . he must remember to ask Daisy if her Miss Raymond really was going to be all right? Not that he felt acute interest in her fate, but he did feel a vague sense of responsibility towards her, because he suspected that his words of warning had not fallen on completely stony ground. Girl could see beyond the end of her nose, and take a hint. Good luck to her.

The wish would have added the final touch to Molly's contentment that evening, as she fussed round a large and rather comfortable bed-sitter in Kilburn preparing a messy Italian supper for Tibbs. But they were not going to stay in Kilburn for ever, because 'Hulton's Comforter' had been finally worked out, and successfully tested, and was going to be produced on a large scale by the firm employing Don.

Years hence, a rich young man with slanting eyes, going over an album of old photographs, was to say: "Yes, my grandfather founded the family fortune . . . that's my grandmother, in all those stoles, or whatever they used to call them. Oh, do you think so? I like *bones*, myself, in a face. At first they didn't even bother to get tied up, but my father's birth changed all that . . . I don't remember her . . . she seems to have been a pretty good ass, by all accounts, but everybody says she certainly did stick to him."

Ella sat by the window while her brother and cousin talked, looking out into the evening. The railway cutting was already in shadow and beyond it the terrace caught the last of the light. 'Tomorrow,' thought Ella, half hearing what the others were saying, 'I will go and paint those houses in Campion Street.'

She had seen them in passing from the top of a bus; two rows of sly little white places with seemingly nothing else in their street but smooth paving stones; no shops, no playing children, no traffic, and they went round in such a sharp curve that the end of the street was concealed by it. Their front doors were fast shut, the heavy scrolls of creamy plaster above their windows looked like lowered eyelids, each house had old iron railings above a steep basement, and each basement its iron gate. 'White cats live in those houses,' Ella thought.

In fact, those friends of Annie's to whom she went on her afternoon off and at Christmas, lived in one of them; Ella had often heard Annie speak of 'going to Campion Street'. Who they were, what they did, how many of them there were, or their ages, Marcia and Ella had never troubled to find out, partly because all Annie's affairs were a matter for indifferent amusement to the Furnivalls but also because Marcia felt, though vaguely, that their old servant had a right to some privacy in a life that had possessed so little.

Ella had been excited to see the name, Campion Street, because for years, hearing it mentioned by Annie, she had imagined it as *rose-coloured*; with no other quality at all. (Rose campions had grown in the garden at Oxford.) But the reality—the two secretive, creamy rows curving off into themselves—was even better. Tomorrow, she would go.

Godfrey was getting up. She trotted across from the window to receive his good-bye kiss; he told her to take care of herself, and Marcia laughed and asked why there was any particular reason that she should begin now? She never had. "I doubt if she knows what it means," she said.

"I do," said Ella. "When I cross the road I look left—then right—then left."

"Like the children," her brother said. "Well"—he put a light hand on an arm of each—"both take care of yourselves. We'll all have a slap-up dinner together, of course, the children as well, before we go. But for the next few weeks I shall be very busy."

When he had gone, and Ella, who liked few things better than sitting up late, had been sent off to bed Marcia lingered for a moment admiring some flowers sent up that morning from the country, and thinking about Godfrey's suggestion that she and Ella should come out to Canada next year on a visit.

The journey would be easy; they could fly (the airliners, even the great Comet IV itself, she knew, were full of seventy- and eighty-year-olds floating cheerfully round the planet—"so much less tiring, my dear,") and Ella would like to paint the pine forests.

No, thought Marcia, she wouldn't. She only wants to paint London. She wouldn't enjoy it, and of course I wouldn't go anywhere without her. Then she thought of that 'where' to which she must certainly one day go without her, alone, and turning out the lamp, went quickly to her room.

Campion Street was even more entrancing to walk down than to see from the top of a bus.

There were curtains at all the tight-shut windows, of dim green, or faded rose, and some with wide blue flowers. The railings above the basements were a pale and ghostly red. Not a soul in sight. It was late afternoon; the light blue and silver spring sky dreamed and floated overhead, sometimes a woman's drawn face looked up from a basement or out of an upper window. 'The children are having their tea,' Ella thought. 'That's a good thing, they won't bother me.' The air smelled of ancient soot, and spring.

She listened to the muted music of the traffic in the faraway main road; it carried along with it the lightly drifting clouds whose shadows ran ahead of her and over the curve of the street whose end she could not see.

When she felt herself to be exactly in the middle of Campion Street, she stopped, and looked about her. Yes, this would do. There was a creamy bit of wall here that abutted on to the pavement, and it would afford the slight shelter she always needed. She leant her satchel against it while she began to unpack her stool.

Through the quietness, she became aware in a moment that someone was calling.

"Miss Ella! Well, I never. Fancy seeing *you* down here, of all people!"

She glanced up impatiently, and felt a tremor of annoyance and fear. Annie's mocking face, Annie's red head, were looking up at her out of the nearest basement. She was standing on the steep old steps, a black coat over her neat blue dress, and a purse in one hand.

"I'm just off to buy a bit of something for our tea . . . what brings you down here?" she asked. "Painting, as usual, I suppose. Or," her voice went up and the muscles of Ella's stomach contracted, "nosiness and spying?"

"Don't speak to me like that," Ella said coldly, going on with her preparations. "I had forgotten your friends lived here."

"I'm sorry," said Annie, with a change of tone. "I didn't mean it, Miss Ella. Look—I tell you what—you come and have a cup of tea with us. You'd like to see the inside of the house, wouldn't you? It's ever so pretty. They got some nice old pieces; you'd like those."

"No, thank you, Annie. I just want to paint the outside of the houses, and the light will be going."

"Oh, come on, don't be shy." Annie came smiling up one step, and put her purse into her pocket, and stood there looking strong and commanding in the fresh spring air, and younger than her sixty-odd years. There was scarcely any grey in her hair and her face was unwrinkled.

Ella, staring at her now, felt how lovely were the tones of black against cream, of blue and dun and soft faded red. She took a rocking hesitating step forward, drawn irresistibly and as always, towards what she felt to be beautiful. How long and tall, too, was Annie's dark shape rising apparently out of the shadowy ground, and beyond it all the colours so soft and calm.

"Come on now. I'll give you a hand. It's a bit steep," Annie said.

The delicate and luring colours spoke with a voice known since girlhood. 'I may as well go,' Ella thought; 'it won't take long and then she'll leave me in peace.'

"All right, Annie, then, thank you," she said, and glanced hesitatingly around. "I suppose my things will be safe?"

"Oh yes, Miss Ella. My friends aren't thieves."

Ella advanced towards the gate that Annie had opened; below it she saw the whitewashed basement with green ferns in pots and a window shrouded in lace curtains. It looked cosy, tidy, peaceful. She put one foot on the narrow step.

"Come on," cried Annie stridently, "don't be a cowardy-custard," and she shot out her powerful hand and gripped Ella's wavering one.

She meant—night after night on her knees for years afterwards, she was to swear with tears that she meant only to give the lightest of playful pulls. But as she felt the touch of the slight bones and delicate old skin, all the starved pain that lived inside her reared itself up in bitter savagery *(oh, the birds calling, and the light on the river)* and she jerked her forward. Then, as Ella stumbled and fell, Annie snatched away her hand and stood aside, and watched her strike the stone basement, screaming and screaming at the top of her voice.

Marcia sat by the bed. There was not much hope that the eyes would open in the unrecognisable face, but there was a little, and she had been told that she could wait.

In a little while, as if Marcia's anguish had impelled them, the black lids moved, and in a moment she was looking into Ella's eyes. They had an annoyed expression, and were a little ashamed too.

"Hullo, my darling," Marcia lightly said.

"Hullo, Marcie. I fell down the steps . . . so clumsy."

"I know, dearest. Annie telephoned. She was in such a state." Ella moved her lips.

"Marcie, I feel *very* bad . . . I must tell you something. Please don't be angry, will you?"

"Of course not." Surprised, Marcia thought it better to say the simplest, most reassuring thing than to protest, *When have I ever,*

*in the sixty-five years that you and I have loved one another,
been angry with you?*

"Well, you see," Ella almost whispered, "I'm a Christian.
I *do* hope you won't mind. It's been ever since I was thirty, no,
thirty and three months, really, and I've had these Thy creatures
of bread and wine at the Early Service and believed *everything*.
Like all the others." She paused. Marcia was completely at the
mercy of agony, but there was room, even at that moment, for
utter amazement. Ella! She tried to find something to say.

"I hope—it comforted you, darling."

"No, it didn't, not really," said Ella, rather crossly. "I liked
being it, but I was always so afraid you'd be angry."

"Never, my dearest. Never with you."

"Oh yes—and I told you four lies, all about going to church. (I
made a note of them somewhere, on the back of a picture—and
the dates—but I don't quite know where it is.) I'm so *sleepy*," in
a surprised voice. Marcia slowly reached out her hand, long and
beautiful, and laid it over the stubby, small, artist's paw lying on
the coverlet. It did not respond to her caress.

"I'm not cross, darling," she began, "not in the very—"

"Marcie, will you try?" Ella thought that she was saying it in
a sensible voice, raising herself on one elbow, but she was lying
flat and her eyes were shut. "*Do* try."

The answer came back to her from a distance so vast that just
to conceive it was unimaginable weariness, and already, even as
she heard, Marcia's voice was dimming off into softest silence.

"I will, my darling."

In a moment, Marcia got up and stood looking at the cracked
and broken thing on the bed. It did not look like Ella any more.
But then, it never had looked much like Ella.

Marcia and Annie, the latter looking the perfect old servant
in good quality black, returned alone together to King Edward's
Road after the funeral, for Marcia had declined Colonel Furnivall's offer to let him accompany them.

"Would you like some tea?" Annie asked, when she came back from her room with the marks of recent tears washed from her face, and her smooth hair made even smoother.

"Yes please." But Annie lingered.

"I should like to say I'm sorry for having made rather a show of myself this afternoon, Miss Marcia. But it all seemed to come over me sudden—being with the family so long, and how we're going to miss her and that."

"It's all right," Marcia said absently. Then feeling that some concession, however small, must be made to a genuine grief, she smiled and added, "Will you make the tea strong, please, because I'm rather tired." She had seldom admitted as much even to Ella. Well, she and Annie were alone now.

"I expect you are, miss," eagerly, "I'll make it really strong."

"Thank you, that will be very nice." Marcia smiled at her. "It has been a comfort, having you with me," she added kindly.

How uncontrolled they always were, she could not help thinking an instant later, as Annie fairly ran sobbing from the room. And wasn't there, too, just an odious suggestion of enjoyment in it all? It seemed a pity that Annie could not have behaved better to Ella during the fifty or so years that they had been closely associated: five minutes' crying did not, to Marcia, atone for half a century of discreet bullying.

Later that evening, when the spring dusk had grown so deep that the lamps must be lit, she put down her coffee cup and got up from the chair beside the flowering plants, and went to the open window.

It was all just the same; the shadows already gathered into the railway cutting before they had completely invaded the trees on the other side of the bank, the terrace floating in the pale orange afterglow, the hint of London smoke veiling the white towers and blocks of new flats still just visible beyond the houses to the south.

Godfrey had asked her to make her home with them in Canada. But she had refused. Her roots were here, and Ella had loved these streets of old, sooty, rain-whitened stone, and painted them. Here Marcia would stay; near the hill that had once been fresh earth where primroses grew and now shut in, built over, poisoned—still faintly retained the memory of its former beauty.

But in her last years there remained something important for her to do: two old virtues to cultivate, and a new one to learn.

'For all that matters in the world,' she thought, standing by the window, 'are duty and courage and love. Art, philosophy and science are toys, but by the other three a human being can live and die.' She had always known about duty and courage; now she must learn about love.

Sitting down at the table, in an upright chair, she drew lamp and book towards her and opened the latter at the Gospel of St. John. Before she began to read, she glanced round the room. It was quite empty. Then, gradually, her wide brows assumed the calm concentration that they had worn when she was a student long ago at Somerville. For this was, to her, a new language.

THE END

FURROWED MIDDLEBROW

Made in the USA
Middletown, DE
25 September 2022

11213380R00139